MENACING MEMORIES

"There is one way to purge our memories, Belle," Jack said, his voice suddenly harsh.

Isabella looked into his eyes, and shook her head slowly. "No," she said. "I have children to consider now, and you have a courtship to pursue."

"This has nothing to do with either children or courtship," he said. "This has to do with old memories and old needs." He brought his body against hers and closed his eyes. "This has to do with you and me, Belle, and with—curiosity, if you like. What are you like now? What am I like? What—?"

But her mouth had come up to meet his and cut off the words. And when they at last paused, their bodies stayed pressed together, their mouths still joined, eyes still closed, digesting what had happened, what was happening. . . .

Isabella could only wonder how a heart so grievously broken once could beat so hard and fast again. . . .

Christmas Belle

CHRISTMAS BELLE

%

by

Mary Balogh

A SIGNET BOOK

SIGNET
Published by the Penguin Group
Penguin Books USA Inc., 375 Hudson Street,
New York, New York 10014, U.S.A.
Penguin Books Ltd, 27 Wrights Lane,
London W8 5TZ, England
Penguin Books Australia Ltd, Ringwood,
Victoria, Australia
Penguin Books Canada Ltd, 10 Alcorn Avenue,
Toronto, Ontario, Canada M4V 3B2
Penguin Books (N.Z.) Ltd, 182–190 Wairau Road,
Auckland 10, New Zealand

Penguin Books Ltd, Registered Offices:
Harmondsworth, Middlesex, England

First published by Signet,
an imprint of Dutton Signet,
a division of Penguin Books USA Inc.

First Printing, November, 1994
10 9 8 7 6 5 4 3 2 1

 REGISTERED TRADEMARK—MARCA REGISTRADA

Printed in the United States of America

Chapter 1

"A man ought to be allowed to choose his own bride. That is all I have to say on the subject," Mr. Jack Frazer informed his mother as their carriage bowled along toward Portland House, thirty miles south of London.

But the trouble was he had been saying the same thing for a week past. And yet here he was, as meek as a lamb and as weak as water, on his way to his grandparents' home for Christmas. On his way to being managed by the most managing female it had ever been his misfortune to know—his grandmother, the Duchess of Portland.

"Then, perhaps you ought to have done it already, dear," his mother said. "You are one-and-thirty and my sole prop and support. Besides, we do not know for certain that your grandmama has chosen you a bride. The invitation was to spend the holiday season with her and your grandpapa and the rest of the family. What is so strange or unusual about that? There was no mention of matrimony."

Jack looked sidelong at his mother. Was it possible that she knew her mother so little after all these years? No, it was not possible, he decided without even having to give the question due consideration. It was just that she wanted to see him married. And so she had urged him to accept the invitation—or summons rather—despite the fact that he had had far more congenial plans for Christmas.

"You are quite sure," his mother asked, the customary anxiety in her voice, "that this particular stretch of road is not frequented by highwaymen, dear?"

Jack sighed, took her hand on his arm, patted it reassuringly, as he usually did on such occasions, and spoke soothingly. He wondered how many hundreds or thousands of times his mother had traversed this particular stretch of road, on her way to or from Portland House. And yet she still lived in terror of having her carriage held up by masked ruffians with smoking pistols.

He could have gone to Reggie's for Christmas, he thought. Reggie had invited a group of amiable fellows to accompany him to his hunting box in Norfolk for a week or two. And a group of an equal number of sprightly Cyprians to accompany them there. Reggie's choice of girls was invariably faultless. Or he could have stayed in town and taken in all the parties there and amused himself with Lady Finlay-Dodd, with whom he had spent an interesting—and sleepless—night less than a week before and with whom he was considering pursuing a full-blown affair.

And yet here he was in a carriage with his mother, on the way to his grandparents' house, to spend the festive season with them and with all his uncles and aunts and cousins and their brood of very young children.

Was he mad? Was he completely touched in the upper works?

"Jack," his grandmother had said to him a month ago, when she had come alone to town for a few days to attend Connie's wedding—Grandpapa's gout had kept him at Portland House. "Jack, it is high time you were married, too, my dear. The Stewart men always marry by their thirtieth year."

"But I am not a Stewart, Grandmama," he had protested.

"If your mama had not married, you would have been," she had said.

He had looked sidelong at her and patted her hand. "If Mama had not married, Grandmama," he had enjoyed explaining to her, "I would be a bastard."

"It is time you were married," she had repeated briskly. "And you may be thankful that Grandpapa had to remain at home, the poor dear. Only I would have stood between you and his wrath if he had heard you utter such a word in my hearing."

"But you are a veritable Rock of Gibraltar and would

have defended me admirably, Grandmama," he said. "A very small rock, it is true, but nevertheless a firm rock."

"You are an impertinent boy," she had said. "You need a wife to teach you to curb your tongue. Now, what do you think of the young buck Constance has chosen? She has taken long enough in the choosing. She is one-and-twenty. In my day she would have been considered long in the tooth already."

That was three mentions of matrimony in connection with himself in one encounter, Jack thought now as the carriage made a sharp turn and his mother uttered her customary cutoff shriek as she realized that it had been occasioned by the turn onto the long driveway to the house rather than by highwaymen diverting the conveyance into a hedgerow. And hard upon those three mentions, little more than a week after, in fact, had come the invitation—the summons.

Grandpapa, it seemed, had conceived the notion that there should be a family Christmas at Portland House, just as in old times, with family members. Dear Maud was to come, and she was to bring Jack. No family gathering would be complete without the presence of dear Jack. And there would, of course, be a few other guests apart from the family.

It was a typical letter from the Duchess of Portland—long, rambling, and devious. Grandpapa, of course, had conceived no such notion. Jack doubted if his grandfather had ever conceived a notion in his life. And yet for so long Grandmama had perpetuated the myth that he was a forceful ogre of a man that perhaps she had come to believe it herself. Three times in the course of the letter she had emphasized the fact that Jack must accompany his mother with the lure of other guests apart from family members. She must realize, then—and quite rightly, of course—that the prospect of a family Christmas was not an overly appealing one for a bachelor of one-and-thirty years. But he knew as clearly as he could see the nose on his face when he crossed his eyes the nature of those guests. Or the nature of one of them, anyway.

Grandmama had chosen him a bride, just as she had chosen Alex a bride five years ago—except that Alex had spoiled things by marrying Anne before he could quite betroth himself to the girl of Grandmama's choice—and just as she had chosen Perry a bride after that and Prue and Hortie husbands. Freddie, of course—that oaf, Freddie—had chosen for himself. Or had been chosen. One had only to look at Ruby to know that she was the sort of woman who might well have done the choosing. One tended to think of Amazons when one looked at Ruby. Not that she was not good to old Fred, Jack had to admit.

"We are almost there, dear," his mother said from beside him in the carriage. "I do believe we are safe from the perils of the road."

"We are safe, Mama." He patted her hand. "But I would have protected you, anyway."

But was *he* safe? And who would protect him? He was curious—he had to admit as much to himself—to know what kind of girl or woman the duchess deemed a suitable mate for him. Doubtless she was just a girl—seventeen or eighteen years of age. Grandmama disapproved of unmarried women beyond the age of nineteen, and even girls of that age she viewed with some suspicion, as if there must be some hidden blemishes that had deterred prospective grooms from leading them to the altar. For a moment Jack thought with some interest of young girls. But only for a moment. Young girls seemed to lose their appeal for him with each passing year. But doubtless this one would be pretty and charming. Grandmama would hardly choose an antidote for her own grandson even if the girl came loaded with a tempting dowry. There was a grain of romance in Grandmama's soul. More than a grain, in fact. She was still, at the age of seventy-something, and after fifty-four years of marriage, almost indecently in love with Grandpapa.

The carriage turned sharply again onto the cobbled terrace before the great double doors leading into the hall of Portland House, and then jolted to a halt. Jack waited for the doors to be opened and the steps to be set down before vaulting out onto the cobbles and reaching up a hand to help his mother down. The doors were opening behind him. At any moment now his grandmother was going to be coming down the steps to greet them. She never failed to greet her guests in person even before they could cross her threshold.

Well, he thought with philosophic gloom, let the party begin. He could, after all, say no to the girl. A quite firm and unequivocal no. Grandmama could not force him to marry her.

Just as a seasoned sergeant could not force a raw recruit to follow orders. Just as a burly chimney sweep could not force a diminutive climbing boy to climb. Just as an executioner could not force his prisoner to place his head in the noose. Just as—Well, he got the message, Jack thought with deepened gloom.

"Maud, dear. Dear Jack," a familiar voice said from behind him before his mother's feet had even touched cobbles.

The drawing room at Portland House sounded fuller than it really was, Jack found when he made his way down there after changing his clothes and washing away the grime of travel. But then it had usually been the way of his family members all to talk at once. And since it had been a long time since they had all been together—a whole month had passed since Connie's wedding—they had all raised the volume and pitch of their voices in a vain attempt to silence everyone else.

Despite himself, Jack felt a wave of fondness for them all. There was nary a stranger in sight.

"Jack." His sister, Hortense, was the first to catch sight of him, and she hurried toward him, hands outstretched. But before he could take hold of them, she had planted them on his shoulders and a hearty kiss on each of his cheeks. "I have won the wager. I knew I would. Zeb wagered that you would not come, the foolish man. He still does not quite know this family even though he has been married into it for almost three years. How are you? You are looking as handsome as ever."

"I am feeling as if my cravat is two sizes or so too small," he said. "Where is she, Hortie?"

"She?" She raised her eyebrows and then dissolved into laughter. "Oh, yes, Grandmama did say that she is expecting guests who are not family. Something to do with very dear friends of hers. The old story. And it has to be you, does it not? You are the only one of us left."

Jack pulled a face and possessed himself of her hands, one of which he raised to his lips. "Is what Mama tells me right?" he asked.

"Oh, yes," she said, glancing down at her elegant high-waisted gown. "But thank heaven for current fashions. I do not expect it to show for another month or two yet. If only there were not the wretched sickness in the mornings again. Have you seen the twins?"

"The twins?" He frowned. "Do you think I took the stairs three at a time to the nursery as soon as I arrived, Hortie? Incidentally, the nursery must be literally crawling with infants this year."

She laughed again. "We have all been rather prolific, have we not?" she said. "You are going to feel left out, Jack."

"Never!" he said fervently and hoped he was not blushing. The idea of paternity could always make him squirm.

"Never fear." She chuckled once more at his discomfort. "Grandmama is a tyrant, Jack, but she is a benevolent one, you know. She chose Zeb for me, if you will recall, and I am still inordinately pleased with him after three years. The twins are longing to see their Uncle Jack."

The twins, his nephew and niece, two years old and possessed of enough energy for sextuplets, had somehow wrestled him to the floor on his last encounter with them and had sat on him and jumped on him and squealed on him— and at least one of them had wet on him. Jack grimaced.

"Damme if it ain't Jack," an unmistakable voice said from the chair beside the fireplace. "Make your bow to Uncle Jack, Bobbie."

It was Freddie, of course, beaming and rather large—he had expanded in girth since his marriage—and as dazzling to the eye as ever with his usual tastelessly bright waist-coat. It was puce today. Old Fred must scour the earth to find fabrics of such luminous shades. Ruby, who had sense enough to compensate for her lack of beauty, might have been expected to have curbed such vulgar excesses of taste, but she had determinedly refused to rule her husband.

Jack's eyes came to rest on the small blond-ringleted infant on Freddie's lap. The child always struck him as surprisingly handsome and almost suspiciously normal. But then Freddie, he supposed, was not really an imbecile. He was just rather slow.

"I am not Robert's Uncle Jack, Freddie," he said. "You and I are cousins. That makes him a cousin once removed or something like that, dear chap. And how can he bow in those skirts? You have not considered leaving him in the nursery with the other children?"

No, of course Freddie had not considered it. Everyone knew how much old Fred doted on his son. Robert did not even try to bow to his first cousin once removed. He was too busy playing with his father's watch fob—and endangering his eyesight by gazing toward that monstrosity of a waistcoat.

"Hello, Jack," Ruby said in her strident, rather masculine voice. "Frederick is afraid that Robert will feel strange in the nursery here and will believe we have abandoned him. His fears will be allayed after a day or so."

"Freddie's or Robert's?" Jack asked with a grin. "That is a handsome new hairstyle you have, Ruby."

"Thank you. Frederick must be allowed to care for Robert in his own way," she said firmly, taking his arm and steering him away from her husband and son. "Frederick suffers from anxieties you would not understand, Jack. He has tender sensibilities."

Jack continued to grin. He was having amusing and quite improper mental images of Ruby and Freddie in bed together.

"Do come and have Anne pour you some tea," Ruby said, leading him in the direction of the tray.

"Ah, Anne." Jack's eyes softened when they came to rest

on the Viscountess Merrick, his cousin Alex's wife, seated behind the tea tray—as she had been on his very first encounter with her four years ago. She was as pretty and as dainty now as she had been then, though she had borne two children in the meanwhile. He had fallen a little in love with her four years ago and had tried to flirt with her since she and old Alex had been more or less estranged at the time. But she had been unwilling to have anything to do with him. She was one of the few women, married or otherwise, who had ever resisted his charm. Perhaps that was why he still had a soft spot for her.

"Jack." She smiled at him. "Will you have tea? I remember your saying once that tea was not quite your cup of tea, but it is that or nothing. You know that Grandpapa will allow nothing stronger during the afternoon."

"Anne," he said fondly, "do you still subscribe to that old myth? If truth were known, Grandpapa would like nothing better than a glass of claret in his hand."

She smiled her pretty, placid smile. Damn old Alex that she loved him as much as Grandmama loved Grandpapa— and had done so even while they were estranged.

"Anne," he said, leaning a little toward her, "I still wish I had been stuck with you in that snowstorm instead of Alex. I still wish I had been the one forced to marry you."

"Nonsense, Jack," she said. "You never change, do you? And of course you grow handsomer by the minute." She handed him his cup.

"Which is as flirtatious a remark as you can ever expect from Anne." Alexander Stewart, Viscount Merrick and the Duke of Portland's heir, stepped up beside his wife and set a hand on her shoulder. "I hear you are for the chopping block this year, Jack." He chuckled with altogether too much amusement.

Jack grimaced. "Is there anyone who does not know?" he asked. "But where is she? And, as much to the point, *who* is she?"

"Upstairs with her entourage, I believe," Alex said. "Had you not noticed that Grandmama is absent? They have just arrived. But her identity is a closely guarded secret, of course. Do you believe that Grandmama, with her well-developed sense of the dramatic, would have divulged that information to anyone in advance of the moment when she will present the girl? Drink your tea while you may, Jack. It may steady your stomach."

"Poor Jack," Anne said softly. "If it is any consolation, it was Grandmama who helped bring Alexander and me back together after that stupidity of a year apart following our wedding." She lifted her hand to rest it on her husband's on her shoulder. "She will probably have chosen well for you, Jack. Besides, you will be quite free to make the actual choice for yourself."

Alex threw back his head and laughed while Jack frowned. Dear Anne. She still had a lot to learn about the family into which she had married.

"I have been in the room for all of five minutes," he said, "and have not yet paid homage to Grandpapa. I had better go and make my bow before his wrath burns me to a crisp."

The two men looked at each other and snickered and snorted as if they were boys again.

"Grandpapa only looks fierce, you know," Anne said quietly. "In reality he is a veritable lamb."

The two men snickered afresh.

The Duke of Portland was a great mountain of a man, who generally sat with legs braced apart, one large hand splayed on each. His huge neck bulged over his cravat. His florid-complexioned face frowned fiercely on the world from beneath bushy eyebrows, which were a shade darker than his white hair. His coughs and wheezes and rumblings could easily be mistaken for signs of disapproval and even rage by those unacquainted with him. The fact that his numerous infant great-grandchildren, whenever they were given the opportunity, liked to climb all over him, combing his hair and undoing the buttons of his waistcoat and doing them back up again and otherwise making free with his person, was evidence enough that all his family members were well acquainted with the fact that he was a sheep in wolf's clothing.

"Well, Jack," he said after his grandson had made his

bow to him, "you came. Your grandmother has been anxious. She would have been disappointed if you had stayed away." He wheezed into a cough. "Your grandmother is not to be disappointed at her age."

It also needed to be added, Jack thought, that Grandpapa was at least as much in love with Grandmama as she was with him. He thought of the picture of them that hung in the portrait gallery, a portrait that had been painted soon after their wedding fifty-four years ago. They had been an extraordinarily handsome couple. Grandpapa had looked much as Alex looked now. And much as he himself looked now, Jack supposed. He and Alex were said to look alike.

"Do I take it, Grandpapa," he asked, "that your words have a double meaning? She was not to be disappointed by my staying away? And she is not to be disappointed in whatever it is she has planned for me this Christmas?"

His grandfather looked at him and harrumphed.

And then Peregrine Raine, the duchess's great-nephew, came to shake Jack heartily by the hand, while his wife, Lisa, smiled at him. For all that Perry had been married for three years, he had only recently got around to performing successfully the duty that Grandmama doubtless considered a married man's primary one. There were no children of his upstairs in the nursery, but it looked as if there would be any day now. Lisa was almost embarrassingly large. Jack was careful to keep his eyes on her face as he bowed to her.

The others were all in the room, too, and Jack nodded to or spoke to all of them over the next fifteen minutes. There were Zebediah, Viscount Clarkwell, his brother-in-law; Stanley Stewart, his grandfather's nephew, with his wife Celia; Uncle Charles and Aunt Sarah Lynwood, Freddie's parents; Great-aunt Emily Raine, Grandmama's sister; Martin, her unmarried son; Claude, her other son and father of Perry, Prue, and Connie, and his wife, Fanny. Then there were Prue and her husband, Sir Anthony Woolford, and Connie with her new husband, Samuel Robertson.

It was all going to be quite dizzying for the newly arrived family, who probably knew none of them except his grandmother, Jack thought. Sorting out names and relationships would take several days of serious study.

And then the drawing room doors opened again, and his grandmother appeared with a group of strangers. It was a sizable group, but Jack's eyes riveted themselves to the only one who really mattered. There was only one young lady in the group.

One very young lady. He doubted that she could be more than a few weeks past her sixteenth birthday. She scarcely looked even that, though she must be. Even Grandmama would not present a younger girl as a matrimonial prospect.

Very young and very, very lovely. She was small and dark and exquisitely shaped. She was lovely enough to stir any man's loins and catch at any man's breathing. But still, Jack thought, shaken, a mere infant. She looked as if she belonged in the nursery. Well, not quite that, he admitted, but very close.

This was the woman—the girl—whom Grandmama expected him to take to wife? The woman she expected him to lie with for the rest of his life? The woman she expected him to get his children on?

Jack wished suddenly that he were a thousand miles away. He thought with longing of Reggie and his experienced Cyprians. He thought of Lady Finlay-Dodd and her mature woman's body and ways. And his cravat felt three sizes too small or thereabouts.

Perry was whistling softly close to his ear. "A looker, Jack," he said. "You lucky dog, she has chosen a looker for you."

Jack did not turn his head to see if Lisa was within earshot. Perry's words implied that Grandmama had not chosen a looker for him. And it was true. Lisa was good-natured and she had brought Perry a very comfortable dowry, but it would be stretching the truth very thin to describe her as pretty. Perry seemed fond enough of her, of course.

Jack tried to keep his mind occupied with such irrelevancies. His grandmother was presenting her dear friend, the dowager Viscountess Holyoke, to the duke, with her son and his wife, the Viscount and Viscountess Holyoke, and their son and daughter, the Honorable Mr. Howard Beckford and the Honorable Miss Juliana Beckford.

His grandmother was conducting matters quite correctly, of course. She was presenting them first to the duke, who must already know at least the "dear friend." And then she turned to present them to Alex and Anne. And so on. He would be among the last, Jack realized, partly because Grandmama would do everything according to rank, and partly because she really did have an unerring sense of the dramatic.

Thinking of which . . .

Jack turned his head sharply and frowned at Perry. "Good Lord," he said, "have I entered my dotage, Perry? Why have I not thought of it until this very moment? You do not suppose Grandmama will have planned one of her amateur theatricals, do you?" He grimaced. Grandmama always organized her family for the performance of some play when she had lured them all to Portland House. The last one had been four years ago on the occasion of her golden wedding anniversary. They had been forced to put on a production of *She Stoops to Conquer* with only two weeks in which to rehearse. Some holiday that had turned out to be. He had had a large part, and his love interest had been Prue of all people. His own cousin! Not Anne, as he had hoped—she had played opposite Alex—but Prue.

Peregrine chuckled, and Jack remembered that Perry was the only one among them—with the possible exception of Freddie—who actually enjoyed the theatrics. But then Perry was easily the best actor among them. He had taken three curtain calls at the golden wedding performance.

But there was no time to think about the happy prospect of Christmas theatricals. The duchess, in her element, was sweeping toward him with her group of guests.

Miss Juliana Beckford was even more exquisitely pretty from close to. Her porcelain complexion was flawless. Her dark eyes had eyelashes to match, and they were large, beautiful eyes. But oh, Lord, she was a little child. He half expected that she would address him as "Uncle Jack," and was almost surprised when she curtsied to him and blushed very charmingly and murmured something about "Mr. Frazer."

He made her his most elegant bow and then wondered if he had breached good manners by bowing less deeply to the girl's mama and grandmama. No, they would be charmed by the contrast. They were looking charmed, as was his own grandmother.

Good Lord, had his valet fitted him out in a trick cravat, one that contracted one full size every half hour? And someone, he thought, had sucked all the air out of the room. And if there was a family eye that was not riveted to his face, he would be surprised to know it.

The girl's brother looked vaguely familiar. And then Jack, concentrating hard on not grimacing, recalled that he had been at Reggie's last gathering, during the summer. And that he had borne off the very Cyprian on whom Jack had had his eye.

"And so our gathering is complete," the duchess announced to the occupants of the room, all of whom had obligingly fallen silent. She had a strange gift for producing silence around her whenever she wished to make an announcement, without ever having to bellow for it. "Or almost complete." She beamed at the duke, who had hauled himself to his feet for the introductions but was now being replaced in his chair by Alex on one side and Stanley on the other. "There is, of course, His Grace's and my surprise guest, who will arrive tomorrow."

A buzz of annoyance arose from those who hated the suspense of surprises. But Jack did not share in it. Somehow he had been stranded in company with his intended bride. He clasped his hands at his back, smiled, and proceeded to charm her.

Chapter 2

Isabella Gellée, Comtesse de Vacheron, was traveling south of London in the luxurious and well-sprung carriage the Duke of Portland had insisted on sending for her convenience. She had her own carriage, she had explained in a letter to the duchess, but Her Grace had written back to say that the duke insisted on sending his own. And there was no changing His Grace's mind once it was set upon something.

"How much farther, Mama?" the thin, dark little girl on the opposite seat asked her.

"We will soon be there," Isabella said with a warm smile for her daughter, who had been very quiet and very patient throughout the long journey, as she always was. People were in the habit of complimenting Isabella on her well-behaved child. She herself sometimes wished that Jacqueline was more mischievous, more restless, more like other children.

There were sounds of sleepy grumbling and complaining, and Isabella turned her smile downward. Marcel was moving his head on her lap and wriggling his shoulders against the side of her leg to find a more comfortable position. He did not wake, but quietened again as Isabella stroked her hand lightly over his fair hair.

Her son had grumbled and complained and bounced and slid and yawned and whined at the length of the journey and the confinement of the carriage. Marcel did not travel well. But true to his normally placid nature, he had finally curled up and gone to sleep. She hoped he would sleep until their arrival at Portland House. Surely it could not be much farther.

It still amazed Isabella to realize that she had achieved the pinnacle of her dreams and ambitions—and even more than that. People were saying—a large number of people, people of fashion and influence—that she was the greatest actress of her time. It seemed an extravagant claim to her, but she was being treated accordingly. Since her return from France in the spring, she had acted in packed theaters to enthusiastic audiences who had stood to applaud her each evening and had forced her to one curtain call after another.

It was her dream come true, the goal for which she had struggled and sacrificed for longer than ten years.

And unexpectedly, she had found that success had bred respectability. When she had fled to France nine years ago, wretchedly unhappy and frightened and bewildered, she had only just begun to climb the ladder of success. She had grown almost accustomed to being treated with scant respect. Even when Maurice had met and married her, she had been shunned—by his family and by the rest of the members of French aristocratic society, who tried to cling to the old standards despite drastically changed conditions. But in France, she had finally achieved recognition as an actress—partly as a result of her talent and hard work and partly as a result of Maurice's influence. She had acted for the Emperor Napoleon himself and had been singled out by him for praise.

She had not really expected her fame to travel with her to England. And she had certainly not expected to achieve respectability in England even though she returned with an impressive title and with the young holder of the title—Marcel had been the Comte de Vacheron since his father's death almost two years ago.

And yet both had come to her.

She had thought to be alone with her children for Christmas, as she had been last year in France. But she had had her choice of two invitations. The Earl of Helwick had invited her to his country home—as his very special guest. He was a handsome, wealthy, and influential man, perhaps ten years her senior. She had been tempted—tempted by the lure of some sort of emotional stability in her life. He wanted her as a mistress, of course, but she knew that now, with her fame and wealth and position, she could command respect. The near-reverence with which he treated her reminded her somewhat of Maurice.

And the Duke and Duchess of Portland had invited her to their country home, where they were to spend Christmas with their family. They had invited her as an honored guest—the duchess had emphasized that point. They would also consider it a signal honor if she would favor them and their family and guests on Christmas Day with a sampling of her acting skills. A program of her choice—for perhaps an hour? They hoped she would not be offended or feel constrained to grant their request. If she preferred merely to relax and enjoy the holiday, they would understand perfectly.

Isabella smiled and set a protective arm about her sleeping son as the carriage made a sharp turn and she could see that they had passed gateposts and were traveling on a private driveway. "You see?" she said to Jacqueline. "We are almost there. You have been a very good girl."

She suspected that the duchess was a strong-willed woman who generally had her own way. And it sounded as if His Grace was something of a fierce tyrant, too. She might regret her decision to accept this particular invitation.

She sobered suddenly, and for the first time since leaving London felt something very like panic flutter in her stomach. What impulse had prompted her to accept when this was the one family of all others that she should most studiously avoid? And she wondered as she had done perhaps a hundred times before leaving if *he* would be here. He was one of the family—the duke and duchess's grandson, in fact. The chances were very strong that he would be here. The duchess had said it was to be a family gathering.

Even if he were not here, she should not have come. But if he were . . .

She patted Marcel's shoulder gently and bent her head to kiss one plump cheek and blow in his ear. "Wake up, sleepyhead," she said. "We are going to be there in a few minutes."

He sat up instantly, yawned, rubbed his eyes, and was fully awake and bouncing on the seat while looking out at the trees and the house just coming into view around a bend.

"Will there be other children for me to play with, Maman?" he asked. "Will we be allowed to come outside to play? Look at the house, Jacquie."

"Yes to both questions, I think," Isabella said, trying to smooth with her hand the ruffled hair at the side of his head and reaching for her reticule and the comb inside. Marcel would enjoy being in the country for a couple of weeks. London offered too many constraints on his energy. It was one reason she was considering beginning a liaison with the earl. He had a country estate.

She should not have come here, she thought again as the carriage turned onto a cobbled terrace before the house and slowed before the great double doors. Good heavens, they were his grandparents! And he might well be here himself.

He spent most of his time in London. She knew that. But she had not set eyes on him since her return in the spring. She had expected he would come to the theater to watch her perform, but he never had. Of course, he had never really enjoyed seeing her on the stage. She had expected to encounter him somewhere during all the months since the spring, but she never had.

Perhaps that was why she had come here. Perhaps she had wanted to force a meeting. But the thought was horrifying. No, not that. She did not want to see him.

Then, why had she come? And why had she returned to England when she was acclaimed in France and could have stayed there to enjoy fame and fortune?

The carriage door was being opened, and one of the Duke of Portland's liveried footmen was setting down the steps. Isabella set her hand in his and allowed him to hand her down onto the cobbles. The diminutive but rather regal Duchess of Portland, whom she had met in London a month ago, was coming down the steps of the house, both

hands outstretched. Isabella smiled and left the footman to
see to handing the children out. Not that Marcel needed as-
sistance. She heard the thud of his feet landing on the terrace.

"My dear, what an honor you do us," the duchess said
graciously. "I do hope you had a pleasant journey. What a
delightful little boy you have and what a prettily behaved
little girl. Do come inside where it is warm."

She was here, Isabella thought, climbing the steps beside
her hostess and stepping into the great hall. There was
nothing she could do about it now. She had not even
brought her own carriage. She must just hope that at least
he was not here.

Or did she wish it?

The duchess's surprise guest was not expected until the
afternoon. Although several of her relatives had asked and
wheedled and begged both at dinner and at breakfast, and
Martin had even been devious enough to ask the duke, ca-
sually enough, over their port, there was no discovering
who it might be. There was no absent member of the family
to make a surprise reappearance, and there was no one else
in need of a bride or groom except Jack, who had already
been provided for in the form of Miss Juliana Beckford.
Who, then?

"Oh, I do hate surprises," Prudence had said after breakfast, speaking for the whole family.

But Her Grace had merely smiled mysteriously and complacently.

And so they had all gone reluctantly about their business.

Jack, knowing that an attack by his young nephew and
niece was inevitable, had meekly given in to being led
away to the nursery by his sister, who had the misguided
notion that she was presenting him with a great treat.

Actually he was rather fond of them, he conceded as he
entered the bedlam that was the nursery at Hortense's side.
And somehow he was reminded of childhood Christmases
and other occasions spent largely in this very nursery, although he and his cousins had been considerably older dur-

ing the times he could remember best—but just as wild or probably more so. With the exception of Stan and Celia's three children, who had arrived almost at the age of reason, all the others seemed to be toddlers or babes in arms.

The Honorable Rupert and his twin sister, Rachel, came toddling and shrieking toward their mother and uncle. And bursting with news, the two of them, despite their limited mastery of the English or any other language. And Prue's Alice and Alex's Catherine came trailing along after them to discover if this prospective new adult playmate was going to prove worth his salt.

Jack was down on the floor on all fours, whinnying like a wounded horse, with Catherine and Rupert on his back and Rachel and Alice trying with some success to dislodge them, when Anne and Miss Beckford arrived on the scene. He could hardly have been looking more undignified if he had tried.

But Anne laughed and told him he was setting a precedent he might live to regret. He would never be allowed to escape if he played so enthusiastically. She bore Juliana off to the other side of the room, where she lifted her son, the Honorable Kenneth Stewart, from the rocking horse on which he had been stranded and merely laughed when he wriggled from her arms and half toddled and half crawled across the room to join the fun with the other small children.

The three ladies sat down to observe the play.

Fortunately for Jack's peace of mind, the duke and Alex soon arrived on the scene with Freddie hard on their heels. Freddie had just finished a brisk morning walk with his son.

"Thank heaven for men's energy," Anne said with a laugh as the play became fast and furious and all four men were somehow caught in the thick of it, including the duke, who was being put to sleep with numerous shawls and pillows. "Juliana, Hortense, how about a stroll in the gardens? It is rather a pleasant day."

Jack felt less inhibited after they were gone.

"At least," Jack commented to Alex when they were on

their way downstairs later, "Grandmama did not call a family assembly this morning to announce a Christmas play and to allot parts. At least we have been spared that, Alex."

"Hush," the viscount said firmly. "Do not even whisper it, Jack. Do not even think it. If Grandmama tries to get us to spend the next week rehearsing a play for her Christmas amusement, I for one am going to commit murder. Murder most foul."

"The trouble is," Jack said, "that if she has planned it, you know, and if she does it, we will all fall meekly into line. She would not do it, would she?"

"Not even a whisper," his cousin said sternly. "Not even a thought, Jack. At least she has done something well. Miss Beckford is an extremely lovely and charming young lady. Are you pleased?"

Jack looked sidelong at him. "Were you pleased?" he asked. "When it happened to you, I mean?"

"Actually I was," Alex said. "I considered Lorraine to be everything I most wanted. Had that snowstorm not forced me on Anne and vice versa, I would have married her and considered myself a fortunate man."

"But you are not sorry for the way things turned out for you?" Jack asked.

"Good Lord, no," Alex said. "But Grandmama does make decent choices. Miss Beckford appears to be a prize."

"Yes." Jack sighed. "I feel as if I am about to rob the cradle, though, Alex. I cannot quite picture myself . . . Well, I do not need to be graphic, do I?"

"Give it time," his cousin said. "Did Hortense rush from the breakfast room this morning for the obvious reason?"

"Yes, apparently she and Zeb have been busy again," Jack said. "And it seems that twins are as common in his family as single births are in most others. Poor Hortie."

"She looks happy enough to me," Alex said. "And it is Zeb who will have all the worry of marrying them off suitably when the times comes."

"Oh, Lord, yes," Jack said. "It makes you wonder why any man goes to the trouble of begetting children, does it not?"

His cousin looked full at him and grinned. "One of these days, Jack, my boy," he said, "you will perhaps understand that the sort of pleasure you have been taking for years and that I took for years before I married Anne can get one stage more pleasurable."

"Yes?" Jack looked interested.

"One does not want to become too graphic with a novice," Alex said, setting a hand on Jack's shoulder and patting it. "It has something to do with the planting of a seed with the full intention of its taking root."

Jack hoped desperately that he was not blushing.

"Now, who can this surprise guest we are expecting this afternoon be?" Alex asked. "What has Grandmama plotted for our delight this time?"

Jack did not much care. He had other things on his mind. A courtship, for example, that was looking somewhat unavoidable as he had known full well it would.

She was very pretty, of course. And very sweet. And it was about time he married, he thought with an inward grimace.

"Yes, Mama," Miss Juliana Beckford said. Her mother had come to accompany her downstairs for tea. She was ready.

"You look delightful, child." Lady Holyoke touched her fingertips to her daughter's cheek and then bent to kiss it. "He is excessively handsome, just as Grandmama promised you he would be, and exceedingly charming. And you must not fret over the fact that he is untitled, you know. He has a large and prosperous estate and a vast fortune, and the Frazers are an old and respected family. If the Duke and Duchess of Portland were willing to marry their daughter to the father, I am sure Papa can feel right about marrying you to the son."

"Yes, Mama." Juliana smiled.

But it was only ever her father who had voiced misgivings over Mr. Frazer's lack of a title—though the fact that he was the grandson of a duke had weighed heavily in his favor. It had never mattered to her. She wanted only an amiable husband, someone with whom she could feel comfortable. She was nineteen years old. She was ready for marriage.

It was true that Mr. Frazer was excessively handsome. He was tall and well formed, and he had the dark good looks to set any female heart to fluttering. And it was true that he was exceedingly charming. After spending some minutes almost alone with him at tea the previous day and after spending the evening in the drawing room partly in his company, she could not find fault with either his looks or his manners. Her grandmother and her father between them appeared to have chosen wisely and well.

Except that she could not like Mr. Frazer. No, it was unfair to say that she did not like him. He had made every effort to be agreeable and had behaved with perfect good breeding. But he was—well, for a start he was so old! No one had thought to mention his age to her, and she could only guess at it. Her guess was that he was at least thirty. That was not so very old. If she was right, he was only eleven years her senior. But there seemed to be a gulf in excess of eleven years between them.

"Everything is progressing quite satisfactorily," Lady Holyoke said as they descended the stairs together on their way to the drawing room. "He has paid you attention, but not too markedly. He is showing admirable good breeding. As are you, my love."

"Yes, Mama. I try," Juliana said.

The gulf between them was most evident in his eyes. His eyes were an old man's eyes—old to her nineteen-year-old eyes, anyway. There was a worldliness, a cynicism, a knowledge in his eyes that set him worlds apart from her. She had felt stripped of her clothes when he had looked at her. It was not that he had done anything improper or even looked too boldly at her. It was just that she had felt that he knew exactly what she looked like without her clothes. It was just that she felt he had a long acquaintance with women and their bodies. And that he was somewhat bored with the knowledge.

It was her own innocence that was at fault, she knew. Although she was nineteen years old, she had the misfortune to be small and to look younger than her years, with the result that Mama and Papa had been reluctant to bring her out when she should have been brought out a year or even two ago. And she had not protested overmuch, being fond of the quietness of home and her life there.

She did not want to marry a man who had lived so long in the world already that he was bored with it. And yet marry him she must. He had been chosen for her by her grandmother and her father, and she had been chosen for him by his grandmother, the Duchess of Portland. And it had been obvious to her that he knew it and that his whole large family knew it.

Juliana wished she had a friend close by, someone in whom she could confide all the teeming emotions she had suffered during the journey and during the day since her arrival at Portland House and her introduction to Mr. Frazer. But there was no one. Mama was out of the question. Howard was her friend as well as her brother, but she did not feel that she could completely open her heart on such a subject with Howard. And everyone else was on the other side of the fence. Everyone else was related in some way to him.

Juliana sighed and then smiled, remembering that she was about to enter the drawing room, about to be on view.

Perhaps the duchess's surprise guest would make things somehow easier for her. It was unlikely it would be another member of the family. That would hardly be a surprise. Juliana was feeling rather overwhelmed by the largeness of Mr. Frazer's family. But she had no way of knowing if the newcomer would be a man or a woman, young or old.

But she must not allow herself to feel overwhelmed, she thought. At least his family was pleasant and friendly. As was Mr. Frazer himself. She was somewhat cheered by the memory of seeing him in the nursery earlier with infants climbing all over him.

Juliana entered the drawing room at her mother's side, smiling. Mr. Frazer immediately detached himself from the group at the fireside and came hurrying toward her.

It was gratifying. She knew she would be the envy of her friends.

Chapter 3

The duchess's surprise guest arrived when everyone was at tea in the drawing room. It was a lady with two children, Martin Raine reported. He had been out of the drawing room when he had had no business being out of it and had observed the arrival, but from too great a distance to be able to identify the lady.

"With two children," Charles Lynwood said, his brow knitting in thought. "Whoever can that be? We do not have another unmarried male in the family to be married off, do we? Except you, Martin. Perhaps Mother has brought her here for you."

He laughed heartily at his own joke, and Freddie joined him since Freddie could never resist the sound of someone else's laughter. But everyone else who had heard—and most had—squirmed with embarrassment for Jack's sake and for the sake of Miss Juliana Beckford and her family. It had been a thoughtless and an excruciatingly tasteless joke under the circumstances. Everyone, almost without exception, rushed into conversation with the result that within moments a dizzying variety of topics was under discussion. And there was a great deal of hearty laughter over even the slightest suggestion of wit.

And yet despite the noise and general hilarity, the opening of the doors brought near silence, and everyone's attention focused on the duchess and the lady with her—as the duchess had doubtless planned.

"You see, my dears?" she said, clapping her hands unnecessarily for their attention. "You see what a splendid surprise I have been keeping in store for you? I know that you have all been speculating on the possibility that I would suggest Christmas theatricals to you and that you have all been holding your breath in hope that I have not thought of it, you naughty people. Well, I did indeed consider it, but it has been in my mind this year that I must allow you all to be lazy and to have a true holiday. Hence my idea. The greatest actress of our time has returned to London from France within the last year. How wonderful it would be, I thought, if I could persuade her and her children to accept an invitation to spend Christmas here with my family and to have her demonstrate for us on Christmas Day what true acting is all about. You will all know the Comtesse de Vacheron, of course. She needs no introduction from me." She turned her head to smile graciously at her guest.

The Comtesse de Vacheron did not indeed need any introduction. The duchess must have been singularly gratified by the effect her announcement and the sight of her guest had on her family and other guests. They all gazed at the famous beauty, the English actress who had gone to France almost ten years ago, when her fame was still on the rise, and there had married a French count. She had returned to England the previous spring at the very pinnacle of fame. And more—she had returned with a title and position. She had social standing, something rarely achieved by any woman in the acting profession.

Having succeeded in persuading the Comtesse de Vacheron to spend Christmas at Portland House with her family was a coup indeed for the duchess. Those assembled in the drawing room politely applauded, almost as if the famous actress had just performed for them. And then they all murmured self-consciously, and some of them laughed.

The comtesse smiled and inclined her head in gracious acknowledgment of the homage. Breathlessly lovely with her tall, shapely figure and golden hair and delicate features, she appeared rather like a goddess from a different universe to her awed audience.

"Come, my dear," the duchess, said, at her regal best. She linked her arm through that of the taller woman and

moved her determinedly into the room. "I shall introduce
my family and guests to you, and then you must make
yourself quite at home."

She followed almost the same pattern as the day before,
taking her guest first across the room to the duke, who was
being helped to his feet by Peregrine and Stanley. Jack,
who had been conversing with Juliana and her brother,
strolled nonchalantly across the room away from them to
stand at the pianoforte, alone. Thus it was that he was quite
the last to be presented to the great de Vacheron. Indeed, it
seemed for a moment that his grandmother might miss him
altogether, but Great-aunt Emily pointed him out, and the
duchess turned to him, a gracious smile on her face.

"And my third grandson, my dear," she said. "Jack
Frazer, son of my daughter, Lady Maud."

The newly arrived guest turned her attention to him.

Hers was a mature beauty. She must be almost thirty
years old, he knew. And yet, in its way her beauty was as
flawless as Juliana's. And more vivid and appealing because of its very maturity. It had been molded by many of
life's experiences and sufferings, not just by youth. She
was far more beautiful than she had been ten years ago.

Jack was half smiling at her when her eyes met his and
held them. Held them for several silent moments.

"Hello, Jack," she said eventually in a soft, melodious
voice that belied the power that voice could achieve on the
stage.

"Hello, Belle," he said equally quietly.

"Ah," the duchess said with brisk satisfaction, "you have
met before. I shall leave you to entertain the comtesse,
then, Jack, while I have some tea and a plate of cakes
brought over."

Jack found himself wishing—fervently wishing—that his
grandmother had stuck to her old tricks and had found a
play for her family to act out at Christmas. He found himself wishing that she had given him the main part, one that
would occupy him during every waking moment between
now and Christmas. It would have been better far than this.

A thousand times better.

"It has been a long time, Belle," he said, the half smile still on his lips.

"Yes," she agreed. Her eyes did not move away from his, as he half expected they would, even to lower to his chin or his cravat. They looked directly back—those wonderful green eyes that could so expressively mirror the state of her emotions. "Nine years. You have not been to see any of my performances since I returned?"

"No," he said. "I have had better things to do with my time."

She did not flinch or change expression. "I need not have asked," she said. "I would have known if you had ever been in the audience. I would have sensed your presence there."

They stood staring at each other for the minute or so that passed before Anne brought a cup of tea for the comtesse and stayed to converse. Jack stood where he was for another minute or two before murmuring some excuse and moving away.

Yes, she was far more lovely than she had been. But then she was a woman now and no longer a girl. And she was somebody now, the Comtesse de Vacheron and the mother of the present count, not just a budding actress.

His first woman.

His first love.

His only love.

He had never repeated the folly.

Isabella was well aware that once one became well-known, even famous, as an actress one no longer acted just upon the stage. The whole of one's public life became in a sense a dramatic performance. It was something she had tried to fight against. She had tried to be herself when in company with others just as she was when alone or with her children. But it was not easy.

For once she was glad of her ability to put on an act, to appear calm and confident and even gracious when she was feeling quite the opposite. The duchess had taken her and the children to the nursery first, where she had introduced them to some of the older children already there, though a seeming horde of curious toddlers had gathered around. Jacqueline had looked calmly accepting. Marcel's eyes had shone.

And then the duchess had shown her to her room and had stayed to converse while Isabella changed quickly and washed her hands and face and had the maid assigned to her care comb her hair. And all the while Isabella had smiled and joined in the conversation and behaved as if her heart was not thumping against her ribs and as if she did not long to rush out through the door and down the stairs and bolt in the general direction of London.

At first when they had entered the drawing room together she had thought he was not there. A quick glance about her had revealed only strangers. But she had felt his presence and then she had spied him across the room close to the pianoforte, even though she had not looked directly there.

These people, all gazing with polite interest at her and then with gratifying awe when they recognized her or when the duchess had informed them who she was—all these people were his family. And she had been his mistress. For a whole year she had lived under his protection. And when she had left him and gone to France . . .

She was more thankful than she had ever been for her acting skills and for her ability to face a roomful of strangers with poise. More than ever now she was here, now she had seen them, now they were real people before her eyes, she knew that she should not have come. And she thought with some regret of the Earl of Helwick and his invitation.

Jack had aged. That was her first impression when she was finally close to him and forced to look at him and even speak to him. He looked every one of the nine years older than he had been when she saw him last. He was no longer a boy, though he had been two-and-twenty even then. He no longer had a boy's slim physique or the open, eager boyish expression that had made him so handsome and so irresistible to her.

And yet he was more handsome now. He had a man's

body, still slim, but powerful, too. His face, hardened into manhood, was still devastatingly good-looking. His hair was as thick and as dark as ever. His eyes—those compelling dark eyes—had changed. There was cynicism in them, mockery that was perhaps turned both inward and outward. And there was a cynical curl to his lip as he half smiled at her. It was not really a smile at all, she realized.

She was able to say his name. She was able to exchange some trivial inanities with him—she did not know what they talked about—and with Anne, Viscountess Merrick, after she joined them. And all the time she felt as if a giant fist had slammed into her abdomen.

She had longed to see him again and dreaded doing so. But she had had no idea what it would really feel like.

Jack!

She had loved him with all the reckless, foolish totality of youth. And she had come to hate him with a matching intensity. No. No, she had never been able to hate him. Never deep down. She had never hated him. She had merely accepted reality and berated her naïveté in not having understood from the start.

And then he moved away, leaving her with the viscountess. The viscount joined them—the family resemblance between him and Jack was remarkably strong—and then Lady Sarah Lynwood and Mr. Martin Raine. She smiled and talked as if she had not a care in the world but felt only delight to be at Portland House preparing to spend Christmas.

She lost sight of Jack. She might have thought he had left the room if there had not been that extra sense she had always seemed to possess where he was concerned. She wondered how he was feeling. Angry that she had come here of all places? Upset in some way at seeing her again? Perhaps a little glad to see her? Totally indifferent? It had been nine years, after all, and she had been only his mistress.

A dainty little hand touched her arm, and she smiled at the very pretty young girl whose name she could not recall.

"I have never been to London," the girl said, "and I have never seen you act. But Howard, my brother, says you are the best actress he has ever seen. It must be wonderful to have talent like yours."

Juliana something. Isabella was annoyed with herself. She prided herself on her ability to remember names even when she had just been introduced to a large number of strangers.

"Thank you," she said. "Acting is something I have always felt compelled to do. Will you be going to London any time soon? For a Season, perhaps?"

"Oh, I think not." The girl blushed. "Unless it is after my marriage. My father has arranged a match for me. It is why we are here. Mr. Frazer . . ." But her blush deepened, and she bit her lip. "Nothing is settled. I should not have said anything. Forgive me."

"I heard nothing." Isabella smiled warmly until the girl smiled ruefully back. "It is rather noisy in here. So, like me, you are not part of the Duke of Portland's family. We appear to be in a very small minority."

"Yes," Juliana said. "I was very relieved to find that the duchess's surprise guest is a lady and a-a young lady. I thought perhaps we might be—friends?" She blushed again.

Isabella continued to smile, but they were joined at that moment by Mr. Howard Beckford—ah, yes, of course, that was the girl's name—and Mr. Peregrine Raine.

She felt as if that giant fist had dealt her another blow. And it served her right, she thought. She had only herself to blame. This was to be a family Christmas and was to include a family celebration of a betrothal.

Jack's betrothal to Miss Juliana Beckford.

The very pretty, shy, and charming young girl who wished to be her friend.

Oh, yes, it served her right.

He had to watch her during dinner and in the drawing room afterward playing court to all his male relatives from Grandpapa on down. Grandpapa wheezed and preened himself, Freddie giggled and damned himself, Perry forgot good breeding to the extent that he planted both elbows on the table at one point and leaned across it to hear what she was saying, totally ignoring Great-aunt Emily on his one side and Hortie on his other.

But then, Jack had to admit, the ladies were all hanging on her every word, too. Just as if she really were some grand lady, much grander than any of them, the family of the Duke of Portland. Just as if she really were the greatest actress of her time.

She was a nobody. She was the daughter of a country schoolteacher. She had gone to London to make her fortune and had gradually made a good enough living out of working in the beds of men like himself. And she had become an actress, an increasingly successful one during the year she was with him. And then she had crowned her success by disappearing abruptly—after their bitter quarrel—and reappearing in France more than a year later as the bride of the Comte de Vacheron. Right in the thick of the Napoleonic wars. She had acted for the emperor himself and had been feted by him and his court. Nothing could have been more calculated to escalate her to unprecedented fame in her native England than the adulation of England's deadliest enemy.

And so here she was at his grandfather's table, his grandfather's honored guest, holding the rapt attention of his grandfather's family, when she had been the mistress of one of the duke's grandsons for a full year. She had been paid to cater to his sexual needs.

Except that it had not been quite like that. Oh, Belle.

But it sickened him to see her there, to see her with his family. How had she dared come? She could not possibly have forgotten that the Duchess of Portland was his grandmother.

Perhaps he meant nothing at all to her. Perhaps she had forgotten about him in the course of nine years. She had known countless other men, after all, including a husband. And yet she had told him that she would have known at any time during these last months if he had been in the audience at any of her performances.

She had also become a skilled flatterer.

He could stand it no longer when the gentlemen joined the ladies in the drawing room after dinner, especially when his sister smiled at him and beckoned to him. She was sitting beside his former mistress on a small sofa.

He pretended not to notice her and crossed the room to the pianoforte, at which Miss Beckford sat, playing quietly for the amusement of her grandmother and his. She made a charming picture, dressed in white, her face the picture of sweet virgin innocence. He could fall in love with her, he thought recklessly, if he set his mind to it. He *would* fall in love with her. She was to be his wife, was she not? For the first time he welcomed the fact that he had been very effectively maneuvered into courting her.

His former mistress and his future wife were in a room together. He wondered if his grandmother would have a fit of the vapors if she knew the truth. But somehow he could not imagine her giving in to hysterics for any cause.

He waited for the music to come to an end.

"Beautiful," he said, smiling. "You have considerable talent, Miss Beckford." She had no such thing. What she had was a typical lady's accomplishment. She played correctly and competently. But there was no flair for music in her.

"Thank you." She blushed on cue while out of the corner of his eye Jack saw his grandmother and hers exchange looks of triumph.

"We must gather in the music room one evening to share our musical talents," his grandmother said, clasping her hands together at her bosom. "I have cherished memories of family musical evenings."

Jack grimaced inwardly. Yes, there had been those, too. Whenever there had been no theatrical performance to prepare, or whenever it had not taken every waking moment of their time, they had been forced to entertain Grandmama and Grandpapa with their musical talents or lack thereof. Prue on the harp, Perry and Martin on the violin, Claude on the flute, all of them on the pianoforte. Most of them sang—solo or duet or quartet or madrigal.

Oh, Lord, the madrigals—he and Alex and Perry with

Prue, Hortie, and Connie—all fa-la-la-ing and hey-nonny-nonny-ing their heads off in six parts. Elizabethan musicians had been a peculiar lot. Surprisingly, Freddie had always had the best voice, but Freddie could only sing solo. If he tried singing even a duet, he invariably went soaring off in unison with the soprano or bellowing downward in unison with the baritone. In his school choir, he had once explained to the unholy mirth of his male cousins, the choirmaster had always placed him in such a way that there was someone singing the same part as he on either side of him and behind and in front of him.

"How delightful that would be," the dowager Viscountess Holyoke said. "Juliana sings even more sweetly than she plays. You would enjoy a musical evening, would you not, my love?"

"Yes, Grandmama," the girl said, her eyes lowered to the keys. Jack had never seen a woman with longer or thicker lashes.

"Splendid," he said. "I shall look forward to hearing your voice, Miss Beckford."

"Thank you," she said again, raising her eyes to his. When she grew up, Jack thought, she was going to slay someone with those eyes. Though he would certainly not want her slaying any other man but him, since she would be married to him before she grew up. The trouble was that by the time she did that he would be half into his dotage already.

"With your permission, ma'am and Grandmama," Jack said, aware that soon he was going to have to turn around and behold the spectacle of Belle holding court, "I would take Miss Beckford to view the portraits in the gallery."

It was a bold move. For an unmarried man to take an unmarried woman who was not his sister or his first cousin to the gallery in Portland House was tantamount to announcing to the family that he was seeking out a private place in which to steal a kiss, but that his intentions were strictly honorable. If his intentions were not honorable, he was more likely to seek out a tree with a stout trunk somewhere outside. Or any secluded place outside. Jack had kissed

Anne four years ago in the middle of the stone bridge across the marshy lake—much to her indignation. And he had kissed Rose a few days later behind the rose arbor—appropriately. Rose! Sweet little Rose. He wondered briefly what had happened to her. He must ask Ruby, her sister.

His grandmother predictably beamed graciously. "What a splendid idea, my dear boy," she said, giving her permission for the stolen kiss. And, of course, for the honorable intentions.

"How kind of you, Mr. Frazer," the dowager added. She would not know, of course, the significance of a stroll in the portrait gallery. Or perhaps she did. Who, after all, would take someone to view portraits in the middle of a dark evening? Perhaps she was thanking him for making his intentions so very clear right from the start.

And was that what he was doing? Deliberately burning his bridges? Deliberately thumbing his nose at Belle?

But then what was Belle to him? When all was said and done, she had been brought here merely to entertain them. A sort of servant in the guise of a guest.

Devil take it, how dared she come here, upsetting him like this.

He bowed to Miss Beckford as she rose from the bench and extended an arm to her. She was tiny, no taller than his grandmother. The top of her head would not even bump his chin if she stood against him. And dainty.

She set her arm along his sleeve, and he smiled at her. And made rather a theatrical exit from the room, he had to admit to himself afterward. Normally he would have slunk out, knowing that everyone would realize where he was going and for what purpose and knowing that later or tomorrow he would have to endure the jocular and ribald teasing of the other males. But he did not slink. He was, he realized in some annoyance when it was too late to replay the scene, making an exit Belle could not fail to notice.

Chapter 4

She was frightened, he thought, looking down at her as they climbed the stairs together. She did not hesitate to follow his lead, and her arm did not tremble against his, but he could sense fear.

She appeared very young to him. He had considered in the course of the day, and particularly since teatime, whether he could be content with one so young: if he could be satisfied with the sort of companionship she would be able to offer, if he could be content with the inexperienced lovemaking she would bring to their marriage bed, if he could be happy with the idea of her as the mother of his children.

And he had concluded that yes, he could be content. Since he must marry soon—he was past thirty already— and since marriage was an alliance more than an emotional union, then she would suit him well enough. Her youth would be pleasant to behold for many years to come.

And yet now he was forced to contemplate the quite unexpected thought—would she be content with him? If she appeared very young to him, did he appear correspondingly old to her? It was a daunting and a humbling idea. He was so accustomed to having women showing their attraction to him—but mostly older women, it was true—that it came as something of a shock to realize that perhaps there was the woman who would not want him.

Perhaps Miss Juliana Beckford did not want him.

He freed her arm when they reached the gallery in order to set down the branch of candles on a shelf, from which it gave light to much of the long room, though not enough light to enable one to examine the portraits. The candles cast long shadows over the walls and across the coved ceiling.

Juliana shivered.

"You are cold?" he asked her, looking at her and knowing that it was not that at all despite the fact that it was December and there was no fire in the gallery.

She shook her head.

He stepped closer to her and set a finger beneath her chin so that she could not lower her head. "You are frightened," he said. "I'll not hurt you. Are you afraid of me?"

"No, sir," she said.

But he could see by the wideness of her eyes gazing into his that she was. And he felt afraid himself suddenly. Dealing with a very young lady, courting her instead of flirting or trying to coax her into his bed, was something new to his experience. Could he be gentle? Patient? And did he want to be? But it was too late to ask that question. It had been too late as soon as he had suggested bringing her up here. There was no going back now.

The thought threatened to bring panic with it until he remembered Belle downstairs in the drawing room. No, he was thankful that this had been arranged for him. And it was about time. And she was sweet and innocent and exquisitely pretty.

"Jack," he said, making the inevitability of it all a little more total. "I wish you would use my given name."

"Thank you, sir," she said and bit her lip.

He smiled. "We are intended for each other, Juliana," he said. "I suppose you realize that."

"Yes, sir." She was almost whispering.

"Do you find the thought offensive?" he asked.

"No, sir."

But it was impossible to know if she spoke the truth. And impossible to know if she was truly frightened or just understandably nervous.

"I brought you up here to kiss you," he said. "My grandmother realized that and yours, too, I believe. It is an acceptable stage of courtship, you see."

"Yes." She was whispering again.

"May I?" He cupped her face gently with his hands and waited for her answer. Her hair was silky. Her skin was petal smooth.

"Yes."

He kissed her, as he had not kissed a woman in more years than he could remember. As perhaps he had kissed Belle at first. Or perhaps not. The first time he had kissed Belle he had also bedded her.

He kissed gently, warmly, with closed lips. It was a kiss of lips only. He kept his body away from hers. He found the kiss mildly arousing. He wondered what it would be like, progressing from stage to stage with her. He wondered if there was a stage at which she would take fright and freeze or panic. He would find out, he supposed, after his marriage.

She did not panic now. Although she did not move at all, even to the extent of setting her hands at his waist or against his chest, her lips remained soft against his and even pushed back against them slightly.

He continued to hold her face in his hands when he lifted his head. "Very sweet, Juliana," he said. "Will you answer a question? Is this being forced upon you in any way? Are you at all reluctant for this courtship?" And could he expect an honest answer?

"It is not being forced upon me," she said. He noticed that she was looking directly back into his eyes. "I am of age for a husband, and Papa and Grandmama have chosen you as an eligible suitor for me."

"And you always do as you are told?" He smiled at her.

"I try, sir," she said.

He would have a sweet and biddable wife. And a lovely one. He would grow accustomed to the idea, he thought. He would be fortunate. He would be envied by other men.

But he was not at all sure that she would become accustomed to the idea.

"There is a whole week to go before Christmas," he said. "I will tell you what my grandmother has planned, though she has not deigned to discuss the matter with me. She plans that you and I will come to an agreement and I will

speak with your father and the matter will be settled in time
for an announcement on Christmas Day. There is to be a
dinner followed by a theatrical performance followed by a
ball. But there is a week between now and then."

"Yes," she said.

"I will wait almost a week," he said, "before making my
formal offer. Until Christmas Eve. I will not tie your hands
before then. If you cannot like me by then, I will shock
both my family and yours by not making the offer at all.
Does that sound fair?"

He knew that the week would avail him nothing. He had
passed the point at which he might have retreated. He had
come to Portland House, he had met and conversed with her,
and he had brought her to the gallery. There was no going
back for him. But he did not want her to be trapped. Perhaps
she already was. Perhaps a way out for her was as impossible
as it was for him. But he would not himself trap her into anything before she had had any chance to get to know him.

"I do not dislike you," she said.

He removed his hands at last, running one finger along
her jaw and beneath her chin as he did so. "Young ladies
who like me call me Jack," he said. "We will give it the
week. I cannot allow my grandmother to have things all her
way. Let her know some anxiety for a few days."

For the first time her smile looked relaxed and genuinely
amused. "Your grandmother, too?" she said.

"Are they not a pestilential breed?" He grinned at her.

"Yes, they are," she said, "Jack."

The effort to say his name aloud was so obviously an
enormous one that he had to check himself from laughing.

"Ah, we make giant strides," he said. "Have you seen
enough of the portraits?"

She nodded, her smile still amused.

"No one will ask you about them," he said, "so you must
not feel that you need to be knowledgeable. No one would
expect you even to have glanced at them. They would despise me heartily if they thought I had allowed it."

He offered her his arm and picked up the branch of candles and led her back to the stairs and the drawing room. It

was a satisfactory beginning, he thought. He liked her, and he believed that with effort and patience he might bring her to like him.

Could he love her? The question was not particularly relevant. But yes, he told himself, he could love her.

He had loved only once before. Totally, passionately, jealously, hopelessly. He had loved a woman who was not in the business of love, a woman who had used him and abused him and finally left him. And a woman he had had no business loving anyway. A woman who could not possibly have been his wife, the mother of his children. He had loved with all of a boy's lack of wisdom and moderation.

He cringed from the thought that she was in the drawing room, that first love of his, that she would be at Portland House over the Christmas holiday, an honored guest of his grandparents.

He was going to love Juliana as a man loved, wisely and gently and . . . Oh, Lord, he thought, he knew nothing about love.

Juliana slipped free of Jack's arm as soon as they had returned to the drawing room and seated herself beside her mother. It took all the training of years not to cringe and not to hide her face. Her mother smiled at her, and Juliana knew from the smile that her mother was well aware of the fact that she had just been kissed for the first time. And it seemed to her as she forced herself to look about the room that everyone there knew it, too, and was politely hiding the knowledge.

He had been unexpectedly kind and gentle. Although she had been terrified at first because she knew very well why she was being taken to the gallery, her fears had calmed. And the kiss had not been nearly as fearful as she had anticipated. Except that she had sensed that he had kissed her with restraint, that he might have done it quite differently. And so she would fear the next kiss and the next. Until her wedding night and the ultimate embrace. Not that she knew what exactly that involved. Her mother would tell her before her wedding day.

He had given her the coming week to be free, to get to

know him without committing herself to him. It was a kind
gesture. He did not know, perhaps, that she would find it
quite impossible now to go back. She had agreed to come
here. She had told Mama and Papa and Grandmama that
she was well content to come and to betroth herself to Mr.
Jack Frazer.

No, she could not withdraw from the commitment. But at
least now she felt better pleased with it. The cynicism she
had seen in his eyes had not made him a hard or a cold
man. She thought it might be possible to come to like him.

But, oh, she wished she did not seem such a child when
she was with him. She did not feel like a child, but she
knew she behaved like one. Was it because he treated her
like a child? He was almost too kind and too gentle. Did he
see her as a child? She cursed her small stature. And she
knew she must have kissed atrociously. She had not known
at all what to do except stand very still and allow it.

She was going to have to do better in the coming week.
She just wished she was not surrounded so almost exclu-
sively by his family.

She looked about her suddenly for the Comtesse de
Vacheron. There was someone, she felt, who might help
her overcome her gaucherie. The comtesse was perfectly
poised, perfectly in command of herself. Juliana admired
her immensely.

But the comtesse was not in the room.

"You have made a good beginning, my dear," her mother
said, leaning close to her ear so that no one else would
hear. "He did not keep you too long away, and you returned
to my side as soon as he brought you back. Well-done. I
knew I would be proud of you."

"Yes, Mama," Juliana said. "I try."

"Damme," Mr. Frederick Lynwood had said when Jack
left the drawing room with Juliana Beckford on his arm,
"but they make a handsome couple, don't they, though?
Brains, you see. Jack has brains and so she likes him."

"And so she should, Freddie, brains notwithstanding,"
Prudence Woolford said. "I used to consider it the cruelest

fate when I was younger that Jack and I were related. One's cousins ought not to be allowed to be so handsome." She sighed. "But then I met Anthony and recovered my spirits."

"And he likes her, too," Mr. Peregrine Raine said with a grin. "As what single man in his right mind would not? She is definitely a looker. Now I wonder what the two of them plan to do in the gallery. Gaze at portraits, do you think?"

"What else?" Viscount Clarkwell chuckled. "We gazed at portraits when we went up there on a similar occasion, did we not, Hortense?"

"Zeb!" that lady protested with a blush. "Of course we looked at pictures. *Are* there pictures in the gallery?" Her eyes widened in feigned innocence.

There was a general burst of laughter from their particular group.

"Jack did not even have the grace to slink out trying to look invisible," Viscount Merrick said. "He had definite plans, and he did not mind if we all knew about them."

"Alexander," his wife said reproachfully. "I think it is too bad that poor Jack's courtship has to be conducted in such a public setting and has to be a matter for general amusement. Just like everyone else's."

The viscount grinned fondly at her while Peregrine chuckled and Freddie followed suit, a little more heartily.

Anne's eyes met Isabella's apologetically. "You will think us all dreadfully vulgar, Isabella," she said. "Poor Jack—the one who just left the room, you know—has had a marriage arranged for him by Alexander's grandmother, the duchess, and everyone is gathered here to witness his discomfort and to tease him mercilessly at every available moment. I think it most unkind. Jack is not nearly as insensitive as everyone believes him to be. And Juliana is a very sweet and pretty girl."

"Damme but she is, too, Anne," Freddie said. "You are in the right of it there. Brains. Anne has brains."

"I hasten to add," Viscount Merrick said, laughing, "that it is benevolent witnessing and benevolent teasing that is proceeding here, Comtesse. We are family, you know, and rather fond of one another when all is said and done."

Yes, Isabella thought, all this definitely served her right. As if it would not have been hard enough to have arrived to find Jack betrothed or married, she was going to have to endure a week as an unwilling witness to his courtship of Juliana Beckford, culminating in his betrothal to her at Christmas, no doubt.

It was going to be impossible to bear. Except that nothing was impossible. She had lived most of her life with that philosophy, and she had proved it true numerous times. It would not be impossible. After all, Jack was someone from her distant past. There had been a marriage since then, family life, great leaps forward in the success of her career. Jack meant nothing to her now.

Nothing whatsoever.

"Families should be close enough to laugh with one another and tease one another," she said with a smile, and noticed all heads turn her way as if she had just made a wise and original pronouncement. She was becoming accustomed to such reactions. It had ceased to amaze her, though it had never ceased to amuse.

"Damme, yes," Freddie muttered. "I wonder if Bobbie was able to fall asleep in a strange nursery tonight. Do you think so, Anne? Maybe I should go and ask Ruby. She is sitting over there talking with Holyoke and his mama."

"The nursery will not be so very strange to Robert by now, Freddie," Anne said gently. "It is his fifth night there, is it not? Did you not arrive three days earlier than the rest of us?"

"As usual." Viscount Merrick chuckled as Freddie got to his feet and made his way toward his wife. "He has such a fear of forgetting appointments, Comtesse, that he invariably arrives a few days early even for the most mundane of occasions and then refuses to go away again for fear that he will forget at the appropriate time."

Isabella joined in the general laughter, tinged with affection for the portly Freddie, who was apparently not as swift as he might be.

She was feeling deeply depressed. Quite inexplicably depressed for someone who had just persuaded herself that Jack meant nothing whatsoever to her. He was in the gallery, wherever that was, with the very pretty and sweet young lady who wanted to be her friend. He was doubtless kissing her at this very moment. He was going to marry her.

Isabella wondered if he was kissing the girl with his mouth and his tongue as well as with his lips. In the old, remembered way. Though until her arrival at Portland House this afternoon and until she had set eyes on him again, she had forgotten—or packed away the memories in a safe corner of her mind that would no longer bring conscious pain. She had stopped remembering how he made love and how he made her feel—until today.

Why did it matter to her now? It did not matter. Oh, of course it did not matter.

Jack Frazer was someone who had played a minor role in a different lifetime.

"Speaking of strange nurseries," she said, getting to her feet and smiling warmly at the people gathered about her, "I have two young children of my own in unfamiliar surroundings. I must go and see that they are peacefully settled, if you will excuse me."

Marcel would be asleep. He could sleep anywhere, that boy. He had his father's placid disposition. But Jacqueline would be anxious and sleepless. She was a highly strung, insecure, sensitive child. Isabella tried hard not to love her more than she loved Marcel. And indeed she did not do so. She would gladly—oh, gladly—die for either of her children to save them from one moment's pain. But Jacqueline needed her love more or her closeness and her reassurance, anyway.

And her guidance. Marcel would go back to France when he was old enough, back to his father's estates, now his own. And he would fit in there, too, and be accepted by the family that had frowned upon his mother. But Jacqueline? She did not know what would become of her daughter.

"Of course. You must set your mind at rest." Viscount Merrick was on his feet and extending an arm to her. "Allow me to escort you, ma'am."

Fortunately—she almost held her breath the whole way—they did not meet Jack and his intended bride on the stairs. And she did not return to the drawing room that evening. She sent her excuses with Lord Merrick when he left her in the nursery, having assured himself that his own children were fast asleep. Jacqueline, on the other hand, was lying awake and needed the comfort of her mother's presence. Isabella pleaded tiredness after the day's journey and the viscount—he asked her to call him Alex—smiled with kindly understanding.

Not that he really understood at all, of course.

"Jack."

Her fingertips were playing up and down his spine, making him feel deliciously relaxed. Her voice was low and dreamy against his ear. "I am going to succeed. I am going to be recognized as the best there is."

She would, too. She had talent—sometimes he had to admit it to himself—and the fashionable world was beginning to take notice of the fact and flock to see her on the stage.

"And independent?" he said, lifting his face from the silky, fragrant pillow of her golden hair and opening his mouth over hers in a long and lazy kiss. "So that you can be free of me, Belle?"

"Yes," she said.

He was buried deep, though spent, in her warm, familiar depths. But he withdrew and moved to her side to lie on his back and stare upward. There it was for the first time—the first open admission that theirs was a liaison that had only practical functions. She made her body available for his sexual pleasure. He provided her with the wherewithal for survival while she built her career. But only while she built it. Once she had reached a point at which she could live independently, she would need him no longer. She would want him no longer.

He had known it from the start.

Except that he loved her with his life, and had imagined in her eyes and in her body as he used it a return of that love.

Poor twenty-one-year-old infant, he thought in self-mockery, sick with unrequited love for his paid mistress. For his first woman. He had hardly known what to do or how to find what he was looking for the first time he had bedded her. And he had shattered in her with embarrassing speed.

He felt his eyesight blur. He felt hot tears on his cheeks. And then, before he realized it was about to happen, he heard the loud sob that would betray his imbecility to her.

Jack struggled upward, dismayed and humiliated, and swung his legs sharply over the side of the bed, flinging back the bedclothes with one arm as he did so. He was on his feet, struggling to draw air into his lungs, looking about him for a route of escape when he came awake.

God! Good God in heaven! He muttered a few more blasphemies aloud and raked the fingers of one hand through his hair.

He had had a hundred women since Belle. Perhaps hundreds. Why the devil had it been her fingers he had felt on his spine in that dream and her hair he had smelled and her body he had been sheathed inside? Why not Lady Finlay-Dodd, his most recent bedfellow?

But thank God for one thing, he thought as he strode into his dressing room and rang for his valet and his shaving water. The reality had been a little different from the dream. In reality he had neither shed tears nor sobbed. He had disguised the hurt he had felt quite admirably. He could still remember what he had said, one hand flung carelessly over his eyes.

"Just be a good girl and give me some advance warning when the times come, then, will you, Belle?" he had said, and he had yawned deliberately, tired after sex. "So that I can have another whore ready to replace you?" The first time he had used that word to her. A word he had used more times afterward, a sure accompaniment to pain.

He had been very badly hurt. And so with all a young man's unsubtle viciousness, he had wanted to hurt in his turn. He doubted if he had succeeded. But he had succeeded in making himself feel ashamed.

He thought very deliberately about Juliana while he shaved and dressed. Sweet child. Sweet innocent. He had felt a definite tenderness, a protective sort of tenderness, for her last evening in the gallery. He was going to convert that tenderness into love within the coming week, he had vowed. He renewed the vow now. And he was going to be gentle with her and convert her timidity into love for him.

He chuckled without any real mirth as he left his room. That old fiend, Grandmama! A few days ago in town he had been free and had even been half contemplating ignoring her summons. He had not realized just how advanced her plans were for marrying him off, though he might have guessed. Certainly Juliana herself seemed to have been brought here on the understanding that a marriage had been arranged. And a mere two days after his arrival—less—he was quite securely caught in the trap that had been set for him.

Not that he wanted to be free of it any longer, of course. He had decided that yesterday.

He paused suddenly when he was still almost at the top of the staircase on his way down. And the lady—the woman—who was on her way up paused, too. And then they both resumed their course. She was dressed for the outdoors. She must have been out walking already. He knew that he had slept late. He had been detained in bed by pleasant dreams! He clenched his teeth.

"Good morning," she murmured as they were about to pass. She did not raise her eyes to his.

He took a step to the side, blocking her path, and she looked up at him. With green and surprised eyes.

"What do you want?" she asked after a few moments of silence.

"Some privacy," he said. "Outside. Now."

She looked assessingly at him as he clamped his teeth together again. "Very well," she said at last, her voice low and self-possessed. She turned to walk down the stairs again, but did not wait for his escort.

His grandfather's head footman always kept a few cloaks secreted away somewhere in the hall. He had one over his arm by the time Jack reached the bottom of the stairs and offered it with a bow. Jack took it and threw it roughly about his shoulders. He was feeling angry enough to commit murder.

Chapter 5

They walked in silence along the terrace and past the rose arbor onto the lawn that led to trees and the stream and the marsh lakes. He did not offer his arm. She made no move to take it.

"Well?" he said at last, his voice steely with fury. "Explain yourself, ma'am."

Her voice was infuriatingly calm and quiet. "I beg your pardon?" she said.

"Don't pretend not to comprehend my meaning, Belle," he said. "What are you doing here? How dared you come here?"

"I am here at the invitation of the Duke and Duchess of Portland," she said. "At their request, I am to put on a performance of my acting skills for their guests at Christmas. In the meantime, my children and I are to enjoy their hospitality for the holiday."

"How much are they paying you?" he asked viciously. "I do not doubt they are making it well worth your while."

He thought she was not going to answer and resisted the urge to grab her arms and shake her until her head flopped on her neck. They were still within sight of some of the windows of the house.

"The duke and duchess are far too well-bred to have offered me payment," she said at last. "Unlike their grandson who is ill-bred enough to ask me such a question."

This was better. He could hear a slight quiver of anger in her voice.

"Their grandson, yes," he said. "I am glad you have remembered the relationship, Belle. And you talk of good breeding? How could you accept the invitation? For all of a year you were their grandson's whore." He flinched after saying the word. He had only ever called her that when he was feeling hurt, he had told himself less than an hour ago.

She smiled slightly as her chin came up. In profile, with her head lifted proudly and that half smile on her lips, she looked incredibly beautiful, he thought irrelevantly.

"Ah, yes," she said. "How could I possibly forget when you called me that more than once during that year? I became very familiar with that word. You have not lost it from your vocabulary, then."

"What would you call yourself?" he asked harshly.

"What?" She raised her eyebrows and thought for a moment. "Widow. Mother. Actress. Woman. Oh, and yes, your word, too, Jack, I suppose. Undoubtedly I whored for you, did I not? You paid me well enough and used me often enough."

Somehow she looked magnificent with lifted head and bitterly smiling lips and flashing eyes.

It was stupid how pain could be almost as sharp in memory as it had been in actuality. Even after nine years of scarcely thinking about her at all, there were still wounds and there was still pain. Anger was ebbing away from him.

"You ought not to have come, Belle," he said.

"No." She had never been one to avoid his eyes. She did not avoid them now. "I ought not. But I did. And I am staying. My children need a home like this and company like this in which to celebrate Christmas."

"Your children," he said. He felt a bleakness to match her eyes, remembering that she had experienced marriage and motherhood in the years since she had been his— woman.

"They are innocent, Jack," she said. "They know nothing of the sordid side of life that adults learn of fast enough and often become involved with. They are children. I will protect them from all that is sordid with my life if necessary. Do not call me *that* in their hearing."

They had stopped walking and were standing face-to-face, well out of sight of the house.

"You are the Comtesse de Vacheron," he said, his voice low and bitter, "and now England's most famous actress. You do not need to augment your income in any other way now, do you?"

"No," she said.

"Was he good to you, Belle?" He did not want to know. He could not think why he had asked.

"Yes." She nodded.

"How old are your children?" He did not want to know that either. He did not want to think of her conceiving another man's children, large with another man's child, rather as Lisa was large with Perry's right now. Not Belle. He did not want to think of Belle that way.

"My daughter is seven," she said. "She was born nine months after our marriage."

The Comte de Vacheron had waited for his marriage bed with her, then. And had then wasted no time at all. He did not want to hear this, Jack thought, and turned to walk back in the direction of the house.

"Marcel is five," she said, falling into step beside him. "He looks very like Maurice and shares his quiet good nature."

Maurice—she pronounced it the French way. The man who had been her husband. The man who had fathered two children on her. It was nine years since he had known her, Jack thought. He really did not know her at all any longer. He must be just a very distant memory to her. So distant that she had not hesitated to accept this invitation to spend Christmas at Portland House with his family. And with him.

He meant nothing to her.

Of course he meant nothing to her.

Just as she meant nothing to him.

"Stay away from me, Belle," he said, "for the next week or so. And stay away from Miss Juliana Beckford. She and I are to be married. Our betrothal is to be announced on Christmas Day. I love her—very dearly. I want you to stay well away from us. Is that clear?"

"I did not seek you out this morning, if you will remember," she said calmly. "Why should I do so, Jack? So that I might be hung with that so-charming label that you are always so eager to drape about my neck? So that I might be reminded of a year I had forgotten and would far rather not be forced to remember? I have a life to live and children to live it with. I will be quite happy to ignore your very existence."

"We are agreed, then," he said stiffly. "It is as well."

"Yes," she said, "it is as well."

He stared ahead as they made their way back to the house in silence. And he clamped his jaws together again, remembering the dream that had sent him hurtling from bed and into wakefulness just a couple of hours ago. He was terrified that he might reenact the final part of that dream. There was a soreness in his throat and up behind his nose that had nothing to do with any impending chill or cold.

He could not remember when he had last cried. He was certainly not going to start again now.

And for what? What was there to cry about?

She would rather not be forced to remember that year of love and beauty and foolish dreams.

Ah, Belle.

He fought the tears.

And walked beside a stranger who had once meant all the world to him.

"Hello," the fair-haired little boy said, smiling sweetly. "I am Marcel Gellée. Who are you?"

Juliana clasped her hands together and smiled back. Oh, he must be the comtesse's son. He spoke with a charming French accent.

"Juliana Beckford, Mr. Gellée," she said, holding out her right hand. "I am pleased to make your acquaintance."

She had come to the nursery because Anne and Hortense—she was beginning to learn their names—spent most of their mornings there, they had told her. And because she liked children. With children there needed to be no pretense.

"That is my sister, Jacquie," he said, pointing to a thin,

dark child, who was reading to Anne's little Catherine. "And this is my friend, Kenneth. He wants to ride on the rocking horse, but I cannot lift him that high and the nurses are busy."

Kenneth Stewart sucked his thumb and watched her. He looked very like his father, Juliana thought. And therefore like Mr. Frazer, too. She wondered if her own children would look so and shied away from the thought. She lifted the infant into her arms and crossed the room to the rocking horse, Marcel trotting at her side and talking almost ceaselessly.

And then he spotted his mother coming into the nursery and ran to meet her.

Juliana had always imagined that a famous person would look different from others, larger than life in some way. The Comtesse de Vacheron looked reassuringly ordinary as she smiled at her son and stooped to kiss him before taking his hand and coming across to the rocking horse.

"Has Marcel been talking your head off?" she asked. "He has a tendency to do that. I thought that moving to England would slow him down for a while, but he learned English in an unbelievably short time."

There was color in the comtesse's cheeks. And her hair looked somewhat windblown.

"Oh, you have been outside for a walk already," Juliana said. "I wish I had known. I would have come with you. I am not a late riser, you see. I have lived all my life in the country."

"I, too, wish I had known." The comtesse smiled.

Marcel was rocking the horse while Kenneth squealed with delight.

"I so desperately need someone to talk to," Juliana said in a rush, and then she bit her lip. Perhaps the comtesse would not be interested in her concerns. She was a great lady. But she was still smiling. She looked warm and friendly.

"You know why I am here." Juliana said. "Everyone knows. It is far more—public than I expected. And I feel so very much more alone than I expected even though my family is here with me and his family are friendly and kind."

Isabella did not answer for a few moments. "But sometimes you feel the need to pour out your heart to someone who is in effect just a friendly stranger," she said. "Is it a match you cannot like?"

"No," Juliana said quickly. "It is perfect in every way."

Again there was a pause. "But?" Isabella prompted quietly.

"Oh, there are no buts," Juliana said with a sigh. "I do not really know what I wanted to talk about. It is just that everyone knows we are to be betrothed, and everyone knew why he took me to the gallery last evening, and even Mama and Grandmama were not outraged but thought it all very satisfactory. Just as if there are no—no feelings involved in such an arrangement. I was kissed for the first time last evening." She could feel herself blushing hotly. "You will think me very foolish for being all a-flutter over such a thing."

"No," Isabella said.

"But it was an event in my life," Juliana said. "And this whole week is an event. I want it to be the most glorious event of my life. I want to be able to remember how wonderful it was. I want to fall in love with him and feel that I am the happiest woman in the world."

"But you cannot?" Isabella asked.

"Is it unrealistic?" Juliana asked. "You have been married, and I believe you must know a great deal about life. There is an air of assurance about you that I admire greatly. Does such a thing exist—love and romance and that feeling that the world is colored golden because there is that special man and mutual love between you and him? Does it exist outside my imagination? Or am I being foolishly naive?"

She watched as the comtesse closed her eyes briefly. They looked rather sad when she opened them again. "Oh, it exists, Juliana," she said. "It does. But so does another kind of love, a quieter, warmer, more comfortable kind. That is what you will learn of life, perhaps, as I have. That there are many kinds of love, each of infinite value in its own way. The one you describe is every woman's dream, and perhaps every man's, too. If we are fortunate, we know it once in our lives, even if only briefly. Perhaps a few people know it for a lifetime."

"I am sorry," Juliana said. "I have made you sad. You felt that way about your husband? I did not mean to awaken painful memories."

But the comtesse smiled at her. "Perhaps you will fall in love with—with Mr. Frazer," she said. "He is very handsome."

"Yes," Juliana agreed, "and kind, too. I did not think he would be because of his eyes. He has world-weary eyes. But he was kind. He told me he will not make a formal offer until Christmas Eve so that if I want to be free of the commitment, I may. I-I like him."

But they were interrupted at that moment by the arrival of a servant requesting the favor of the Comtesse de Vacheron's presence in the duchess's private sitting room.

"I hope I have not bored you," Juliana said anxiously. Suddenly it seemed unpardonably presumptuous to have burdened the great actress with her own girlish turmoil over her first kiss.

"Not at all," Isabella said with a warm smile. "We all need friends, Juliana."

"And so you must tell me what you will need to assist you in your performance," the Duchess of Portland said. "Anything in the way of props or costumes, that is. I have seen you act, my dear, and know that even if you dressed in a sack and stood on a bare stage, you could bring any audience in the world to its feet or dissolve it into tears. But I am quite sure it would be uncomfortable to wear a sack and stand in the middle of a bare stage."

"Thank you for your kind words of praise, Your Grace," Isabella said. "I hope I will deserve them on Christmas Day."

A wheezing sort of rumble brought her eyes to the mountain of a man—the duke—who was seated beside the fire in the duchess's private sitting room. It was easy, looking at him, to believe that he was the tyrant of a man she had been led to believe he was.

"I have not seen you act, Countess," he said. "The gout keeps me at home. But if Her Grace says you can bring an audience to its feet or dissolve it into tears, then it is so. Her Grace is not given to flattery."

Isabella felt chastened and curiously touched. Despite appearances, she had the feeling that she was in the presence of a rare phenomenon—an elderly couple deeply attached to each other. Jack's grandparents. She hastily closed her mind to the thought.

She turned it gratefully to the familiar world of her work. After the deeply disturbing encounter with Jack, she had hoped to make a quick visit to the nursery to greet her children and then retreat to her room for an hour or two to lick her wounds in private. Perhaps this was better. She did not need to think about the past. She had buried it long ago. And she did not need to think of the present. Juliana Beckford was a sweet girl. Jack would be fortunate to have her as a bride. She wished them happy. She really did. She had her work, and when all was said and done, it had always meant more to her than anything or anyone else.

Except Jack. The thought came unbidden and was ignored. And except for her children.

"I thought to perform some excerpts from Shakespeare," she said. "Not too many and not too lengthy. I am sure that your guests will be eager to begin the dancing quite soon after dinner. Perhaps three? I believe you suggested an hour. There are some glorious female parts in Shakespeare."

"*Romeo and Juliet* has always affected me deeply," the duchess said. "Juliet has some very moving speeches in the play."

"If you will pardon me," Isabella said, "I will avoid that play, Your Grace. Juliet is fourteen years old and thinks and behaves like a fourteen-year-old. I am always made rather uncomfortable when I see her part assigned to a sea-

soned actress, as it almost invariably is. I am almost thirty
years old."

The duke rumbled. "You look ten years younger, Countess," he said gallantly.

Isabella smiled warmly at him. She liked him, grim and
forbidding appearance notwithstanding.

"I rather fancy Portia's courthouse scene in *The Merchant of Venice*," she said. "And Desdemona's death scene
from *Othello*. And perhaps a scene from *The Taming of the
Shrew*. There is rather a nice contrast among the three parts,
I believe."

"Splendid!" The duchess clasped her hands to her
bosom. "Oh, quite splendid. I can scarce wait. Can you, my
love?" She turned to beam at her husband. "But how can
you do it alone, my dear? Will you not need some support-
ing actors?"

"Ideally," Isabella said, "I suppose I should have a Shylock and an Othello and a Petruchio at the very least. But
you could hardly invite a whole company of actors here. I
will manage without, Your Grace. Perhaps someone could
be persuaded to sit beside the stage and read certain
speeches that are essential to the flow of the relevant
scene."

The duchess, who had sat down beside her husband, got
to her feet again with the energy of a young girl. The deep
rumblings that came from somewhere inside the duke's
chest were a chuckle, Isabella realized suddenly.

"Now you have started something, Countess," he said
and rumbled again.

"But, my dear," the duchess said, "you do not know, do
you? This family has a long history of performing theatricals. We have many accomplished and experienced actors.
It will be no trouble at all to persuade some of them to act
with you. Any of them would be honored and delighted."

The duke's rumblings had brought on a coughing fit, and
the two ladies were forced to sit and watch him in some
concern for a few moments until he recovered.

"You are quite right, my love," the duchess said to him
as if they had spent those moments in conversation with

each other. "The last time we had a play performed here—
it was *She Stoops to Conquer,* my dear, on the occasion of
our fiftieth wedding anniversary—there was almost a family mutiny. And I promised that it would never happen
again. But it was such a resounding success that I have regretted that promise. This would not be the same as breaking it. You would do all the significant acting, Lady de
Vacheron. Our own actors would be almost in the way of
props."

Isabella smiled. "I would hate to be the cause of mutiny,
ma'am," she said.

"Nonsense!" the duchess said briskly. "I will only have
to mention this downstairs, and all my nephews and nieces
and grandchildren will be fighting duels for the honor of as-
sisting you. Leave it to me, my dear."

The duke patted her hand when she sat down again, and
then curled his fingers about it to hold it in his great paw.

"Well," Isabella said, "it would certainly help, ma'am.
Just a very few rehearsals for those concerned would be
sufficient. I would not expect them really to act or know
their lines by heart. I would not willingly cause anyone
great inconvenience, especially at Christmastime."

"My dear," the duchess said, "you do not know my family and their extreme pride in their acting. Oh, this is going
to be many times more wonderful than I imagined. Is it not,
my love?"

The duke rumbled.

Isabella had something very definite to think about when
she left the duchess's sitting room. And although she had
looked forward to the relaxation of a type of holiday, she
rushed thankfully back to work now. As she had always
done. Her work had always been extremely important to
her, but she knew, too, that sometimes she had used it in
order to escape from boredom or unhappiness. Occasion-
ally she had used it in order to stay sane, in order to give
herself a reason for going on living.

She had a great deal of work to do. She must view the
ballroom and become accustomed to its size and its atmosphere and acoustics. She must plan simple costumes and

props. She knew already the parts she would act, but she would need to polish them up. And she would need to decide what other characters and speeches were essential to the scenes she had chosen. She had promised to give the duchess a list after luncheon. And then she must decide how many rehearsals would be necessary for each scene and when they were to be held.

Oh, yes, there was a great deal with which to occupy herself for the coming week—less than a week already. She would not have to think. She would not have time for thought.

Her fellow actors were to be drawn from the duke and duchess's family. Who? she wondered. Who were their best actors?

Jack was a member of the family.

But Jack, even if he was one of the best, even if he was asked, would refuse a part. *Stay away from me, Belle,* he had said to her just that morning.

She need not worry about that, at least.

Chapter 6

"I have a premonition," Claude Raine said. "A dark and gloomy premonition."

"No," Hortense said. "It cannot be that. It must have something to do with the Christmas preparations. There will be all the greenery to gather and the ballroom and drawing room and dining room to decorate."

"And the hall," Celia added.

"It is more than that," Claude insisted. "I have a premonition."

"It had better not be what you think it is, Claude," Alex said, "and what we all think it is. I have sworn to do murder over that."

"Isabella has been invited here to do the acting," Anne said, her voice quietly reassuring. "We were told we could relax."

"Grandmama did mention a musical evening last night," Jack said, grimacing. "It is probably that."

But Claude stood in the middle of the morning room, looking thunderous and shaking his head. He had a premonition, and a mere musical evening was not important enough to have brought it on.

They had been summoned, all of them—all of the duchess's family, that was—to the morning room immediately following luncheon, and they had all arrived there, obedient and darkly grumbling.

They turned and fell silent when the duchess herself appeared, a diminutive and smiling tyrant whom any one of the men could have picked up with one hand and crushed to powder. Instead of which she had been allowed to run loose for years, tormenting them and ruling and blighting their lives. Or so Martin Raine was heard to whisper to Maud Frazer.

The duchess clapped her hands for silence, a habitual but totally unnecessary gesture.

"I have a treat in store for you, my dears," she said.

There was a collective groan from her ungrateful relatives.

"Absolutely not, Grandmama," Jack said boldly. "I refuse point-blank to do whatever it is you have planned for me on the grounds that you brought me here for another purpose entirely. Besides, you once accused me of being too lazy to walk out of my own shadow. You were quite right."

The duchess waited patiently for this brazen speech of insurrection to come to an end.

"And so you were, dear boy," she said. "You were fourteen years old and all your cousins had been taken to the stables as a treat to help groom the horses ready for Stanley and Celia's wedding, and you fell asleep in the hay."

"We punished him suitably for that offense, Grandmama," Alex said. "We rolled him in the manure pile. Don't you remember?"

Freddie giggled. "Damme but we did, too, Alex," he said. "And got our backsides tanned for it by Grandpapa."

"There is some justice in the world," Jack said.

The duchess clapped her hands for order again. "Some of you," she said, "not all, unfortunately, are going to have the extraordinary honor and pleasure of acting with the Comtesse de Vacheron." She beamed at them all with benevolent goodwill.

A few of her relatives looked interested. Most groaned. Jack turned cold.

"Not me, Grandmama," he said. "I have other interests to occupy my time. As you are well aware."

"Sit down, Jack," his grandmother said kindly. He had got to his feet during the previous speech. "You are one of our best actors, and one of the handsomest. Besides, one of the surest ways to impress a lady is to act out a romantic part before her very eyes."

"We all remember, Jack," Stanley said, "how all the ladies were falling all over their slippers and frock hems and fans to be noticed by you at the ball following our last play. Not that matters are much different ordinarily," he added dryly.

"Grandmama." Jack had remained on his feet. "I am not acting with the Comtesse de Vacheron. That is my one and final answer." And it was, too. This was one matter on which she was not to be allowed to have her way.

"You would have our honored guest feel slighted, Jack?" she said.

"To be honest with you, Grandmama," he said, "I do not really care how she feels. After all, she is only a—"

She looked at him with haughtily raised eyebrows, waiting for the completion of his sentence. Everyone else looked at him with heightened interest.

"—An actress," he said lamely.

"But a great one, dear," she said. "And a French countess, too. I will not have her snubbed in my house because she is on the stage. Grandpapa would not have it. Grandpapa invited the comtesse here, and he will insist on absolute courtesy being shown her."

Grandpapa invited her! Hell!

"You will show her absolute courtesy, dear?" his grandmother asked him kindly.

He sat down again. "Yes, Grandmama," he said, the meek schoolboy again.

His mother, he noticed, was fanning herself with a lace handkerchief.

The duchess smiled at him. "The dear comtesse will have the main part in each excerpt, of course," she said. "But it will be impossible for her to act alone. I assured her that my family members would like nothing better than to assist her by playing the other parts in her chosen scenes. All the scenes are from Shakespeare plays."

This time the collective groan was so muted as to be more of a collective sigh.

Freddie sighed more loudly than the others. "I would have liked a part, Grandmama," he said. "But I don't have the brains. I can never remember my lines, and even when I do, I cannot remember when to speak them. All I had to do last time was laugh."

"And you did it exceedingly well, Freddie," his grandmother assured him. "This time you can try the part of Gratiano in *The Merchant of Venice*. All he really does is crow with delight when he sees Shylock being bested by Portia at the trial. The comtesse will be Portia, of course."

"Damme," Freddie said, not quite speechless. "Well, damme."

Martin was to be Antonio, the merchant of Venice, Stanley was to be Bassanio, Portia's husband and Antonio's friend, and Peregrine, the family's star actor, was to be Shylock.

"I like it," Perry said, grinning and rubbing his hands together. "I have always fancied the part of Shylock. He is so deliciously, greasily evil."

"Well, you have it, dear," his great-aunt said fondly.

"Alex is to be Petruchio in two short scenes from *The Taming of the Shrew,*" the duchess announced.

"Good Lord," Alex said. "What was that I said about committing murder?"

"No, dear," his grandmother said. "You do not murder her, dreadfully vulgar as she is at the start. You wed her and then tame her."

"Hm," her grandson said.

"There may be a few other small parts," the duchess said. "I will keep Prudence, Constance, and Hortense in mind, and Anthony, Zebediah, and Samuel."

Zeb muttered something under his breath.

"I would rather not, Grandmama," Hortense said. "And I have a very good reason. Perhaps two." She glanced at her husband and blushed.

"Perhaps Anne . . ." Alex began hopefully.

But the duchess held up a hand. "I need Anne for the part of Emilia in *Othello*," she said.

"Oh, Grandmama," Anne said, "I am no actress."

"This is your fault entirely, Anne," Claude said. "You learned your part so thoroughly last time and rehearsed so conscientiously and acted so convincingly on the night, that you assured yourself a spot on Aunt Jemima's star list forever after. Don't complain now."

Jack waited in cold despair. It was so obvious as to be almost like a fist about to collide with his nose.

"And you, Jack, dear," his grandmother said at last, turning to look quite steadily at him, "are to be Othello in Desdemona's death scene. Who better to play the part of such a misguided and passionate lover than our handsomest and one of our most accomplished actors?"

The devil! Oh, devil take it.

"Oh." Prudence sighed and then chuckled. "How fortunate the Comtesse de Vacheron is, Jack, even if you do murder her in that scene. I was your love interest in the last play. Remember?"

"When Miss Beckford sees you as Othello, Jack, she will swoon quite away with terror and pity," Peregrine said. "Kisses in the gallery will be nothing to this."

"Kisses in the gallery?" Alex said with a frown. "Who has been stealing kisses in the gallery? Never you last evening, Jack. I thought you went up there to show Miss Beckford the portraits."

"Has someone been stealing kisses in the gallery?" Hortense asked with a little shriek. "My brother, Jack? This is too much for my delicate feminine sensibilities and for my even more delicate condition." She did a fair imitation of a swoon into Peregrine's arms.

Jack got to his feet and walked very deliberately to the door. He turned with his hand on the knob to glare at his raucously amused family.

"You can go to hell, the lot of you," he said, and left the room, closing the door with ominous quietness behind his back.

Hortense shrieked again. "Did someone just say a naughty word?" she said, and launched herself backward into Perry's arms again.

"Hortense," Anne said quietly, "he was not joking. He meant it."

Hortense sat up, her face suddenly serious.

"Grandmama," Alex said, "I think this courtship business has Jack rattled."

"It is about time, dear," she said complacently. "Jack has taken nothing seriously for years. Now, Claude. As usual, dear, you must be our theatrical director. Not that the comtesse will need directing, of course. The very idea is an insult to her. But everyone else will. You will see to it?" It was not really a question despite the inflection of her voice.

"Of course, Aunt," he said meekly.

Ruby had decided to walk over to the rectory in the village to visit her parents, taking Robert with her. And wherever his beloved Ruby and Bobbie went, Freddie must go, too, of course. And since no one had anything particular to do for the rest of the afternoon and it appeared that the coming days were going to be busier than anticipated—though they might have guessed that the duchess would think of something to occupy their every waking moment, Martin commented to Maud—a large group also decided that it would be a good idea to pay their respects to the Fitzgeralds. And to take their offspring to be introduced and admired.

Jack did not join them. He was feeling rather ashamed and rather sheepish after his outburst in the morning room. It would be said that he could not take a teasing when he had always been the prime teaser of the family. It would be said that he was not a good sport.

He would have returned to London without further ado, he thought, and pursued Reggie and his Cyprians into the country if it had not been for Juliana Beckford, who had been led to believe that a very definite marriage had been arranged for her. He could not abandon her and humiliate her in front of her own family and his. Besides, if he left Portland House now, after his outburst, he would never be able to face any of them again.

He found Juliana in one of the salons with her mother and a group of older ladies, including his mother, begged permission to remove her from their company for a while, and was graciously granted it. Older ladies had a very special way of smirking when a courtship of which they approved was in progress. He bore off his lady to the conservatory.

He took her hand in his after he had seated them among the potted ferns, and looked down at dainty fingers with short, clean nails and smooth skin. Her hand was lost in his own. A child's hand. She looked exquisitely lovely in an unadorned pale blue wool dress that accentuated her shapely slimness. He wanted to gather her up into his arms and protect her from all harm for the rest of his life. He wanted to fall in love with her.

"You are to act with the comtesse," she said. "You must be very excited. Howard says she is a magnificent actress, that all the fashionable world flocks to see her every performance in town."

Excited. What a strange word. He did not believe he had been excited about anything for years and years. He smiled. "So they say," he said.

"You have not seen her for yourself?" she asked, her eyes wide.

"Not for many years," he said. "But she was good even then."

He had resented her talent a little. Oh, no, it had been more than just a little. He had resented that look of sparkling exhilaration with which she had sometimes rushed into his arms after a particular success and her expectation that he shared her hopes and dreams. He had wanted her to be wholly dependent upon him. He had dreaded her independence. And he had hated the adulation of other men. And her capitulation to that admiration.

"Your mother and your aunt and great-aunt say that you will do well acting with her," Juliana said with a smile. "I think you will, too."

"Do you?" He smiled back at her, touched by her open charm.

"You look like a romantic hero," she said.

"Do I?" Did she classify Othello as a romantic hero? He raised her hand to his lips, kissed the back of it, and then each finger one at a time. She watched him, her face flushed.

"Yes," she said.

"You have never been to town?" he asked. "Or to the theater?" But of course she had not. She must have been in the schoolroom until very recently. Perhaps until last week.

She shook her head and swallowed as he turned her hand over to kiss her palm.

"You are expected to marry," he said, "before you have had a come-out and a Season and a chance to be admired and to look about you. Do you resent that?"

"No," she said. "I have never wanted a Season."

"And yet," he said, "you are exquisitely lovely. Is it fair that I have no competition? That I have the chance to win you so easily?" He had had a great deal of competition once upon a time and had lost. But on that occasion, of course, he had been vying for the favors of an actress, not for the hand of a young lady of quality. "What do you want?" he asked her. "What do you hope for from life?"

She watched as he set his palm against hers and spread his fingers along hers. The contrast in size was almost laughable. And the delicacy of her skin made his appear sun-bronzed.

"To have a quiet and pleasant home," she said, "and a kind and amiable husband. To be able to please him and make him comfortable. To have a few children."

Oh, Lord. He was terrified suddenly. They were such very modest hopes. But could he possibly be the man to make her dreams come true? A quiet home? An amiable husband? Submitting himself to being made comfortable by her? He had images of her tripping toward him with his slippers whenever he came in from outside and rushing up to his chair with a cushion for his back and a stool for his feet every time he sat down. She was going to be a sweet and perfect wife for someone—for him.

She was looking at him a little anxiously, and he laced his fingers with hers and clasped her hand warmly.

"And you?" she said. "What do you want of life?"

Something to take away the lethargy and the boredom.

Something to make it alive again. Something to make it worth living. But where was that something to be found? In women? In carousing? In gambling? In attending more and more parties and balls? He had tried them all, yet his life was becoming emptier with every year that passed. Perhaps it was time he tried something different.

He lowered his head and took her lips with his—lightly and lingeringly. He would not part his lips or taste her with his tongue, though he considered doing both. He would not outrage or frighten her.

"You," he said, pulling back a couple of inches and looking into her eyes. "I want to make you happy, Juliana."

Briefly, speedily hidden, there was a look of fright in her eyes. He had spoken too fervently. He drew back and smiled at her.

"I think I should go back to Mama now," she said.

"Yes." He got to his feet, still smiling, and took both her hands in his to assist her to hers. "I must not keep you away too long. I would not harm your reputation by even one jot, Juliana."

He wondered as she stood before him, a dainty doll of a little beauty, how one made love gently. Gently enough not to hurt and not to frighten or disgust. It was something he was going to have to learn on his wedding night and practice for the rest of his life. Perhaps that was what his life needed, concern for someone else instead of an endless search for personal pleasure—or for what he had once known and lost.

His relationship with Belle had started gently, too. He had often seen her walking alone in the park, a quietly yet neatly dressed and breathtakingly beautiful young girl. He had started to go there every day just in hope of catching a glimpse of her. And finally he had come upon her seated beside the Serpentine, watching the swans. He had sat beside her in silence for five minutes or so. He had been very young and very gauche. And then they had talked. For two whole weeks they had talked almost daily. She was a working girl, she had told him. She had seemed eminently respectable. He had not touched her in those two weeks, only admired her with his eyes and dreamed of her at night with a young man's ardor. He had been deeply in love with her before he had seen her on the stage one evening, acting a minor role, but attracting all the attention—in the form of whistles and ribald remarks—from the pit.

He had been first stunned and then angry. She had deceived him. Everyone knew that actresses were also whores. She had made a fool of him. The following afternoon he had taken a room at a somewhat shabby inn before going to the park. And he had taken her there—as he had expected, she put up no resistance—and lost his virginity with her there, an embarrassingly fumbling performance about which she did not either complain or sneer.

After getting up from the bed and dressing and standing facing the window while she dressed and pulled the covers back over the bed, he had offered to set her up in her own establishment, and she had accepted. He had still been in love with her and had wanted to lay his gentleness, his concern, his devotion at her feet. He had wanted to redeem her, to rescue her from the necessity of selling her body to multiple buyers. Poor fool of a boy. And yet for a year—or for almost a year—he had found a happiness he had not known since, but had sought restlessly. Happiness and anxiety and ultimate betrayal.

It would be different this time. This time the lady of his choice was not an actress.

It looked and sounded as if the house was under invasion as Jack led Juliana into the hall on their way back to the salon. The double doors to the outside stood open, the hall was filled with people, and everyone was talking or shrieking or bellowing at once. The family had returned from the rectory.

Ruby was instructing Freddie to set Robert down since he was quite capable of walking up the stairs on his own legs, but Robert was clinging stubbornly to his father's hair, and Freddie was good-naturedly indicating his pain. Connie was loudly protesting that she and Sam had not brought up the rear merely so that they might steal kisses unobserved, and Sam was declaring smugly that they had no need any longer to steal kisses. Lisa was complaining that the walk had exhausted her with all the extra weight she had to carry with her. But she shrieked her protest when Perry offered to carry her upstairs to her room, and told him smartly to behave himself. Alex was laughing as he set Catherine's feet on the floor, and Prue's Alice rushed to take her place on his shoulder. Prue was scolding and explaining to her daughter that Uncle Alex already had Kenneth on one shoulder and that was enough. Zeb was bellowing at the twins to stop shoving each other or he would lay a hand to each of their backsides, and then bobbed and feinted in front of them, shadowboxing, until they shrieked with laughter.

It was a typical scene of mature dignity at Portland House. Jack looked down apologetically at Juliana. "This is not exactly the quiet home of your dreams, is it?" he said.

And then he was assaulted by a grinning near-stranger who slapped his shoulder and pumped his hand.

"Jack," he said. "How are you, old fellow? Just as handsome as ever, I see, making the rest of us poor mortals want to crawl back into our holes. Why did you not come calling with everyone else? Despite the crush—the old house was almost bulging on all four sides—Mama remarked on your absence. But then Mama always did have a soft spot for a pretty male face."

"Fitz!" Jack returned the handshake and the grin. Bertrand Fitzgerald, the rector's son, had always romped with them during their childhood visits to Portland House as had Ruby, Addie, and Rose, his sisters. He had always been the boys' partner in crime. "It must be all of—four years?"

"Ruby's wedding," Bertrand said, "to the blushing bridegroom. Present me, Jack?" He glanced with open interest at Juliana.

Jack was recalled to good manners and introduced the two of them. She curtsied, and he made an elegant bow.

"One predictable thing about old Jack here," Bertrand said, smiling at Juliana, "is that wherever the prettiest young lady is, there he is close by."

Juliana blushed and lowered her gaze.

"And look whom we have here, Jack," Hortense said, emerging from the noisy masses with another young lady in tow. "Addie was the only one not at home. She is off spending Christmas with her husband's family."

"Rose!" Jack stretched out both hands to take one of the rector's youngest daughter's in his. "Just look at you. Tell me who the fortunate man is who carried you off to the altar and I shall challenge him to pistols at dawn." He could remember flirting quite outrageously with the seventeen-year-old Rose during his last visit to Portland House. She was just as pretty now, though perhaps not as blushingly so.

"Jack," she said. "No one has."

Bertrand was explaining relationships to Juliana and asking about her journey.

"What?" Jack said. "Has the male world gone mad? So you are still at home in the rectory?"

"I am a governess," she said, "at the same house where Bertie is steward. The family was going away for the holiday, so we were granted a two-week leave."

Rose. Placid, blushing Rose a governess. When Freddie had married Ruby, he had vowed to find husbands for his sisters-in-law. He had succeeded with the passably pretty Addie. What had happened with the delectably lovely Rose?

Someone mentioned tea, and there was a minor stampede for the staircase and the drawing room.

"Come," he said, taking Rose's hand and placing it on his sleeve. "Come upstairs and have a cup of tea, Rose, though I daresay your mama poured at least six for everyone at the rectory less than an hour ago. You must tell me how someone so pretty manages to keep order in the schoolroom."

It was only as he led her in pursuit of everyone else that he remembered Juliana. He noticed with some relief when he glanced over his shoulder that she was coming on Fitz's arm with Hortie chatting at her other side. It was so difficult, he thought, to concentrate all one's mind and attention on one lady and to give up one's natural inclination to flirt with the nearest pretty woman.

Changing his way of life, changing himself, was not going to be easy, he realized with an inward sigh.

Chapter 7

Bertrand and Rose had been persuaded to stay for dinner, though their mother would be expecting them back at the rectory, they both protested. It was the duchess's pronouncement that the duke would be annoyed if they refused that finally decided them. It was not good for His Grace's gout for him to be annoyed, apparently.

Jack walked home with them afterward, glad of some fresh air and of the quietness of the walk home again after stepping inside briefly to pay his respects to the rector and Mrs. Fitzgerald and to sample the latter's trial batch of mince pies. She always made a trial batch a week before Christmas, she explained, just to make sure that she had not forgotten from the previous year how to make them just so.

Tomorrow rehearsals were to begin for the theatrical performances. And it seemed that he was stuck with the part of Othello, Jack thought, despite his protests and despite his childish burst of spite in the morning room. He wondered if Belle had had anything to do with the choice and guessed not. She had made it quite clear to him this morning that she was as anxious to avoid his company this week as he was to avoid hers.

Now that she was respectable and even more than just respectable, he supposed that it was only natural that she not want to be reminded of a time when she had needed his protection and had sold her body in exchange for it.

He did not want to think of Belle. And he did not want to have to go to the drawing room, where she would inevitably be the focus of attention as she had been yesterday and as she had been at tea this afternoon despite the presence of fresh visitors from the rectory. It was to escape the drawing room that he had decided to walk Fitz and Rose home.

It was with some relief, then, that his lagging footsteps stopped altogether as he was passing the music room and heard music from within. It must be Juliana playing the pianoforte. If he was fortunate, she would be alone and he would be able to resume his courtship of her. But even if she were not, it was unlikely that Belle would be part of her audience. He would spend the rest of the evening here rather than in the drawing room.

But it was not the pianoforte that was playing, he realized as soon as he had turned the handle and pushed the door ajar. It was one of the violins. It would be Perry or Martin, then. All the better. He would be able to relax with some congenial male company.

But it was neither. He closed the door quietly behind his back and strolled slowly across the room toward the pianoforte, on which a single candle burned. Beside the pianoforte, holding a violin far too large for her beneath her chin and playing it with a bow that looked almost as long as she was tall, was a thin, dark-haired child. Her eyes were closed, and the movements of her body suggested that she was totally absorbed in the music she was producing. Beethoven. With surprising skill and feeling for one so young.

Jack stood very still, his hands clasped at his back, until she had finished. She still kept her eyes closed, as if listening to the dying echoes of the music.

"Beautiful," he said softly.

Dark eyes, far too large for the thin face, flew open and the violin slipped from beneath her chin as she took several hasty steps back and away from him.

"No, no," he said, not moving. "I am not going to hurt you. Who are you?"

She was breathing quickly and noisily. "Jacqueline," she said. "Jacqueline Gellée. I meant no harm. I knew I would not be able to sleep. I can never sleep."

Belle's daughter. With a French name like the boy, Marcel. He felt a heaviness about the heart for a moment. "It is a wretched feeling, is it not?" he said. "Insomnia. That is the word for it. I suffer from it myself sometimes. You are talented. Do you have lessons?"

"No." She shook her head.

"Who taught you that particular piece?" he asked.

She shrugged her thin shoulders. "I heard it," she said. "I think it was at Papa's." She spoke with a slight French accent.

He raised his eyebrows. "And have you heard other music?" he asked. "Do you play anything else or is that your party piece?"

"I have heard more," she said.

"Play something for me, then," he said, strolling closer to the pianoforte and resting one elbow on it.

She stood very still for perhaps a whole minute, staring at the carpet ahead of her before lifting the violin to her chin again and raising the bow. She started to play without looking back at him. After a few moments she closed her eyes again, and he knew that she had forgotten his presence. She played Mozart a little too quickly, a little too aggressively, but surely with more flair and feeling than he had ever heard before. It was a remarkable performance.

"Child," he said quietly when she was finished and had opened her eyes and become aware of him again, "you should be having lessons."

But unheard by either of them, the door had opened at the other end of the room and someone else had come inside.

"Jacqueline!" a shocked and angry voice said. "Whatever are you doing?"

Isabella had spent the afternoon out walking—again—with her children. There was an imposing triple-arched bridge across the marshy lake some distance away, she had been told. It had been built by the present duke for his duchess soon after their marriage. Apparently there was a picturesque view of the house from above the central arch.

She was feeling wretchedly guilty for coming. Perhaps

she might anyway have accepted the duchess's invitation since it had offered both her and the children a chance to spend Christmas in the country and amid what would probably be congenial company. But she knew in her heart of hearts why she had really accepted, though she had denied full acceptance of the fact to herself until now.

It was probably Jack, she admitted to herself, who had drawn her back to England. She had been pining for a sight of him. But he had not called on her, as she had hoped he would, and he had not attended the theater for any of her performances, as she had fully expected he would. And yet she knew he was in London.

She should have left well enough alone. Pride should have kept her well away from him. Despite her present respectability and the dizzying heights of success to which she had risen, she knew that to him she would always be merely the woman he had employed for a year as his mistress.

It was only at first, in her dreadful naïveté, that she had believed it was a glorious romance they were involved in. Even after he had taken her to that inn one afternoon and had hurt her badly and then disappointed her because nothing had happened for her except the pain and the shock— even after that, she had thought it was love. She had thought he had taken her under his protection because he had perceived how poorly she was forced to live and how little she usually had to eat and had wanted to care for her. She had not made any real connection between the protection and the sex. Even though he had paid for her lodgings and for a servant and had given her money for food and clothes and even some luxuries, she had not thought of herself as a mistress.

She had thought he loved her as she loved him. She had thought that in time . . . What a poor foolish innocent she had been. She had been quite incredibly naive.

Why had she never been able to put that year of her life behind her? Despite the callousness and even cruelty he had shown her toward the end, despite her realization of the true nature of their relationship, despite the years since and

Maurice and his adoration and kindness, despite her escalation to undreamed of success, despite it all she had never been able to purge her emotions of that year.

She should never have come. She should never have brought her children here.

And yet they were enjoying themselves. Marcel, placid and happy wherever they went, skipped along at her side during their walk, telling her that his new friend, fourteen-year-old Davy—he must be Stanley and Celia Stewart's boy, Isabella guessed—had told him they were all to go out gathering greenery to decorate the house tomorrow or the next day.

"And I am to carry holly, Maman," he said in his eager, piping voice. "And Davy is to show me how not to prick myself and bleed all over."

Five-year-old Marcel considered anyone from the age of one to eighty-one who deigned to notice his existence to be his friend.

"My friend Kenneth shared his milk with me at breakfast," he added. "I am going to read stories to him later. He is only one year old. I can read, Maman. I can see the pictures and remember the stories you have told. And I know some words."

Maurice must have been just like Marcel, in both looks and nature, at this age, Isabella thought. She hoped Marcel would be like his father at the age of forty. But she hoped he would live longer. Poor Maurice. She had been fond of him.

"And you, chérie?" She had smiled down at her daughter with the old familiar ache of love. Jacqueline was walking quietly at her side, holding her hand. "Are you enjoying yourself?"

"Yes, Mama," the girl said. "I helped the nurse dress one of the little girls this morning. And I brushed Catherine Stewart's hair until it crackled. She liked it. She said her mama brushes it for her every night but her nurse does not take time over it in the morning. Her mama smiled at me and thanked me when she came to say good morning to Catherine and Kenneth. She said to call her Aunt Anne."

Such a strange, solemn little child. Isabella was never sure if she was happy or not.

And she was never sure when Jacqueline would cause her untold anxiety. Later in the evening, an hour after she had gone to the nursery to tuck the children into bed and kiss them good night, she excused herself as she had done the evening before in order to go up to check on them. There was more than one nurse up there, of course, but she always liked to check for herself.

Marcel was asleep, one chubby cheek resting on his curled fist, his mouth half-open. Jacqueline's bed was empty but she was not out in the nursery, where no fewer than three nurses were having a comfortable chat over a cup of tea. They had not seen the child leave—they all leapt to their feet in some consternation when they knew she was missing.

Isabella knew that Jacqueline would not have left the house. Nevertheless, by the time she had looked in every conceivable place where her daughter might be, she was feeling sick with worry. It was nighttime and dark outside. What if the child was just not to be found? What would she do? Panic clawed at her. She was going to have to go to the drawing room to beg for help.

And then she came to the music room. She knew it was the music room. The duchess had given her a personal tour of the house earlier. It seemed hardly worth looking in there, she thought, her hand going to the knob. But even as she turned it, before she opened it and saw light, she knew. Of course. Why had she even considered looking elsewhere? She should have known.

Relief—knee-weakening relief—at seeing first the light of a single candle inside the room and then the small form of her daughter on the far side of the pianoforte, holding the inevitable violin and bow, quickly gave place to other feelings when she saw the man reclined on one elbow at the pianoforte.

Jack.

Oh, dear God. Dear Lord God. Fear clutched at her, a

blind and unreasoned fear. She had been mad to come here, to bring her children here.

And then relief and fear converted to anger. Furious anger.

"Jacqueline!" she hissed. "Whatever are you doing?"

Jacqueline jumped with alarm and made a futile attempt to hide both violin and bow behind her back. Jack pushed himself indolently to a standing position.

Isabella hurried across the room, her eyes on her daughter. "I have been frantic," she said. "You were not in your bed, and the nurses had not seen you leave, and this is a strange house."

"I could not sleep, Mama," the child said, stepping closer to the pianoforte in a further attempt to hide what she held.

"Then you should have lain in bed until you did," Isabella said tartly, her anger fanned by the man who stood silently a few feet away. "I will not have this, Jacqueline. You cannot wander about a strange house at night in your nightgown talking with strangers."

Jack did not move.

"And what do you think you are doing in here and with *that*!" she said, pointing an accusing finger at the violin. "You know you are not to play it, Jacqueline. That you are never to play it. You are a naughty, disobedient child."

Two tears were trickling down her daughter's cheeks.

"I asked her to play something for me," Jack said quietly. "No harm has been done. Insomnia cannot always be cured by lying still and willing sleep to come."

Isabella had a sudden shocking memory of Jack's insomnia. Sometimes he had used to come to her in the middle of the night, tired and irritable, and beg her to put him to sleep. He had used to tell her on the mornings following such episodes, with his characteristic lazy chuckle, that her particular lullabies always rocked him to sleep like a charm.

She did not look at him or show any indication that she had even heard him. "Go back to your room and your bed," she told her daughter. "I will follow you there in a few minutes' time. And be thankful that you have escaped a sound spanking." She had never spanked either of her children and had shed tears on the few occasions when Maurice had. She could not understand the force of her anger now.

"Yes, Mama." Jacqueline's voice was thin and pathetic. Isabella wanted to sweep her up into her arms and weep with her.

"And put that thing down," she said coldly. "Don't let me see you with it or any other ever again, Jacqueline. Do you hear me?"

"Yes, Mama." The child had to reach up and stand on tiptoe in order to set down the violin almost reverently on the pianoforte. She turned and left the room, head down.

Isabella's heart ached. But fury had not yet waned.

"How dare you!" She looked at Jack for the first time, her eyes flashing. "How dare you!"

He had clasped his hands behind him. He looked steadily back at her. "How dare I what?" he asked.

"How dare you be alone with my daughter," she said. "How dare you speak to her."

"Belle," he said quietly, "she is seven, you told me this morning. A seven-year-old child. What do you think I am?"

She glared at him. She recognized from long ago the only sign of anger in him—the hardened jaw.

"Do you think I am a child molester?" he asked her.

She drew a slow breath.

"This is my grandparents' house," he said. "She is a guest here. I am their grandson. Besides all of which, she is a child."

He had put her in the wrong, exposed her anger for the unreasonable emotion it was. She could feel hatred like nausea in her nostrils.

"I do not want you near my children," she said. "Especially not my daughter. I do not want you to speak to them or look at them. I do not want you in the same room as them. I do not want them to know your face or your name. Do you understand me?" And yet she had brought them here, she thought, knowing that he might well be here. Hoping that he would. Dreading that he would.

He was still infuriatingly calm and still. "Is this the point at which I would rise to my feet if I were not already on them, Belle?" he asked. "And applaud with wild enthusiasm and shout, 'Bravo!' Or is there more to come?"

She drew slow breaths to calm herself. "Stay away from them," she said. "They are my children. I would die for them."

"Bravo," he murmured.

She took a couple of steps toward him. "Jack," she said urgently. "Please. Please, do not ever use that word in their hearing. Don't call me that when they can hear. Let them continue to think of me as—"

"My God, Belle." He had closed the remaining distance between them and grabbed her upper arms. Painfully. "You have some strange notions about me."

The shock was so much greater than anything she could ever have expected that all she could do was gaze, frozen, into his eyes. She could feel his hard, heavily muscled thighs with her own, his chest with her breasts. She could feel his breath on her face and smell the cologne he had always used. There was a rush of familiarity as if all the years between this and their last touch had fallen away without trace.

"Please, Jack," she said. She was not quite sure for what she pleaded. She gazed into the familiar dark eyes in the familiar narrow, handsome face, surrounded by the familiar thick, dark hair.

Jack. Ah, Jack.

She lifted her face mutely for his kiss. She expected his kiss. But he did not kiss her. He stepped back from her after a few moments and released his hold of her arms. He walked around the pianoforte and picked out a tune on the keyboard with one finger.

"Belle," he said, "why is she not having violin lessons? She is extraordinarily talented."

"No, she is not," she said quickly. "It is just that Maurice encouraged her too much. It amused him that she could pick out a tune on his violin almost before she could walk. He had one specially made for her, one small enough for her to hold. She used to play it when she should have been playing games like other children. It was nonsense. I forbade it after his death."

She listened to herself and felt the lameness of her explanation. She hid her fear. She did not owe him an explanation, anyway. She was the child's mother.

He lowered the lid over the keyboard and regarded her in silence for a while. "I have never heard a child play with that kind of passion," he said. "It was almost as if she could not stop herself from playing. You have wealth enough now surely to hire the best teacher available to instruct her. She needs the best."

"What do you know of her needs?" She could feel anger returning. "What do you know of children? She needs to be happy and carefree. She needs to play and be a child. She needs to sleep at night. She does not need to be a freak."

"A freak?" He frowned. "I would have thought that you of all people would recognize talent, Belle, and the necessity of nurturing it. At a guess I would say her talent is as great as yours in a different field and could lead to as much greatness and recognition."

She did not want that said in words. Did he not realize she was the very last person to want a talented child?

"Are you jealous of her, Belle?" he asked quietly.

"You know nothing," she said fiercely. "You and your easy, coddled life. You for whom everything has come without effort. Who has always had whatever you wanted whenever you wanted it."

She could have become a teacher or a governess. Or she could have married one of the young men of her own class and background who showed an interest in her before she went to London. But no, she had always been driven by the need to act, by the obsession to prove to herself and the world that she could be the best of the best. She knew all about driving talent. And she knew where it led. It led to a world where women—ladies—were not expected to tread. It led to a world where women were assumed to be of loose morals. It led to the sort of liaison she had known with Jack. It led to the sort of ostracism she had suffered from Maurice's relatives when he had broken the conventions and raised her into a different world. And it led to loneliness. Always loneliness. She could not remember a time when she had not been lonely, except perhaps during the first months with Jack, when she thought she had found her happily-ever-after.

Jacqueline had a chance to be a lady despite her mother's background. She had a chance for a normal life, for a happy life. If everyone would just keep their—damned violins out of sight.

"She is having pianoforte lessons," she said. "Playing the pianoforte is a far more suitable accomplishment for a lady."

"Does she play well?" he asked.

"She is competent," she said. "She is only seven." But she had no interest in the lessons and no interest in practicing. And she played with wooden correctness.

"Belle." He searched her eyes. "You are making a mistake."

"Who are you to tell me how to bring up my children?" She could hear her voice shaking. "Who are you?"

He shook his head slowly. "Only a man who once lived with a woman who was driven by her talent. A man who resented it and wanted to curb it and finally had to recognize that it was beyond his control," he said. "And a man who now has to admit that it was better so. I have not seen you act recently, Belle, but the world is agreed that you are something quite beyond the ordinary."

She remembered how Jack had wanted her to give up the stage, how he became furiously angry if he attended the theater when the unruly gentleman spectators in the pit had cheered her more outrageously than usual, how sometimes after such performances he would make love to her almost violently. He had not seemed to understand at the time that acting had not been simply a job to her.

But someone should have stopped her. Her parents should have stopped her. No. They had tried and failed.

"I must go to the nursery," she said. "I must see that she is safely back in bed."

"Yes," he said. "Go." But his voice stopped her as she

turned. "Belle, don't spank her. Insomnia is a terrible affliction. And wanting something so badly it hurts is not easy to deal with, either. Especially for a child."

She looked back over her shoulder at him. How dared he, she thought again wearily. What did he know about parenthood? What did he know of the dreams and the fears a parent felt for a child, especially a child who was not quite what one expected a child to be? What did he know about the ache of love about the heart one felt for one's own children? Or about the greatest fear of all, the fear of doing it all wrong and forever blighting the child's life?

She did not say anything. What was the point?

And yet his words weighed heavily on her as she climbed the stairs to the nursery.

Jacqueline was lying in bed with reddened eyes and cheeks. She had her eyes closed, though Isabella knew she was not sleeping. She bent over her and touched a hand lightly to her forehead, smoothing the hair back. And then she leaned down impulsively and gathered the child up into her arms. Thin awkward little Jacqueline, so different in coloring and physique—and in nature—from Marcel. So very dearly beloved.

"Chérie," she said. "I was frightened when you were gone. What would I do without my little girl? And then I was so happy to see you safe that I became angry with you. I did not mean to make you cry. Forgive me."

"Mama," her daughter whispered, "that gentleman said it was beautiful. He asked for more. He said I should be having lessons."

That gentleman. Ah, Jack, Jack.

"He said the same thing to me," Isabella said.

There was a little silence. "Mama—"

"We will see when we go home after Christmas," Isabella said. "Maybe we will give it a try." She laid her daughter back down on the bed, tucked the blankets warmly about her, and smiled down at her. "Will you go to sleep now?"

"Yes, Mama," Jacqueline said. But as Isabella turned to pick up her candle and leave the room quietly, she spoke

again. "Mama," she said, "I thought I would die when we
came from France and you would not let me bring my violin."

"We can always have another made," Isabella said, her
heart sinking. "A little larger because you are getting to be
a big girl." But to be played only at specified times. To be
strictly controlled.

Jacqueline gave her one of her rare smiles.

She felt, Isabella thought as she made her way downstairs, as if she had been outmaneuvered by Jack. She had
been so determined to make Jacqueline forget the violin, to
save her from herself. And yet now it seemed that she had
given in.

That gentleman. Oh, how strangely painful it had been to
hear her daughter call him *that gentleman.*

Chapter 8

Jack sat down on the pianoforte stool, pushed back the lid again, and began to play, softly, absently. Strangely, it had frequently been his way of coping with insomnia. Music.

Music or sex. Sex more often than music since he grew up. He had learned with Belle the sweet drug of spilling his energy into a woman's body and drifting into sleep in the cradle of her arms. He had used other women since for the same purpose. But it had never been as sweet as it had been with Belle.

Her body was riper, more mature, as was to be expected. And just as capable now of sending his temperature soaring. He wondered if she had felt him harden into instant arousal when they had touched. Perhaps he had removed himself from her and found the cover of the pianoforte in time that she had not.

He thought of the thin dark little girl who was her daughter and of the ungainly picture she made with the too-large violin beneath her chin. And of the music, unpolished but pulsing with emotion that had made her seem beautiful. Belle's daughter. He had felt drawn to her because she had come from Belle's body. And de Vacheron's seed.

He had been too young, too gauche, too inexperienced with life to cope with Belle's talent. He had tried to ignore it, to snuff it out, to lure her away from it, to draw her into a life in which he would have replaced it. It had angered him, frustrated him, puzzled him. He had hated the fact that she was an actress.

Could things have been different? he wondered. If he had been proud of her acting abilities as well as of her? If he had encouraged her, openly acknowledged her as his woman, perhaps even married her? His mother, his grand-parents would have had an apoplexy if he had married an actress and his mistress. But if he had done what de Vacheron must have done and thumbed his nose at convention? If he had been the one to father her children?

Would it have made a difference? Could he have ignored the jealousy he had always felt of the men who had gone before him as her protectors or casual customers? Could he have turned a blind eye to the men, the admirers and hangers-on at the green room of the theater, who had had her while she was under his protection? He had always known about them, and she had openly admitted it at the end—during that last bitter quarrel, his last meeting with her until yesterday.

If he had accepted her need to follow her dream and had had patience with her need to be worshiped physically as well as from afar by other men, would she have settled down eventually? She appeared to have done exactly that after disappearing for a year or more and then resurfacing in France. No gossip about her had come from France, only word that she was growing in fame, patronized by the Emperor Napoleon himself. And since her return, he had not heard her name being linked with any man's, even the richest and most prominent of society's bucks who habitually drew their whores and mistresses from the green rooms and boasted openly of particular conquests.

His grandmother would not have invited her to Portland House if there had been a breath of scandal surrounding her name.

Had he been older, more experienced, more patient, could things have been different?

Probably not, he concluded, ending the piece of music he had played so absently that he scarcely knew he had played. Even now, at the age of thirty-one, when she meant nothing at all to him, he burned with rage to know that other men had used her body even while he himself had been keeping her and loving her.

No, he could never have shared her with other men. He

was not sure he could have shared her with a career. If he took a wife—when he took a wife—he would need to know that he was the only man ever to have known her body and ever to know it. And he would need to know that he came first and last and everything in between in her life. As she must with him.

He thought determinedly and a little grimly of Juliana, about whom he seemed not to have thought at all for a long time. He had flirted with Rose during tea and dinner, and had then walked home with her and Fitz. And since returning . . . Hours and hours seemed to have passed since his return. He did not have any idea what time it was. Midnight? Later?

The door opened, and Peregrine's head came around it.

"This is where you are hiding," he said, pushing the door wider. "You look like a lovelorn swain, Jack. She is in the drawing room, old chap, doubtless awaiting your return with palpitating heart. And charades are about to begin. Your team is in dire need of your skills. My team has the comtesse—when she comes back down from the nursery. You may want to concede defeat now and save yourself and your team a few hours of grief." He leered and winked.

Jack got to his feet. "Concede defeat?" he said. "Never, Perry, old boy. Not until I feel someone's booted foot on my chest and someone's sharp sword point at my throat. And even then if your face is close enough, I may spit in your eye. Charades, you say? I do believe I am somewhat invincible at the game. Lead the way."

Peregrine chuckled and disappeared again.

The following day was to be a busy one, its activities all carefully organized by the duchess. One could tell that Christmas was drawing closer, her family members agreed among themselves. The duchess would see to it that all of them and her other guests enjoyed every single moment of every day of the holiday—enjoyed it on her terms, that was. Grandmama could never conceive of the notion that for many people—for most people—Christmas was for being lazy and for feasting, Alex told a group of people who were already of the same opinion.

There was to be a general rehearsal in the morning for all the appointed actors so that they might be given their parts and find out exactly what they were to do. During the afternoon, every able-bodied person was to go out into the park to gather greenery for decorating the house—it would be so much more enjoyable to do it themselves than have the servants do it, the duchess explained. And when they returned, they were to do the decorating.

Anyone who had time to spare—"Ha!" Martin commented eloquently to Maud—could practice in the music room or the drawing room for the concert with which they would entertain one another on the evening of Christmas Eve, before going to church.

Most of the family attended the rehearsal, if it could be called that, in the ballroom. Theatricals always drew their reluctant interest at any time. But this time the lure of seeing the Comtesse de Vacheron in her own milieu was irresistible. As also was the prospect of seeing everyone else make cakes of themselves, Hortense commented to her husband.

Juliana would perhaps have gone to the ballroom too had her brother not taken her aside after breakfast.

"I am for a walk this morning," he said. "Perhaps I will go as far as the village and pay my respects at the rectory. Would you care to come, too, Julie?"

"To the rectory?" she said. "But we have not been introduced to the rector and his wife, Howard. Ought we to go unaccompanied?"

"A rectory is a place anyone can call at without a prior introduction," he said. "Besides, we met Fitz and Miss Fitzgerald yesterday."

His tone was too casual. She knew her brother too well to be deceived.

"Oh," she said with a laugh, nudging his shoulder sharply. "She *is* rather pretty, is she not? But she is a governess, Howard. Papa would not approve."

"Good Lord, Julie," he said in some exasperation, "I am not planning to offer for the woman. But do you realize how few unattached females there are at Portland House? You. That is it. And you are my sister."

She thought. It had not really occurred to her until now that this Christmas might be dull for Howard. But he was right. Or almost right.

"And the Comtesse de Vacheron," she said.

He snorted. "She must be four or five years older than I am," he said, "and she has two children. Besides she is—daunting."

"Yes." Juliana had to agree that she would probably appear so to Howard. Certainly Juliana could not imagine the comtesse engaged in a flirtation with him. "But I like her. She is friendly." She linked her arm through his as they proceeded upstairs. "Miss Fitzgerald is pretty. And I can understand your reluctance to call upon her alone. Let us call on her together then, Howard."

Truth to tell, she thought, as they walked briskly toward the village half an hour later, she was glad to be out alone with her brother, with whom she could relax completely. She was making every effort to accept the present situation for what it was and to grow to like Mr. Frazer. On one level she was succeeding. He was a surprisingly likable person, and he had been kind to her. On another level she was finding matters more difficult. He was too self-assured and worldly for her. She felt gauche and childish with him.

It was good to be out, striding along with Howard, talking and listening without having to make any mental effort at all.

It turned out, in fact, to be an incredibly pleasant morning. Mrs. Fitzgerald, after curtsying and looking rather flustered while Mr. Bertrand Fitzgerald was introducing them, insisted on having tea brought to the parlor with mince pies—her trial batch, she explained—and muffins and scones. And the rector himself came from his study and sat down with them and conversed civilly while they ate and drank.

And then Howard, looking significantly at his sister,

willing her to agree, suggested that perhaps Fitz and Miss
Fitzgerald would care for a stroll outside since the air was
fresh and brisk, even if the heavy clouds did make it appear
to be rather a raw and cheerless day.

It looked as if they might have snow for Christmas, the
rector commented.

"Dress warmly, dear," Mrs. Fitzgerald directed her
daughter.

When they were outside, Howard took Miss Fitzgerald
on his arm, as Juliana had expected. She took Mr. Fitzgerald's, and the four of them set off along what remained of
the village street and out along a country lane that was bor-
dered on one side by the moss-grown wall of Portland Park
for some distance and then proceeded into more open country.

But Juliana did not mind being paired with a strange gentleman. He was a good-looking man rather than handsome,
with a good-humored face. He might be eight or ten years
older than she, but she did not feel intimidated by the age
difference. And he was the son of a clergyman and worked
for his living as an estate steward. There was nothing in
him to make her feel awed and tongue-tied and too young
for her years.

He asked her about herself, and she found herself able to
talk about her life, unremarkable as it had been for the nineteen years of her existence. He told her about his work,
which he obviously found both interesting and challenging.
And he told her about the Duke and Duchess of Portland's
family—about the boyhood games he had played with the
younger generation and the mischief he had got into with
them. He had her chuckling and entirely at her ease in no
time at all.

Howard, she saw, was getting along famously with Miss
Rose Fitzgerald, who appeared to Juliana to be both sweet
and pretty—and a mere year or two older than herself. Indeed, after the four of them had stopped for a while in order
to gaze at a distant prospect of Portland House through the
trees, Juliana found herself walking with Rose and talking
with her as one friend to another, just as if they had known

each other for years. It was easier to talk with Rose than with the comtesse, Juliana realized, perhaps because they both talked. She realized that Lady de Vacheron was a kind listener, but had really not talked to Juliana at all.

Rose talked about her pleasure at being home for two whole weeks. And about her fondness of the children under her care. And about her loneliness, which would be acute if her brother were not employed in the same house.

She smiled apologetically at Juliana. "How dreadful of me to confide such a thing," she said. "I have certainly not admitted as much to anyone else, even Mama. Some people are easy to talk to. You are, Miss Beckford. Forgive me for burdening you with my own problems."

"Call me Juliana," that young lady said impulsively.

"Juliana. Thank you. I am Rose."

They chattered eagerly and amicably until Howard, who had been talking with Mr. Fitzgerald, brought the four of them together again and soon led Rose ahead once more. Juliana hoped he would not flirt too outrageously with her over the rest of the holiday. She liked Rose and did not wish to see her hurt—and Rose had admitted to some loneliness. Howard had been to university and had spent some time in town. Juliana suspected that he had learned a thing or two there about flirtation, although there was not quite the worldliness about him that there was about Mr. Frazer.

She suspected that Mr. Frazer had done more than flirt with women. And she blushed deeply at the shocking and improper thought.

As she walked back home through the park with Howard a little later, Juliana felt a great deal happier than she had felt before they left and very definitely refreshed. She shut her mind firmly to the thought that she wished they did not have to go back to Portland House.

"By Jove," Howard said, "the prospect of another week and a half here suddenly seems considerably brighter, Julie. You would never guess that Rose and Ruby Lynwood are sisters, would you now?"

The family all descended upon the ballroom after breakfast with a great deal of witty conversation and laughter and bravado. But something of a transformation took place when they entered the ballroom to find Claude and the Comtesse de Vacheron already there, standing together in the middle of the floor in quiet conference together.

Beautiful as she undoubtedly was, the comtesse was not dressed this morning either to dazzle or to intimidate. She wore a simple wool dress of a dark green, and her golden hair was combed back from her face and twisted into a simple knot at her neck.

And yet they were painfully aware that she was the great de Vacheron, who had acted for that Corsican monster, the Emperor Napoleon, and had been praised by him and bowed to by him and even knelt to by him if the story was to be believed. And she had been applauded by Prinny himself, who had risen to his feet to do so and caused everyone else in the theater to follow suit. She had had a reception given in her honor at Carlton House.

The family, entering the ballroom, were awed by the knowledge that some of their number were going to have the effrontery to try to act with her. They ranged themselves sheepishly about the perimeter of the ballroom.

"As if our body weight is needed to hold up the walls," Peregrine muttered with a self-conscious snicker to Connie and Sam.

"Just like a crowd of raw bucks, still wet behind the ears, at our first ball," Alex said to Jack out of the side of his mouth.

And then both Claude and the comtesse looked up. Claude frowned, and she smiled.

It was still morning. If he were at Reggie's now, Jack thought, he would doubtless still be abed. Not alone, of course, and not necessarily asleep. But abed. He would give anything in the world to be there. And not just because he was here courting his future bride. Not for that reason at all, in fact.

Belle and Perry had led their team to victory at last evening's charades, of course. It was grossly unfair that they had been on the same team. She had been brightly gay just as if that scene in the music room had not happened. But then so had he.

"What on earth are you all doing over there?" Claude asked. "You look as if you are waiting for a firing squad to open fire."

There was a burst of embarrassed laughter, and they crept a few feet closer. All except Jack, who turned slightly so that his left shoulder joined the right against the wall. He crossed his arms over his chest.

He had hated the fact that she was an actress. Hated it. And though he had seen her act many times, he had rarely been willing to admit that she was good. She was pretty. It was her beauty that had drawn the attention of her audience. It was the opportunity to feast their eyes upon her and the chance of meeting her in the green room and hiring her services for the rest of the night that had drawn the male part of the audience. There had been nothing more to it than that. Or so he had tried to persuade himself at the time. He had been rather mean-minded over the whole situation.

He should never have bedded her that first time, knowing that she was an actress. If he had only lusted after her, perhaps. But not given the foolish state of his heart. He should have walked away from the theater after seeing her on the stage and stayed away from the park for the rest of that particular spring. He could have avoided that whole impossible year.

She laughed now. "I promise," she said, "that I do not bite."

More self-conscious laughter from the family.

"And I hate taking you away from your holiday," she said, "and putting you to work. I explained to the duchess, though, that you need not commit your lines to memory or even act overzealously. Provided you give me with my cues, I promise to do all the hard work myself."

Good God, Jack thought, his eyes narrowing, she was as clever as his grandmother. The obvious response broke in a chorus from his gathered relatives.

"But it has always been our greatest pleasure to act," Perry said, "much as we pretend to grumble about it. And how could we face ourselves in the mirror afterward if we did not act to the best of our ability and learn our lines so that we do not need to be prompted even once?"

"Learning lines is not so difficult if one sets one's mind to it, Isabella," Anne said. "And acting is not so impossible if one thinks of the character one is portraying instead of about oneself."

"Damme," Freddie said, "I learned my lines last time and remembered when to say them. If I can, anyone can. I have no brains, Comtesse."

"Oh, Freddie," Anne said with the sort of kindness that usually amused and touched Jack all at the same time, "of course you do, dear. You just think a little more carefully and deliberately than most people."

"We certainly do not want to mar your performance, Isabella, by being quite unprepared ourselves," Alex said. "And a little hard work never hurt anyone, I suppose."

And Alex was the one who had been going to commit murder most foul, Jack thought in disgust.

"We will doubtless appear the merest amateurs to you, Comtesse," Claude said. "But by Christmas Day, everyone will know his part and will act it as it was meant to be acted, or I will want to know the reason why."

"Well." Isabella clasped her hands at her bosom and smiled dazzlingly about at everyone. "How splendid." Her eyes briefly met Jack's across the room.

Claude had decided that they would read through each of the three chosen excerpts so that he could get a mental image of what he hoped to achieve with the amateurs. They would appoint definite rehearsal times for each after that.

The scene from *The Merchant of Venice* came first, followed by that from *The Taming of the Shrew*. Jack watched, somewhat removed from the rest of the impromptu audience. He still stood against the wall, arms crossed.

She was not really acting at all, he thought, merely reading the part. And yet she made all the others, Perry included, look and sound not only as if they had never acted before, but as if they had never read aloud from a book before. And although she read quietly, she became different persons, each quite different from Belle herself. She became the confident, intelligent, clever Portia in the court scene and the angry, sullen, tart-tongued shrew in the second. But they were going to perform two short scenes from *The Taming of the Shrew*, she and Alex. In the second the shrew had been tamed to a quiet, obedient wife. Belle became the tamed shrew.

One wondered, Jack thought with grudging admiration, how she would appear in these parts on Christmas Day, when she would be really acting them.

And then everyone was looking his way, and there were faint cheers and jeers. It seemed it was his turn. God! Perry had been right. Despite all their grumbling at lost leisure time, they had all secretly enjoyed the family theatricals. But how could he participate in this particular one? How could he act with Belle?

He pushed his shoulders away from the wall, uncrossed his arms, and strolled across the ballroom floor with what he hoped was convincing nonchalance to take the book Claude was holding out to him.

"You are my last hope, Jack," he said gloomily. "Let's see if you can read and not sound as if you learned the alphabet only yesterday. A fine week I can see this is going to be."

Claude always scolded and fumed his way through rehearsals, and claimed at the end of it all that his stomach would never be the same again.

"It will all come out well, as it did last time, Claude," Anne said soothingly. She, of course, was in the scene, too, in the part of Emilia, Desdemona's maid and Iago's wife. "I had the main part last time, Isabella, and I had never even seen a play performed."

He had to instruct Desdemona to go to bed, dismiss her maid, and await his return from seeing a guest home, Jack saw at a quick glance through the scene. And then he had a longish rest while Desdemona got ready for bed and talked sadly with Emilia about fidelity and about death, while she sang her sad song about Barbara. And then he returned to murder her, loving her and hating her and believing in the lies about her that Iago had told him. The scene was to end with her death.

He had always despised Othello. How could any man who claimed to love so deeply have believed those lies without checking them and double-checking their truthfulness? And yet it was sad enough. A man loving even as he killed and then discovering too late—only barely too late—that he had killed unjustly. If killing could ever be just.

"Jack?" Claude sounded impatient.

Jack coughed and read his opening lines. The heavy-handed husband giving orders he expected to be obeyed.

And then she became Desdemona—sweet, innocent, obedient, and yet in no way weak. She sensed death coming. She sang about it and tears caught at her voice as she did so. She knew that her husband was angry with her, though she did not understand the reason. And yet she obeyed him with a quiet dignity and courage, sending Emilia away and waiting alone for she knew not what.

He had to kill her. It was the only way. All had been spoiled. She was not the sweet innocent he had taken her for. Honor would not allow him to keep her when he knew her soiled. And yet he did not want to do it. He knew that once he had put out the light of her life, as he phrased it, he would not be able to relight it as he would a lamp. He procrastinated, offering her a chance to say her prayers and clear her conscience before she went to meet her Maker. He did not want to argue with her. He did not want to hear her lie. But he delayed too long. She forced some of his discoveries from him and then denied them. And so he killed her after all in a rage of disillusion and hurt.

And when Emilia returned to the room after the deed was done and after Desdemona had revived sufficiently before dying to clear him of the blame for her death and to take it upon herself, accusing herself of suicide, he would not avoid the blame.

"'She's like a liar gone to burning hell: 'Twas I that kill'd her,' " he said softly.

There was a smattering of applause. Zeb set two fingers to his lips and whistled.

"Well." Claude sounded surprised. "That at least sounds as if it might not be a total disaster." He turned to the group at large and informed the actors when they would be expected to return for their next rehearsal. "Only the actors from now on," he said. "No spectators to distract us. And one excerpt at a time. None of you can say you are going to be overworked, except perhaps the comtesse. I do not want to hear any grumbling."

"Grandpapa will be out for our blood if we try," Hortense said, and laughed merrily at her own joke.

"That is hardly an exaggeration," Alex said, setting an arm loosely about his wife's shoulders. "Do you remember the scolding he gave us, Anne, when we could not act properly together because we were not on the best of terms with each other?"

"It was you he scolded, Alex," Claude said. "There was nothing wrong with Anne's acting, as I recall."

Alex grinned. "Quite right, of course," he said. "To the nursery, love?"

Chapter 9

Jack closed his book while everyone filed out of the ball-room, intent on having some private time before luncheon and the hunt for greenery. He was feeling somehow be-reaved and strangely trapped inside the play they had been reading. Why had he leapt to such obviously ridiculous conclusions about her? Why had he not given her a chance, a real chance, to defend herself? Why had she not forced him sooner to explain himself, as soon as she had sensed that he was unhappy, angry, bewildered? Why at the end had she not raged against him more firmly? Why had she not screamed foul murder so that Emilia might have re-turned in time to save her?

And why was he feeling bereft over a mere story? Over Shakespeare of all things?

He was the last to leave, he realized when he finally looked up from the book. Except for Belle, who had strolled across the ballroom to gaze from one of the French windows.

He hesitated.

"Why did you come?" he asked her. He had not at all planned the idiotic question. He had to half yell it across the room.

She turned her head to look at him as he strode toward her.

"Why did you come?" he asked again when he could do so at normal volume.

"Is that not the same question as 'How dared you'?" she asked. "I answered it yesterday, Jack."

"Why did you come?" He persisted with his question.

"Did it have anything to do with me, Belle? Did you have any expectation that I would be here? Any fear that I would? Any hope that I would?"

She was looking back into his eyes, as she usually did. "You mean nothing to me, Jack," she said. "Nothing at all."

They had grown expert, the two of them, in the last few months they were together, at fighting each other, at wounding, without ever using physical violence. She had not forgotten the skill. Neither had he.

"I never did, did I?" he said. "I was just your bread and butter, Belle, your way of feeding yourself while you climbed the ladder. And you gave me a year of pleasure in bed without the necessity of my having to hunt for it nightly."

"Yes," she said, holding his eyes. "Yes, we gave and took equally, Jack."

He felt ashamed and angry as he had always felt after such exchanges. Why had there been such a need in him to hurt her? Did one always want to hurt what one loved?

But he did not love her now. That was long in the past.

"Did you love him?" The words hung in the air between them. He was appalled to realize that he had spoken them.

He thought for a moment that she would not answer him.

"Of course I loved him," she said. "Very dearly."

The same words he had used yesterday to describe his feelings for Juliana.

"I did not know you wanted marriage," he said. "I did not know you were willing to settle for one man."

"Knowing it would have made no difference to you," she said. "You would not have married your mistress, Jack. That was all I ever was to you."

He was arrested by an idea suddenly. "Would you have married me?" he asked. "If I had asked you? Would you?"

"It is an academic question, is it not?" she said. "But no. The answer is no. I suppose you were right to say that you were my bread and butter. I cannot think why else I stayed with you for a full year. Everything I was and everything I dreamed of you held in contempt."

He suspected that she had always been a little better at

this game than he. Probably because he had been more vulnerable than she. Even now, it seemed. He felt as if she had
lashed his face with a whip. It was not true. He had loved
her. She had been his life. Yet she would not have married
him—even if he had asked. But he had never thought of
asking.

"Yes," she said, "I loved Maurice. To him I was a person
worthy of respect as well as admiration. I found him irresistible—after you."

She had improved with time. The whip stung again.

A year after Belle, two years after Belle, six years after
he had still grieved. He had still sought to recapture or forget his feelings for her in the bodies of countless courtesans
and ladies of easy virtue.

He would recapture them in innocence, he thought now,
suddenly remembering Juliana. Why was it that he could so
totally forget her for long stretches of time? Yes, there was
Juliana.

"As I love Juliana," he said. "I find her worthy of respect
and admiration."

Her eyes—her beautiful green eyes, which could melt
with tender passion—turned blank. He knew with a feeling
of some satisfaction that she had understood the implied insult. He hoped it hurt—just a little.

"And of your time?" she said. "Perhaps you should seek
her out, Jack. I stayed deliberately after everyone else had
left. I am working, difficult as it may be to understand. I
need to think my way into these parts, into these scenes that
are to be acted out in this room. I need to test the acoustics
and feel the atmosphere. I would prefer that you went
away, rude as it seems to ask such a thing of you in your
grandparents' home."

He turned on his heel and strode from the ballroom without a backward glance.

At first Isabella had decided not to join the family excur-
sion to gather Christmas greenery. Her invitation to Portland House had been a kind one, and she was certainly
being treated as an honored guest rather then as any type of

employee. But still she felt rather awkward. It was such a close, boisterous family. She was an outsider, much as they had welcomed her. She would keep herself somewhat apart as often as she could.

She was feeling, far more than she had expected to, the impropriety of her presence here when she had once been Jack's mistress. Nine years had seemed a long time—until she saw him again. Now it seemed as if it all might have happened yesterday. Her feelings were raw again.

But when she went to the nursery after an early luncheon to suggest another walk to the bridge and perhaps all the way into the village with the children, they stared at her blankly, and Marcel's eyes became cloudy and then stormy.

"But we are going for holly, Maman," he said. "I am going to walk with my friend, Davy. I told you I was going."

Children, of course, could not understand the concept of family, the idea of intruding where one did not quite belong. But they did belong—they had been invited here. And she must never forget that Marcel was the Comte de Vacheron. Meeting Jack again, talking to him, had done terrible things to her, she realized. She was reverting to the feelings of inferiority and inadequacy he had engendered in her.

She smiled at her son and looked at her daughter. "And you, Jacqueline?" she said. "Do you want to go gathering greenery, too?"

"Yes, please, Mama," the child said.

Anne was in the nursery and had overheard part of the conversation. "Oh, Isabella," she said, "did no one think to tell you that the children are going gathering, too? Even the toddlers? Of course Marcel and Jacqueline must come. It is to be more by way of an outing than a work party. Wagons are to be sent to carry home everything that is gathered and to bring hot drinks. I believe there is even to be a bonfire."

"Ye-es!" Marcel clapped his hands and bounced on the spot while Anne laughed.

"Freddie has ridden over to the rectory to fetch Bertrand

and Rose," Anne said. "Dear Freddie. He is so very fond of Ruby's family and hates to see them miss a treat."

It made Isabella feel better to know that other people who were not strictly part of the family were to join the party. And she must go, of course, if her children were to go. It would be unfair to expect other adults to keep a watchful eye on them while she stayed at home or otherwise occupied her time.

And so she set out a little more than a half hour later and felt all the pleasure and pain of being a part of a large family gathering. Pleasure because she saw happiness and exuberance all around her and was not made to feel like an outsider—Stanley and Celia walked on either side of her and Peregrine soon joined them, alone because his pregnant wife had stayed at the house with some of the older people to rest. Pain because she had never really belonged to such a group herself. Her mother and father had always lived far from their own families, and Maurice's family had shunned him after his marriage to her.

Sometimes she felt that she would give up everything for that elusive sense of belonging. She would submerge her personality beneath that of the group just for the peace of being a part of it. But she knew that she would never do so. It had always been her fate to be different, to pursue her own dreams even at the expense of personal happiness.

She thought with a stabbing of pain of last evening and finding Jacqueline in the music room with a violin and bow in her hands. She had thought the child would forget about the instrument after it had been left behind in France and after she had been given a few pianoforte lessons. But, of course, she had not forgotten. And so all the old dread had come flooding back to Isabella. Was Jacqueline to be a freak, too? Like her mother? Why could she not have been more like her father, who was quite without driving ambition?

Her eyes instinctively sought out her daughter. She had been with little Catherine at the start, walking beside Alex and Anne. She was no longer there. She was—ah, she was talking with Jack, who had Juliana's arm drawn through his and who was looking indulgently down at Jacqueline.

And then Isabella's stomach lurched with anger and alarm. He stretched out a hand in invitation. Jacqueline looked gravely at it.

No. Isabella willed her daughter to listen to the silent, distant command. *No, walk away. Walk with the other children. Come and walk with me. No, Jacqueline. No!*

Jacqueline raised her hand and placed it in his. He smiled and said something to her.

"I do believe it is going to snow," Celia said, looking up to the heavy gray sky. "It is certainly cold enough."

"That seems like a distinctly pleasing prospect with Christmas coming," Peregrine said. "There is nothing like having snow to frolic in at Christmastime. Snowmen, snowball fights, snow angels, sledding and sliding and all that. Would you not agree, Comtesse?"

Isabella turned her attention deliberately away from Jacqueline and Jack, walking hand in hand ahead of her. She smiled brightly. "Absolutely," she said. "And I do wish everyone would call me Isabella."

"Isabella." Peregrine stopped to sweep her a bow.

They were walking toward the lake. The real lake, where they had used to boat and swim and picnic during the summers, not the marshy lakes where the bridge was. After an hour or so, the duchess had told them, she would have the wagons sent to pick up their loads and to bring them steaming pitchers of chocolate.

If he was fortunate, Jack thought, he would be able to take Juliana walking beside the lake until they lost themselves among the trees. He wanted to be alone with her again. Just to converse. And perhaps to kiss. Undoubtedly to kiss. He wanted to concentrate on his courtship of her. He wondered if he would have been so eager to fall in with his grandmother's plans if Belle had not turned up as one of her guests. But it did not matter. The fact was that it was time he married and that he could not expect to find a prettier or a sweeter or a more biddable girl.

Girl! The word leapt to mind before he could replace it. It was the only possible objection he could have to Juliana, and a strange objection it would seem to anyone he had cared to confide it to. The younger she was, the better. The easier it would be to mold her to his ways. The longer he could expect her looks to last. The more years she would have to breed his children, especially if she had the misfortune to bear him daughters before the coveted son.

Jack set out from the house with Juliana on his arm. She looked very fetching in a green, fur-lined cloak and hood. He proceeded to entertain her with an exaggerated account of his family's embarrassment and awe at being in the presence of greatness in the ballroom during the morning. He did not spare himself, but described the way he had pressed against the wall even after everyone else had summoned the courage to take a few steps forward, wishing that he could become a part of it or even push through to the other side. He did not, of course, explain his real reason for feeling thus.

"I am sure you do not need to feel inferior," Juliana said. "Her Grace has told me that you are one of the best actors in the family."

Yes, his grandmother would have told Juliana that, along with a description of how handsome he looked in costume, he did not doubt, and of how all the ladies in the audience routinely swooned at sight of him treading the boards. Grandmama was not likely to relax her efforts until he was walking away from the altar with the girl.

Girl! He wished he knew exactly how old she was, but he could scarcely ask her.

A few children zoomed past, coming dangerously close to being tripped over. One of them stopped and smiled cheerily at Juliana.

"You are Miss Beckford," he said. "I remember. I do not know this gentleman. I am Marcel Gellée, sir."

Belle's son. Fair and rather stocky, with the promise of pleasing looks. He resembled his father, she had said.

"Jack Frazer at your service, Mr. Gellée," Jack said while Juliana smiled and greeted the child.

Marcel zoomed off again in pursuit of Rupert and Rachel and Stanley's Kitty.

And then Jack's attention was distracted by an awareness of someone else walking beside him. He looked down.

Dark eyes were gazing up at him from a thin face.

"Jacqueline," he said. He felt a pang at the sight of her, at the memory of her absorption in her music the previous evening, and at the memory of Belle's anger with her.

"Mama said she will see," the child said.

"Did she?" He smiled at her. "Do you know Jacqueline, the Comtesse de Vacheron's daughter, Juliana?"

"It is a lovely French name," Juliana said. "Yes, we have seen each other in the nursery."

"She will see about what?" he asked.

"About giving me lessons," the child said.

"Ah," he said. "And when parents say they will see, they almost invariably mean yes, do they not?"

Her eyes gazed very directly into his, rather reminiscent of the way Belle always looked at him. There was faint hope in them. "Do they?" she said. "Promise?"

Lord, he had said the wrong thing.

"Will you ask Mama?" Jacqueline asked him.

He already had. And she had resented his interference, as he supposed she had every right to do. But her daughter was gazing up at him with all of a child's trust in the sort of magic adults could perform without even having to wave a wand.

"It is that important to you?" he asked. But he answered his own question. She was Belle's daughter. Of course it was important to her. And music was important enough to him that he could understand. "Yes, of course it is. And it should be. I will have a word with your mama."

She did not smile or look excited or press thanks on him, as he would have expected. But he had noticed last evening that she was a very grave little child. A curiously appealing child. He rather enjoyed being climbed upon and molested by the infant children of his sister and cousins, but he had never before felt the appeal of older children. Not since he had been one of their number, anyway.

He did not want her to go away. He felt strangely touched by her trust in his ability to sway Belle in her favor. He held out a hand to her, his fingers spread. He would not force her to the dullness of walking sedately with the adults when there were children roaring around using up their energy quite recklessly even before they had reached the lake and the trees.

When she took his hand, he closed his own about it, and felt its smallness. She was Belle's child, he thought, and she had sought him out and taken his hand.

"A lady at either side of me," he said. "My head has probably swelled by two hat sizes." And he turned to Juliana and explained to her that Jacqueline could play the violin better than anyone he had ever heard. Which was an outright untruth if he paused to think of all the professional musicians he had ever listened to. But he meant it anyway, and so it was not really a lie. He felt no doubt at all that she had the potential for greatness.

"Oh," Juliana said, "then you will have to play at the duchess's concert on Christmas Eve, Jacqueline."

If the children had had the size and strength to match their enthusiasm, Stanley remarked dryly later, when they had reached the lake and had dispersed among the trees, the land would have been laid flat and barren long before the wagons appeared. But fortunately the holly was too prickly and the pine boughs too thick and the mistletoe too high on the oak trees to become endangered species.

Alex and Zeb, Peregrine and Howard Beckford broke off holly boughs and handed them into eager children's arms with strict admonitions to be careful. Even so, Kenneth opened his mouth and bawled as soon as his finger touched a sharp tip and took refuge in his mother's arms for one full minute before wriggling to get down again. And Meg, Stanley's oldest girl, scolded Davy for loading Kitty's arms too full. Marcel was eagerly keeping pace with his older friend, carrying armfuls to pile in the open, where the wagons would pick them up. He sucked on a bleeding finger without any complaint.

Sam, Freddie, Anthony, and Bertrand were cutting down pine boughs and organizing the ladies and more of the children in teams to drag them to set beside the growing pile of holly. Robert, Alice, and the twins had joined hands around the trunk of one of the pine trees and were circling it and chanting their own version of "Ring Around the Rosy," which their nurses had played with them during the morning.

Jack had gone in search of mistletoe, taking Juliana with him. But the girl definitely did not know the rules of courtship or even flirtation, he thought when she pointed out some admirably healthy clumps of the parasite growing on an oak tree that was scarcely out of sight of the masses. But then one did not really need to be out of sight when mistletoe was involved, he supposed.

"Now," he said, looking first upward and then down at the high gloss of his boots. "Can I get up there and down again without falling and breaking my head, do you suppose?" He smiled at her. He knew all about the effects of arousing a woman's protective instincts.

He was not disappointed. Her eyes became instantly anxious. "Do be careful," she said.

"I promise," he said, "that you will not have to catch me."

He could have been up and back in no time at all. But why waste the chance to have her attention focused fully on him? He inched his way up, allowing his booted foot to slip at one point, thankful that his male cousins were too far away and too busy about their own pursuits to observe and jeer.

"There is absolutely nothing to fear," he said, when he had reached a branch on which he could sit with some comfort. He looked down at her upturned face, eyes wide with fear for his safety. "There is really no danger at all."

"Do be careful," she said again.

Perhaps, he thought, gathering the mistletoe and dropping it to the ground at her feet, they could walk farther into the trees when he had climbed back down. He felt the definite urge to press onward with his courtship, and what

better opportunity would the week have to offer? Perhaps if
he could give her a thorough kissing this afternoon he
would not find his mind wandering away from her again.

Damn Belle for coming here to Portland House, he
thought. Oh, damn her. He did not believe for one moment
that she had been unaware or even careless of the fact that
he would be here, too, to celebrate Christmas with his family. She had jumped at her invitation. She had wanted to
spend the week here in company with him. She had wanted
to thumb her nose at him, showing him how great she had
become without his help. She had used him to get her feet
firmly on the ladder and then she had climbed to the top
very easily on her own.

Damn her!

He slithered in good earnest during the descent and
landed on the ground more hastily and heavily than he intended. But the effect was gratifying. Juliana had both
hands to her mouth as she took a step toward him.

"Did you hurt yourself?" she asked.

He grinned at her. "Not at all," he lied, wincing inwardly
at one sore knee and one scraped palm. "Now, let me see if
this mistletoe was worth going up after." He bent to pick up
a sprig. "What do you think?"

She took another step closer, quite unsuspecting. Really,
the girl was a total innocent. Or perhaps she was inviting
the inevitable.

"I suppose the only way we can know for sure is to put it
to the test," he said, raising his eyes to hers and slowly raising his arm above her head.

Her lips were cold against his own, as were her cheeks.
He set his free arm about her waist and drew her against
him. She was tiny and warm and felt satisfying feminine.
Perhaps they would not have to move farther into the cover
of the trees. He was, after all, holding mistletoe above her
head less than a week before Christmas, and everyone
knew that he was courting her, that their betrothal would be
announced before the holiday was over. Her brother was
not likely to slap a glove in his face if he saw.

Jack parted his lips to warm her and touched his tongue to her lips.

She pushed hard at his chest and took a step back. For a moment, until she schooled herself to hide her feelings, there was panic in her eyes.

He had told himself that he must be patient and gentle, Jack thought, lowering his arm. But how patient and how gentle could he be? He had the distinct conviction that she would stiffen into total rigidity when he topped her on a bed on their wedding night. Unless she could school herself to a sense of her duty for that occasion, that was. Undoubtedly she would open to him sweetly enough. He would just have to be—patient. And gentle.

"I am sorry, Juliana," he said. "You do not know about such kisses?"

"I, er, I thought I heard someone calling," she said, looking back over her shoulder. "I did not mean to—I am sorry."

But someone was coming to save the moment. That solemn little daughter of Belle's again.

"Ah, Jacqueline," he said. "Have you come to help carry the mistletoe? I have just been testing it with Miss Beckford. Do you know what it is for?"

"Yes," she said. "We always make a kissing bough at home."

"Do you?" He grinned at her, relieved that she had interrupted a romantic moment gone slightly awry. "I tested it on Miss Beckford. Shall I test it on you, too?"

"Yes," she said solemnly, and raised her face to him as he hoisted the mistletoe over her head.

He had intended to peck her cheek, but she had puckered her lips. He kissed them softly instead and then smiled again, still stooped over her. "It does work very nicely, does it not?"

"Yes," she said, and bent over the bundle to lift it into her arms. "Aunt Anne says the wagons will be here soon. The gentleman who is her husband is lighting a fire."

Jack offered his arm to Juliana. "The thought of a fire and hot drinks is irresistibly enticing, is it not?" he said.

But before she took his arm and before Jacqueline had
had a chance to straighten up again, he glanced toward
where the fire would be and saw Belle standing among the
trees, very still, one hand to her mouth, looking at him. She
turned sharply even as he caught sight of her and hurried
back to the others. He followed more slowly with Juliana
and Jacqueline.

Chapter 10

There was a merry gathering about the fire. After the wagons had been loaded with the greenery, they all stood about the crackling flames, drinking chocolate that was still comfortingly hot, warming their hands on the cups, stretching them out to the blaze. And they sang Christmas carols afterward, while the servants packed the empty cups and jugs into a box, loaded it onto the back of one wagon, and drove home. Christmas suddenly seemed very much closer, they were all agreed.

"Only a few days to go," Kitty said wistfully.

"How many sleeps?" Marcel wanted to know.

The children were the first to become restless. Most of them trailed after Davy, the eldest, down to the lakeside to throw stones to smash the ice forming about the edges. Stanley and Celia and Freddie followed them to make sure that no one tried to step onto the thin ice.

Constance and Prudence started on the walk home with their husbands. Bertrand and Howard went to explore the boathouse, taking Rose and Juliana with them.

Jack moved up beside Isabella. "Come," he said curtly. And then, in case any of those left close by were within earshot, "Would you care for a stroll beside the lake before starting back? There are some rather picturesque views."

They had been standing at opposite sides of the fire for close to half an hour, conversing with those on either side of them. Their eyes had not even met. But tension pulsed between them. They might as well have it out before returning to the house, Jack thought grimly. And clearly she was of the same mind.

"Thank you." She took his arm. "That would be pleasant."

They walked in silence along the old path beside the water. Soon enough they would be hidden from the fire by the trees, bare as most of them were of leaves.

"I saw the expression on your face," he said at last, surprised at the sound of suppressed fury in his voice, "despite the distance. It is Christmas, Belle, and I was holding mistletoe. For God's sake, men kiss their grandmothers beneath mistletoe. Or infants in arms."

He was further infuriated when she said nothing.

"I kissed a seven-year-old child beneath the mistletoe," he said, "and your looks and your silence make me feel like a child molester. I resent it, Belle. Good Lord, I resent it. Juliana was there, too. I had just kissed her at far greater length."

"I am sure you had," she said, her voice tight.

"And I resent being put on the defensive," he said, "feeling that I must justify even what I do with the woman to whom I will be betrothed next week."

She turned on him. "And I resent your resentment," she said. "I came here with my children for some relaxation. I came for a holiday. I came to celebrate Christmas with a family at the gracious request of the head of the family. I resent the fact that you are spoiling all that."

"No!" He caught at her arm and swung her back against the trunk of a tree. He set a hand on the trunk beside her head and stepped closer. "You came here because it is my family, Belle. You came here because you knew I would be here. You came to show me what you had made of yourself without my help. You came to show off your respectability and your fame and the children you had from a lawful and impressively eligible marriage. You came to show me what you showed me every day for a whole year, that all you ever needed from me was my money."

Her head was pressed back against the trunk. "I gave a great deal in exchange for that money," she said.

"Oh, yes." He set his free hand on the other side of her head. "You gave your body very openly, Belle, and whenever I asked for it. I have never had it better, you may be gratified to know."

"I gave more than that," she said. "Or rather you took more than that. You took all my self-respect and all my self-confidence, Jack. You made me feel like a nobody. And I allowed you to do that. I earned every penny you ever spent on me."

He was immeasurably hurt. And angered. He had loved her! And she had betrayed him. "And so you came here to show me that I was wrong about you," he said. "That was why you came. Admit it, Belle."

Her eyes roamed his face. "If you say so," she said at last. "Yes, if you say so, Jack."

"Well, you have made your point," he said. "Are you satisfied?"

"It was such a long time ago," she said. "Nine years. I was curious, I suppose. A whole year of my life had been given to you. And there were some good memories. More good than bad, perhaps. I found sometimes that I could not remember what you looked like. I wanted to see you again. I wanted to—to forgive you, perhaps. I am not sure you really meant to hurt me. And you did not succeed even if you did mean to."

He stared at her. "You wanted to forgive me?" he said. "After what you did to me, Belle? After—after all those other men who came to worship you in the green room while you were supposed to be my lo—, my woman? You wanted to forgive me?"

She closed her eyes. "It does not matter," she said. "It was foolish of me to come. More foolish than I realized when I decided to accept the duchess's invitation. It was a long time ago, Jack, and we did not really care for each other even then. It was a business arrangement. I do not really know why things have been as they have for the last few days. It is foolish."

"Perhaps," he said, his voice harsh, "there is one way to purge the memories, Belle."

She opened her eyes to look into his, and shook her head slowly when she saw what was in them. "No," she said.

"No, Jack. I have children to consider now, and you have a courtship to pursue."

"This has nothing to do with either children or courtship," he said. "This has to do with old memories and old needs." He brought his body against hers and closed his eyes. "This has to do with you and me, Belle, and with—curiosity, if you like. What are you like now? What am I like now? You are right. There were good times. We could still be good together. Perhaps we could forget the bitterness of the ending if—"

But her mouth had come up to meet his and cut off the words.

His body pressed hers to the tree, one of his legs pushing between her thighs. They explored each other with hard, desperate hands, and ravished each other with fierce, demanding mouths and tongues. He felt her ignite with a need and a hunger to match his own—for perhaps a minute, perhaps two.

And then they both paused, bodies still pressed together, mouths still joined, eyes still closed, digesting what had happened, what was happening. He lifted his head away and looked into her eyes. Bleak eyes.

"I am sorry," he said softly.

"There can be no more good times, Jack," she said. "There was too much bitterness. And it was too long ago. I am sorry, too. Sorry that I came, not realizing that it would be like this."

Like this. Unchanged. Still yearning, aching with love for her. Still bewildered by her unattainability. He had paid for her, and he had used her body for a year. He had loved her and guarded her and been jealous and angry and hurt. He had raged against her, called her names, tried to hurt her, belittle her so that he might somehow bring her down to an attainable level. She had been his paid mistress and yet as far beyond his reach as the sun and the stars.

"I am sorry," he said again. "Sorry for the disrespect. I am sorry, Belle." He pushed himself away from her, turned his back on her. "But you never need fear for your daughter in my company. I feel an affection for her, just as I would feel for a niece or a-a daughter. If you have ever believed anything I have told you, believe that."

"I do." Her voice was flat, toneless. "I do, Jack. Do you want me to return to London? I shall make some excuse and leave tomorrow if you wish it. I was wrong to come. None of this is your fault."

"Perhaps," he said, "we should prove that we can behave in an adult, rational, civilized manner. Stay, Belle. My grandparents are inordinately pleased to have you. And so are all the others. And your children need company for Christmas." He turned back to her. She was still leaning against the tree, looking at him with troubled eyes. "We had better be getting back to the others." He offered his arm.

She did not take it, but she fell into step beside him.

"I, ah, I have been persuaded to have a word with you," he said. "About the violin lessons. Apparently you have said you will see, but it is not clear if that means yes, no, or maybe."

"I suppose," she said wearily, "it means yes. I wanted to protect her from the sort of life I have led, Jack. I wanted her to be normal. I wanted her to marry when she is old enough and settle down with a husband and children in a comfortable home."

"Perhaps she will," he said. "She is merely a child wanting to play a violin."

"You listened to her," she said. "And I heard in your voice last night that you realized the truth. No, she will do as I did. She will be compelled to go as far as she can with her talent."

"Is that bad?" he asked. "You need not have done so, Belle. You might have stayed with me. Or presumably you might have settled to comfortable obscurity with de Vacheron. It was your choice to reach for more. It will be hers to do likewise—or not."

"You do not understand, do you?" she said. "You never understood. I did not have a choice. The compulsion to pursue my dreams came from deep inside me and drove me on. I always wanted to act, and I always wanted to be as good as I could be. But I wanted everything else, too. I wanted love and passion and . . . Oh, what does it matter? I could not have everything. I am a woman, and if a woman does not choose marriage and motherhood to the exclusion of all else, she must be either an embarrassing oddity or else—or else a whore."

Why, he wondered, had she never spoken like this to him ten years ago? Why was he suddenly feeling that he did not know her at all? That he had never known her?

"Jack," she said, "I wanted Jacqueline to be different. I wanted to protect her from all that. Oh, why can we not shape our children into the people we want them to be? I love her. You will never know how I love her."

He took the arm she had refused to set through his and linked it with his own. He covered her hand with his.

"Then love her, Belle," he said from instinct alone. He was quite out of his depth. "It is all you can do, my dear. Love her and love her. No matter what."

As perhaps he should have done with Belle.

Her eyes, he could see when he glanced at her, were glistening with tears.

The children were still playing down at the lake. Some of the adults were still trying to draw comfort from the embers of the fire. Jack caught Alex's eye, and his cousin raised his eyebrows.

Juliana had made a decision during the afternoon. She was going to take command of her own life. She was nineteen years old, and it was time. She had been shy of life and of people and so had kept away from both, and allowed her mama and papa and her grandmama to arrange her life for her. She had allowed life to happen to her according to their plans.

It was not that she planned to rebel exactly. What would she do if she decided that? She knew nothing of life and the sorts of choices it might be able to offer her. She admired Rose Fitzgerald enormously for having the courage to reject two marriage offers and decide to become a governess instead. Rose had told her that during their morning walk. She could not imagine herself doing likewise. She would hate being a governess.

But she was ignorant and gauche and did not like those qualities in herself. She was deeply shamed and embarrassed at the way she had reacted to Mr. Frazer's kiss at the oak tree—to *Jack's* kiss, she told herself deliberately. He was her betrothed or almost so, and there had been nothing improper in his kissing her even without the excuse of the mistletoe. She had no idea if his way of kissing had been proper, but it probably was. They had been almost in sight of the others, after all.

It was just her stupid ignorance that had made her jump back in shock and make an utter cake of herself in the process. She had almost cried with relief when Jacqueline had come along to help with the mistletoe.

And then she had run off with Howard and Rose and Mr. Fitzgerald at the first opportunity to see the boathouse and the boats in the hope that she could avoid having to walk back to the house with Mr.—with Jack. It had been a dreadfully childish thing to do. As had been her exuberance and her enjoyment of the half hour that had followed and the walk back to the house.

She had found herself wishing that it was Fitz—he had asked her to call him that—who was her chosen bridegroom. Not that he was a particularly handsome man and not that she felt any particular attraction to him. It was just that he was easy company, easy to talk with, easy to laugh with. He was so very totally unthreatening.

But he was not her chosen bridegroom. Jack was. And she could see nothing wrong with the choice apart from the foolish gaucheness she always felt in his presence. He was handsome—and that was an understatement, charming, kind, attractive—yes, he was undeniably that, wealthy, a landowner, young—well, youngish. He was everything she could possibly dream of in a husband. She had been well pleased, if a little nervous, when she had first been told that she was to marry him.

But the trouble with her was that she liked to hide behind dreams and avoid reality. The dream of Jack had been far more comfortable than the reality. The reality of that kiss— just a kiss!—had thrown her into a panic.

It was time she took control of her own life, she decided when she was in her room after returning home, getting ready to go back downstairs to help with the decorating. She was tempted not to go at all, but that would be too typical of her and would solve nothing. If she was ashamed to face Jack now, it would be only harder to do so if she stayed in her room until dinner time.

She was going to marry Jack, she told her image in the looking glass as she smoothed out the imaginary wrinkles in her dress. She was going to marry him, not only because Papa and Grandmama had planned it that way, but because she wanted to. She was going to learn over the next few days to be as comfortable with him as she was with Fitz. She was even going to fall in love with him. She had always dreamed of marrying a man she loved. And she was going to treat him over the next few days, and for the rest of her life, as a woman would treat a man.

She was not a child. She was nineteen years old. Most women of her age were married already. She was not going to behave like a child, then. She was a woman.

And so when she made her way to the ballroom and found it full of people milling about, stepping gingerly around piles of greenery and over boxes of ribbons and bows and bells, she ignored her first instinct, which was to join the group that included her father, Howard, Fitz, and Rose, and looked about until her eyes alit on Jack, who was standing in the middle of the floor with Viscount Merrick and Mr. Lynwood, staring upward.

She did what was perhaps the hardest thing she had ever done in her life. She crossed the room toward them, touched Jack's arm, and smiled into his eyes. "How may I help, Jack?" she asked.

He looked surprised, but he smiled back, and his hand came across to cover hers and hold it against his arm. She resisted the urge either to pull away or to lower her gaze. He really did have quite splendid dark eyes. Perhaps there was some cynicism in them, but there was genuine warmth there, too.

"Just by standing there and looking pretty," he said. "But I daresay that would be rather tedious for you, would it not?"

She could hardly believe that a reply came immediately to her mind. She spoke deliberately. "That depends upon what there is for me to look at," she said. He was in his shirtsleeves. She had only just noticed that.

His eyes warmed with surprised interest. "Actually," he said, "I am about to ascend to the heavens. It seems that ribbons and bells hanging from the chandeliers are an absolute essential, and I have been elected to put them there. We usually send Freddie, but Freddie has been pleading advancing years and advancing girth."

"I say," Freddie said, "that is not quite it, Jack. It is just that Ruby is afraid I will hurt myself, Miss Beckford, and I do not like to make Ruby anxious."

"Besides," Jack said, "if Freddie were to remove his coat, we would all have to behold the full expanse of that waistcoat. It might cause collective blindness. How would you describe that particular shade, Fred, my lad? Is it *sunshine* yellow or *mustard* yellow?"

"Damme," Freddie said, looking down at himself, "but it is a fine color, is it not? Glad you like it, Jack."

Alex laughed and slapped a hand on his shoulder. "If you ever appeared in a subdued waistcoat, Freddie," he said, "we would all wonder what was ailing you. I am glad Ruby has not turned you sober."

Juliana smiled at Jack. She still had her hand on his arm.

"If you care to watch me climb the ladder," he said, "I shall contrive to make the climb seem more difficult and dangerous than it really is."

"As you did at the oak tree?" she said, making an effort not to flinch at the mention of the scene of her humiliation.

His eyes focused fully on her, amusement deep in them. "I did not fool you?" he said. "I must be slipping—no pun intended. How did you know? Have my acting skills deteriorated?"

"Howard and I climb trees all the time at home," she said. "Or we did until a few years ago, anyway."

"The devil!" he said. "So I made a prize idiot of myself, did I?"

She was actually enjoying herself. This really was not so difficult after all. "I will not tell anyone," she said.

"Perhaps," he said, patting her hand and finally removing his own, "you would select some of the largest and prettiest decorations and bring them over here for Alex to hand up to me. Would you? Women invariably have better taste in such matters than men."

Everyone was busy, Juliana could see as she made her way to the nearest box of ornaments. Some of the items were being dragged away to the drawing room and the dining room, holly and boughs and decorations were being hung about the ballroom, the comtesse and Anne with a few of the children were making a large kissing bough, which was to be hung in the drawing room, toddlers were darting about, shrieking with glee, and the duchess stood in the midst of it all, directing operations like the colonel of a regiment.

Juliana made her selections and took them back to the center of the room, where a tall ladder had been set up beneath the largest of the three chandeliers. Alex and Freddie held it while Jack climbed, with far greater assurance than he had shown when climbing the much safer tree a few hours before. Juliana smiled at the memory and at the way she had just admitted to him that she had known what he was about.

It had felt good to tease him and laugh with him. It really had felt good. Perhaps her new decision was not going to be difficult to implement after all. She stood watching. Without his coat and waistcoat he looked broader-shouldered, narrower-hipped. And whatever he did for exercise had certainly succeeded in giving him powerful thigh muscles. She could see them tautening beneath his tight pantaloons as he climbed. And she could remember how they had felt when he had drawn her against him as he kissed her.

The realization that she was deliberately watching him when he was in a state of some undress, that she was deliberately appreciating his attractiveness shocked her for a moment, and she lowered her eyes and made to move away. There was that very real maleness about him that had frightened her from the start. But she stopped herself in time and looked back up and allowed her eyes and her imagination to roam.

This was not a dream situation she was in. It was reality. If they were to be betrothed at Christmas, Papa would want the wedding soon after, probably in the spring. In a few months' time she was going to be this man's wife. She was going to have to share her bed with him whenever it pleased him to come there. She was going to have to become familiar with that body.

And really it was a very attractive body. She felt a quickening in her breathing and a strange tightening in her breasts and a throbbing ache between her legs as she gazed. Yes, very attractive. It would not be at all difficult to fall in love with him. Surely she was more than halfway there already.

By the time Jack was finished and had come down the ladder for the last time, everything else appeared to have been done, too, apart from the clearing away and tidying up. He smiled at Juliana and looked about him.

"There," he said. "Instantly it is Christmas. I believe we have done rather well. Shall we peep in on the dining room and the drawing room to see how they look?"

He set a hand lightly on her shoulder and guided her toward the doorway. Her mother and his, she noticed, were standing together, and both were smiling and nodding approvingly.

Well, let them think they had accomplished this, she thought. In a way they had. But it was her courtship now, and Jack's. It was no longer something she was letting happen to her because it was the right and dutiful thing to do. It was something she was making happen because it was what she wanted.

"I wonder what the kissing bough looks like," she said. "Anne and Lady de Vacheron were working very hard at it. They were going to have it hung in the drawing room." She could feel herself blush, but she forced herself to look at him.

"We must certainly go and see," he said.

Chapter 11

It had been impossible for Isabella to escape to her room after their return to the house. Marcel had danced about her in the hall while Davy and his sisters looked on, begging her to make a kissing bough, as they always did. And even Jacqueline had come to hold her hand and look pleadingly into her eyes.

"I have told Davy and Meggie and Kitty that you make prettier kissing boughs than anyone, Maman," Marcel said.

Three of the older ladies, including Jack's mother, who had spent the afternoon in the attic sorting through boxes of Christmas decorations, overheard Marcel, and Lady Maud smiled indulgently.

"You certainly must oblige us, my dear Comtesse," she said. "I shall tell Mama that you have volunteered."

And so she was forced to go to the ballroom like everyone else. But it was just as well, she decided as a group of children gathered about her and Anne came to help with the kissing bough. She had offered to return to London tomorrow, and he had said no. He had suggested that they try to behave as rational, civilized adults. And he had reminded her that she was there at the express invitation of the Duke and Duchess of Portland.

She and Jack had confronted each other. They had got everything out into the open—all the awkwardness of being here together, all the anger and suspicion. Now they could proceed to enjoy their separate Christmases even though they must do so beneath the same roof.

"I am going to enjoy this," Anne said as they moved to the part of the ballroom the duchess had designated for the making of the kissing bough. "Oh, I do so love Christmas. It is the most wonderful time of the year. And everyone seemed to be of the opinion this afternoon that it is going to snow before the night is out. I hardly dare hope."

Isabella gathered all the greenery and decorations they would need, and set about directing her rather large and eager army. The children talked excitedly about snow and snowmen and skating and Christmas presents and Christmas pudding.

Yes, it was a wonderful time of the year, Isabella thought, and she could not have chosen to spend it with a friendlier family. Last Christmas they had been alone together, she and the children. It was the time she had most missed Maurice.

Jack was climbing a tall ladder in the middle of the room to hang decorations on the chandelier. Juliana was standing at the foot of the ladder, watching him. Owning him. They belonged together. It would be the most wonderful Christmas of all for them.

Isabella concentrated on helping Kitty tie a bow in the red ribbon she had threaded about the bough.

He had removed his coat and waistcoat. He looked impossibly attractive in just his shirt, pantaloons, and Hessians. He did not look so very different. And he had not felt so very different either. In fact, there had been a startling familiarity in the feel of his body and his mouth.

"No, no," she said to Marcel. "Let's not put all the mistletoe together in one clump. Try putting little sprigs in various places all over it. Yes, like that." She lifted a hand to ruffle his hair. "Good boy."

She had wondered nine years ago if it would be possible to live without Jack. Despite everything, the temptation to stay with him until he was the one to turn her off had been almost overwhelming. But she had known that even if it was going to prove to be impossible to live without him, it was certainly impossible to continue living with him. He had never respected her. He had only ever wanted one thing from her. And he had been becoming increasingly bad-tempered and unreasonable and jealous. Things could only have become worse.

The vestiges of her self-respect had driven her away. And she had found that indeed it was possible to live on; not just to survive but to live, to begin a new life, many times better than the old.

She had always despised the pangs of nostalgia for Jack that she had never been able to kill. She still despised them.

"There," Anne said, "it is finished. How very splendid it is. Is it not lovely, Jacqueline?" She hugged the child with one arm about her shoulders. "What a clever mama you have. Where is Kenneth? Oh, there he is with Prue and Alice. He is quite safe. Shall we take the bough to the drawing room?"

Oh, yes, Isabella thought, getting to her feet. Anywhere but the ballroom. He belonged to someone else now. And even if he did not, she would not want any involvement with him. It was too late for that. No, it was not that it was too late. The time had never been right for her and Jack. Their relationship had been a mistake from start to finish.

The drawing room was already crowded with adults and children, who were transforming it from classical elegance to a colorful, fragrant Christmas wonderland. Lady Sarah Lynwood and Jack's mother were setting up a Nativity Scene in the window, and everyone else was busy with the other decorations. But almost everyone stopped work to admire the kissing bough, and almost everyone gathered around to watch it being hung in the middle of the room. Zebediah and Howard Beckford and Anthony hung it, following Isabella's directions.

And then they all stood around, gazing admiringly up at it. It really was one of her best efforts, Isabella thought, though of course she had had plenty of help.

"All the credit must go to Isabella," Anne was saying. "I have never made one before."

The duke had come into the room, Isabella saw, and was standing close to the bough, leaning heavily on a cane. Jack had also come in, Juliana on his arm. He was still without his coat and waistcoat.

"Then the countess must be the first to be kissed beneath it," the duke said gruffly, sounding rather as if he were sentencing someone to cruel and unusual punishment. "Ma'am, step forward if you will and allow me to do the honors."

Isabella was coming to realize that the duke's gruff exterior hid a warm and rather gentle man. She stepped forward and smiled her public smile—the one that she knew dazzled those about her. She was acutely aware of Jack and the kiss they had shared without benefit of mistletoe just a few hours before. And of the sweet young girl on his arm.

"The honor will be all mine, Your Grace," she said, holding her face up for the duke's smacking kiss and then setting her hands on his shoulders to kiss him back. She laughed as someone—Peregrine, she thought—whistled.

"So that is what the kissing bough is for," someone said with a laugh as Isabella took the duke's arm and helped him move from beneath it. "What an interesting notion."

And Howard Beckford took their place, drawing Rose Fitzgerald with him. He kissed her soundly, and she blushed rosily.

"Careful, Beckford," Mr. Bertrand Fitzgerald said, "or I will demand to know your intentions." But he was grinning broadly, Isabella could see.

Everyone was very merry. And several more people had to try out the kissing bough—"just to see if it works," Alex said, chuckling as he kissed Anne.

"I wonder," Isabella heard Juliana say, "if any of those sprigs of mistletoe is the one you held over me earlier."

If the duke had not still been holding Isabella's arm to his side, she would have moved away, perhaps even have left the room. But she could not move.

"Now, would I recognize it if I saw it, I wonder," Jack's voice said, sounding amused. "I must confess that I had other matters on my mind at the time. Shall we go and see?"

"I really think we ought," she said.

Juliana, it seemed, had got over the shyness and reluctance she had felt at first. Doubtless Jack's charm had worked its magic on her, and she was fast falling in love with him.

Isabella had to watch as they kissed beneath the kissing bough to the sound of several whistles. It seemed to her that it was rather a deep kiss—as it ought to be. In a few days' time, they were going to be officially betrothed.

The duke made the familiar rumbling sound in his throat that Isabella was beginning to recognize as laughter. "In my day," he said, "we would not have released a pretty gel so soon, Countess. Not when we had mistletoe to allow us to take unwonted liberties. Stroll over to my chair with me, my dear, if you will, and I shall have Stan and Perry help me down into it."

All feeling of Christmas had disappeared by the time Isabella had complied with his request. She had to look determinedly about her to recapture some of it. And then Marcel was pulling at her hand.

"I want to kiss you, Maman," he said. "Last year you said I was the man of the family now."

"And so you are," she said, smiling down at him and allowing him to pull her beneath the kissing bough again. Bending to kiss his puckered lips, she felt the familiar almost painful rush of love for him—and for Jacqueline who was standing close by.

It was the most meaningful love of her life, her love for her children. She must never forget that. And Christmas was coming. She must make it a happy one for them. When all was said and done, they were the only persons who really mattered in her life.

"Billiards, Jack?" Alex set a hand on his cousin's shoulder later in the evening, after some people had wandered off to the music room to prepare musical items for the Christmas Eve concert and almost everyone else had settled to cards in the drawing room. "We both have lines to learn and rehearsals to attend tomorrow. We have to snatch every opportunity for relaxation that presents itself."

Jack followed Alex to the billiard room only to find that relaxation was not the purpose of going there after all. Alex wandered to the window and stood staring out at snow falling against the darkness. Jack even knew why he had been brought there. The two cousins had been close as boys. Sometimes they could almost read each other's minds. He had known, for example, four years ago that he had no real chance with Anne because, despite appearances, Alex loved her.

"Grandpapa is still head of this family," Jack said warily. "You are not going to try to assume his role before you are entitled to it, are you, Alex? You are not about to read me a lecture?"

"I am a *member* of this family," Alex said without turning. "That is enough. I care about family feelings and family honor. You are not going to embarrass us all over Christmas, Jack."

"And how might I accomplish that?" Jack asked, pretending not to understand. He hated it when Alex played the part of respectable citizen. There had been a time not so long ago when Alex had been as wild as he. They had even vied for some of the same women. Alex had usually borne off the prize, damn him. "By kissing Juliana too enthusiastically beneath the kissing bough? That is what a kissing bough is for. I noticed you making free with it with Anne."

"Jack," Alex said, "she is very lovely. Quite extraordinarily so, in fact. And there is a sort of magnetism about her that draws one's eyes to her when she is in the same room."

"Anne would not enjoy hearing you say that," Jack said. He did not even need to ascertain that it was neither Anne nor Juliana about whom they were speaking.

"My feelings for Anne are deep and secure enough that I do not have to pretend not to notice beauty in other women," his cousin said. "I can understand that you are dazzled, Jack. And, of course, although she is eminently respectable, she is an actress and there is a tendency in some men to assume that therefore—"

He got no farther before he was spun around and two iron-hard hands clamped onto the lapels of his coat and half lifted him from the floor. His back slammed against the window frame.

"You had better not complete that thought," Jack said, his voice like steel, "unless you want to be swallowing or spitting teeth for the next hour."

Alex said nothing. Jack's hands gradually relaxed and dropped to his sides. They stood staring at each other, Jack breathing rather hard.

"I do not suppose you asked Grandmama to find you a bride," Alex said. "Perhaps you did not even fully realize when you came here that she had found you one and that you were expected to pay court to her here over Christmas and offer for her before the holiday is over. Grandmama does have a tendency to be high-handed and to act unilaterally on such matters. But the fact is, Jack, that the girl was brought here with expectations and that you showed almost from the first moment that you were ready to answer them. If you had not done so, no one could have blamed you even though there might have been some embarrassment. But you did."

"I fully intend to marry her," Jack said, looking steadily at him, "if she will have me. I believe she will."

"And have the Comtesse de Vacheron on the side?" Alex asked quietly. "To entertain you while you wait for your bride? Is it to be your room or hers tonight, Jack?"

Jack punched him on the jaw, and his eyes clenched with pain as the back of his head bounced off the window frame.

"You will defend yourself or apologize," Jack said from between clenched teeth. "You have insulted a lady even if she is not present to hear. I took her strolling beside the lake. She is a stranger to the area. I am familiar with it. Does it make her a scarlet woman that she came with me?"

"Jack." Alex fingered his jaw gingerly. "I took Anne walking, too—or started to. I thought to catch up to the two of you. Fortunately Anne was pointing out something across the lake when I saw you. I believe—and hope—that she saw nothing, though she must have wondered why I cut short our walk so abruptly. I did see, and my eyes could not have been deceived about what I saw. It was not a Christmas embrace. Not by any stretch of the imagination."

Jack's fists dropped to his sides. "It is none of your business," he said, his voice flat.

"On the contrary," Alex said. "There is a young lady here who would be badly hurt and humiliated if the truth were known. And there are two families here—one of them my own—who would be deeply embarrassed. And my family would be dishonored. Oh, yes, it is my business. You will wait until you are off family property, Jack, before continuing with your whoring. I make no apology for the interference. And if you raise those damned fists again, you will feel mine right between the eyes. We will see how both ladies like you with two black eyes."

Jack stretched his fingers at his sides and clenched them again.

"Perhaps it is foolish of me to feel disappointed in you, Jack," Alex said. "But I do. And I must confess I am disappointed in the comtesse, too. I had the impression she had more class."

"I hate the sort of glib judgments that are so often made by the respectable," Jack said. "You saw with your eyes and thought you knew the whole of it, Alex. You know nothing. I loved Belle once—a long time ago, before her marriage. You think me incapable of love, of course, but she was my life for a whole year. You did not know. No one knew. She was too important to me to be flaunted in front of my friends. But suggest one more time that there was something sordid in her behavior this afternoon and it is all over between you and me, family notwithstanding."

Alex closed his eyes again briefly. "She was your mistress?" he said. "What a coil. But it cannot be resumed, Jack. Not here."

"Fool!" Jack said. "Of course it cannot be resumed when she is who she is and when I am on the brink of contracting a marriage with someone else. You do not need to fear for the damned family honor, Alex. I am going to marry Juliana, and I am going to make a marriage of it, too. That is family tradition as well, is it not, though it took you a year or two after your own marriage to live up to expectations. My whoring days are at an end."

Alex passed the fingers of one hand through his hair, but paused when they reached the back of his head.

"You have given me a devilish large egg back here, Jack," he said. "And doubtless a bruised jaw, which I am going to have to explain away somehow. Good Lord, when did we last fight? And I did not even have the satisfaction of getting in a punch this time. I used to pride myself on being able to draw blood from your nose within the first minute of our fisticuffs."

"And you always got cracked and sore knuckles for your pain," Jack said. "Shall we play a game of billiards since we made the effort to come here?"

"If you can stand being whipped," Alex said, shaking his head as if to clear it and then wincing. "I believe I have a sizable winning record over you, Jack."

Jack selected a cue and thought of Juliana. And of Belle. And felt slightly sick.

The snow had fallen thickly all night and was still falling softly during the morning. It blanketed everything outdoors, making of lawns and flower beds and paths and driveway one uniform expanse of white. And it hung heavy on every branch of every tree.

"If that is not the loveliest Christmas scene you ever saw," Constance said, her fingers laced with Sam's as they joined the rest of the family in the breakfast room, "I would like to know what is."

No one chose to argue with her.

Perry and Martin and Freddie were scheduled to spend the morning in the ballroom rehearsing their scene with Isabella. Several of the others eyed the outdoors with some enthusiasm.

"Soft snow," Stanley said. "It is always the best for making snowmen."

"And for snowballs," Jack added.

"And we really have no choice in the matter anyway," Zeb said. "Hortense and I peeped in at the nursery on the way down to see if anyone was awake. Tell them, Hortense."

"There was not a child who was not shrieking," she said, "unless it was perhaps Jacqueline. And there was not one who was not bouncing and demanding to be taken outside now if not sooner. Zeb had to make his usual threat of slapped bottoms—though he never carries it out, do you, love?—in order to get them to agree to eat breakfast first."

"And to get dressed first," her husband added.

And so less than an hour later—considerably less—all of the children without exception spilled out of doors at a run, and an admirable number of adults followed in their wake.

"Of course," Jack remarked to Juliana, "having real children in the house always gives one an excuse for behaving childishly when something as irresistible as a good snowfall comes along."

They started with a brisk snowball fight in which the adults made themselves open targets and roared and then grinned when hit while the child with the lucky aim squealed and crowed with delight and then turned and ran for fear of retaliation. And then they divided into four teams for the building of snowmen. Whoever built the largest, Alex declared, would have as a prize the right to boast about it for the rest of the holiday.

Jack, Juliana, Stanley, and Celia had Marcel, Jacqueline, Davy and Robert as helpers. Jacqueline and Davy built with the earnest intention of winning the prize. Robert seemed more intent on burying himself in the snow. Marcel talked as he worked.

He was rather a sweet child, Jack thought, good-naturedly lending an ear to the constant prattle. He remembered Belle's telling him that she did not want him anywhere near her children. But they had had it all out yesterday and had succeeded in treating each other with perfect civility since.

Except that he had dreamed about her again last night, he remembered suddenly. She had been beside him in bed, the side of her head cradled in her hand, propped on her elbow, her golden hair spilling over his shoulder and tickling him. She had been laughing, laughing with pure merriment until he had lifted one arm, set his hand behind her head, and brought her mouth down to his. Then she had stopped. And so had the dream. He had woken up, aching with emptiness.

It was a memory from the early days. He had almost forgotten that they had used to laugh a great deal, usually over the absurd stories he always stored up to tell her. Much of the laughter had disappeared later in their relationship.

"And we came over in a big ship," Marcel was saying, "and everyone was sick because the water was swaying. But I was not. I looked after my maman and Jacquie because I am the man of the family. That is what Maman says. My papa is dead, you know. I like being the man of the family, but sometimes I wish I still had a papa. I used to ride on Papa's shoulders. I can remember. Papa used to talk French."

Their team were the winners by virtue of an elongated head, which Davy squeezed to the desired height as he sat astride Stanley's shoulders.

"Well, Davy, my lad," his father said, "you may boast in the nursery until all the other children are ready to hurl their milk at you, and I will boast in the drawing room until I have tea tossed at me. Tea that has been allowed to cool, it is to be hoped."

Robert emerged from his igloo to cheer the fact that he was a winner.

It was time to go back to the house. They all had red noses and fingers. Gloves and scarves and coats, too, were largely caked with snow.

Marcel trotted along beside Jack and Juliana. "I will ride on your shoulders if you wish," he said to Jack.

Jack stopped and looked down at him. He read some wistfulness in the child's voice. Did he miss his father dreadfully? He must have been no more than three years old when de Vacheron died, but he remembered him. And the child was asking him to do with him what he remembered his father doing? Jack felt a curious tugging at his heart. He bent down, picked up the little boy, and swung him astride his shoulders.

Marcel talked all the way home. Jacqueline, Jack noticed, walked quietly at his side.

He was rather touched. And also rather dismayed. He hoped that Belle would not be looking out of any of the windows to observe them. It was true that Juliana was at his other side and the children had obviously got to know her in the nursery, but it seemed that it was to him they had attached themselves.

But that was not the worst of it. When they got back to the house, Jack lifted Marcel down to the floor and the child raced off to join some of the other children, who were being herded upstairs by Ruby with the promise of hot milk. Something tugged at Jack's greatcoat.

Jacqueline was gazing up at him with huge and pleading eyes. "May I go to the music room?" she whispered.

Oh, good Lord!

"Have you asked your mama?" he asked.

"She says I can have lessons," she said. "She says she will buy me a violin again. Please may I go and play? Please?"

There was no sign of Belle or of Perry, Martin, or Freddie. They must still be at rehearsal.

"You will miss the hot drinks," he said. "Would you not prefer to wait and ask your mama later?"

But she shook her head, and her eyes filled with sudden tears. "Please?" She was still clinging to his greatcoat. "Please take me. Please?"

How could he resist her? She had twined herself quite firmly about his heartstrings, quiet and solemn as she was.

He held out a hand for hers. "Just for a short while then," he said. "I do not suppose it can hurt."

She smiled at him then, and he had the strange impression that she had made him her slave for life.

Chapter 12

She forgot him soon after they had entered the music room, of course. Jack had expected it. She took one of the violins reverently from its case, smoothing one hand over its polished wood surface, running one finger lightly along the strings. Jack strolled to the pianoforte and sat down on the bench. She was gazing at the instrument with the sort of absorbed tenderness he might have expected her to give to a favorite doll.

And then she lifted the violin beneath her chin, picked up the bow, and began to play.

Jack was somehow reminded during the following half hour of a starved man finally presented with unlimited food but only a limited amount of time in which to eat it. She played everything a little too quickly, and she scarcely paused between one piece of music and another. It was as if she feared that after this morning she would never again be allowed to play.

Jack let her play, gradually forgetting his uneasiness lest Belle catch them there, gradually forgetting the passing of time. The child had a great deal to learn, and yet in some strange way, Jack felt, she would have as much to teach her teacher as she would have to learn from him. Perhaps more.

He felt a kind of awe at being in the presence of such raw, undeveloped talent. And a definite tenderness at watching that talent pouring out of a thin, small child.

She stopped finally and sighed with contentment before opening her eyes and looking at him. She lowered the violin from her chin.

"Thank you," she said.

"It was my privilege, Jacqueline." He smiled at her.

"Do you play?" she asked.

"The pianoforte," he said. "I believe if I had been a girl I would have been encouraged to play more, and I would have practiced more. I was told that I had more ability than most. But I was a boy, and it was not the thing to play on the pianoforte all day long."

She set the violin down on the pianoforte as she had done a few evenings before and came to sit beside him on the bench. "But if you had really needed to play," she said, "it would not have mattered what other people said."

Ah. *Needed*, not wanted. Out of the mouths of babes . . .

"You are right, of course," he said.

"I have pianoforte lessons," she said, "but I do not really enjoy them. I have to think all the time about my fingers and where they go on the keys. I do not have the chance to feel the music. I can only hear it."

And she did not have to think about her fingering on the violin?

"What do you want to do when you grow up?" he asked. "Do you want to play the violin for other people? Or will you be content to play just for yourself and your family?"

She thought for a moment. "Mama took me to a concert once," she said. "It was before we came from France. There was a violinist, and he played very well. He is famous, though I cannot remember his name. Everyone clapped and clapped after he had finished. But I was not pleased. He knew that he played well, and he played so that people would see him and hear him and say how good he was. He made himself more important than the music." Her brow was puckered in thought. "I wanted then to be able to show everyone there how that music should have been played. But I could not, of course. I do not know how to play well."

Ah. Poor Belle, Jack thought. Her worst fears were going to be realized. The child was going to be driven by the need to create beauty and perfection with her violin. She was never going to be satisfied with the ordinary, the mundane.

Just as Belle had been driven in a different way? he wondered. Was he understanding in Jacqueline what he had never understood in Belle? Had he learned so little about her in a year of living with her?

He touched a knuckle to Jacqueline's chin. "You play very well, child," he said. "And already you play for the music and not for applause. Shall I escort you back to the nursery?"

She looked wistfully from him to the violin. "Will I be able to come back?" she asked. "Will you bring me back again?"

"Tomorrow," he promised, "unless your mama expressly forbids it. We will find an hour when no one else is using the room."

"Thank you," she said, and got down from the bench to put the violin away in its case.

Jack reached out a hand for hers, and she took it. They left the room and walked upstairs together in silence. They had escaped detection after all, he thought.

But the door of the nursery opened as they approached it, and Isabella stepped out.

She sighed. "I was about to come hunting," she said, looking down at Jacqueline. "Where were you?"

"I invited her to the music room after we returned from outside," Jack said. "I asked her to play for me."

"It was my fault, Mama," Jacqueline said. "I asked to be taken. I begged. I said, 'Please, please.' "

A fine pair of abjectly sheepish conspirators they made, Jack thought with a wave of inner amusement. But Belle felt it, too. He saw it behind her eyes, though her expression did not change. Belle's feelings had always been easy to read in her eyes.

He and Jacqueline were still holding hands, he realized.

"Well," Isabella said, and Jack could tell from the opening word that she had weakened, "just be careful not to make a nuisance of yourself, Jacqueline."

"It was my pleasure and my privilege to be able to listen to her," Jack said.

Jacqueline slipped into the nursery and closed the door behind her. Jack and Isabella eye each other warily.

"How was rehearsal?" he asked.

"Peregrine is good as Shylock," she said. "Freddie has learned all his lines by heart, but he was nervous this morning and kept speaking up in the wrong places. He will learn."

"I would not count on that if I were you," he said with a grin and offered his arm.

They walked downstairs together—in dangerous proximity, Jack realized when she touched him. But they had decided on civilized living, and it was civilized for a man and woman walking together to have their arms linked.

"Belle," he asked her impulsively, "why do you act?" The question sounded extremely foolish once it was out.

"Why?" She looked at him. "I thought you knew the answer to that, Jack."

"For the fame and the fortune?" he asked. That was what he had always believed. She had loved the adulation of audiences, especially of the men in those audiences, and she had loved the thought of becoming wealthy so that she could live independently of men like himself and be more discriminating in her choice of lovers. He really had believed that. He was no longer sure. In fact, he was almost sure that he must have been wrong.

"It is flattering to be famous," she said. "I must admit it. And I will not deny that it is comfortable to have money in some abundance. It was rather frightening not to know quite where my next meal was coming from before you—took me under your protection. But it is more than that. Far more."

"What?" he asked. But he thought he knew the answer now—nine years too late.

"I act because I have to," she said. "Because I read a part, and I have to bring it alive. I cannot be content just to read and imagine or to watch someone else perform that part. I have to do it myself. I have to get inside that character's skin and inside her head. I have to make her heart beat in my bosom. I have to show her as she really is, not just as she appears on the written page. No, I was wrong a few moments ago, and I was right yesterday or whenever it was I said it. You never did understand, did you, Jack? You thought I did it because I liked to be praised. And because I liked to have gentlemen flock to the green room after my performances."

"Belle," he said, "why do the young never talk and never listen? Why must they live on emotion rather than on reason? Why did I not really understand that about you until now?"

"You wanted to possess me," she said. "You had paid well for me, and thought you had ownership of me."

"But I never did." His smile was cynical. "I did not even have exclusive possession of that for which I paid, did I, Belle? I will not take full blame for the bitterness of those last weeks. You were whoring with other men."

"Ah, yes." Her lips tightened, and her eyes hardened. "We always come back to that word, do we not, Jack? Sometimes I regret . . . Oh, never mind."

"Sometimes you regret what?" He set one hand beneath her chin and his thumb against her bottom lip. They had reached the bottom of the stairs some time before and had stood there, facing each other.

But she had no chance to answer. The door of the drawing room opened and Alex, Zeb, Anthony, and Howard Beckford came out, all talking at once, it seemed. Jack dropped his hand as they all greeted one another. He avoided Alex's eyes.

It should have been possible in a houseful of people, Isabella thought, to be able to avoid one particular person if one wished. Especially when there was a mutual desire to avoid.

But it did not seem possible. And perhaps they were not really trying hard enough. She might have gone into the nursery with Jacqueline. He might have gone in there to greet his nephew and niece when he saw that she was not going. But they had walked downstairs together, and they had not even kept their conversation brief or on safe, neutral topics.

And then, of course, they could not avoid each other during the times appointed for rehearsal of the scenes from *Othello*. Their first rehearsal was during the afternoon.

It did not go well. Isabella had planned not really to act in any of the scenes until the last rehearsal and the performance itself. She did not want the other actors to feel intimidated by her. She knew that most of them were already embarrassed and fearful of making fools of themselves. But at least during the morning rehearsal, she had pictured herself as Portia and recited her part accordingly. This afternoon she could not even do that.

This afternoon she was Isabella, talking with Jack, and then speaking sadly with Anne, thinking about Jack. She was thinking about how Jack had tried to control her, about how he had been jealous and angry and accusing—just like Othello. And so when she spoke to Anne, Desdemona to Emilia, she could not for the moment identify with the meek, accepting, obedient Desdemona. She wanted to side with the more feisty Emilia. And yet in one line she spoke, it was Isabella as well as Desdemona speaking. Emilia could imagine herself being unfaithful to her husband, it seemed, if the price was high enough.

"'Beshrew me, if I would do such a wrong for the whole world,'" Isabella said fervently. And yet even then she could not lose herself in the part. She could feel Jack's eyes boring into her from where he stood several feet away. And she could imagine the cynicism with which he listened to the words.

Claude tried to instruct Anne on the way to play her part. Anne was, of course, miscast as the tart-tongued Emilia. She was far too quiet and too sweet and too little able to identify with a dramatic character so different from herself. But she knew all her lines quite faultlessly and her cues, too.

Jack was good. Isabella would never have suspected him of being a good actor, perhaps because he had seemed to despise the theater and all it stood for while they had been together. He was a little wooden, of course, and he did not know his part well at all. While she lay with closed eyes, feigning sleep, Claude twice had to tell him to move closer, to lean over her.

"Good God, man," Claude said in exasperation, forgetting for the moment that there were two ladies present, "you have to bend over her and kiss her. You cannot kiss her from ten yards away."

And finally she could feel his body heat close to her right arm, and then she could feel his breath on her face. She tried again as she listened to the words he was speaking to become Desdemona, to make him Othello in her mind. But he was Jack, his voice a little stiff and tripping over a few of the words, but full of pain, too. He was clearly having no problem acting.

" 'When I have pluck'd thy rose,' " he murmured to her, " 'I cannot give it vital growth again; It needs must wither. I'll smell thee on the tree.' "

He was Othello, she thought firmly, telling himself that he must kill her but not wanting to do so, and knowing that once the deed is done it cannot be undone. And yet he was Jack, telling her that it was the end, that he did not want it to end, that once it was ended there could be no coming back together for them. And there was truth in those words—he was about to marry someone else.

Ah, Jack.

"Are you waiting for Christmas to come and go?" Claude asked irritably. "That is your cue to kiss her, Jack."

"On the night," Jack said. "I'll do it at the performance, Claude."

"Now," Claude said. "Good Lord, Isabella is not going to screech ravishment. This is a play, man. Then act."

It was good advice, Isabella thought, keeping her eyes closed. She could not remember another time when the old magic had failed. Acting a part had always been the surest way to escape from problems or unhappiness. It had always been a sure way to escape from herself.

His lips touched hers softly. They were parted. He kissed her four times in all, according to the text, and she stirred and gradually awoke.

" 'Who's there? Othello?' " she asked drowsily.

"'Ay, Desdemona,'" he said.

"'Will you come to bed, my lord?'" she asked him, and their eyes somehow locked.

She knew that he was finding the scene as difficult as she was. His eyes went to his book and did not leave it while he read his part and listened to hers.

And so he threatened and accused and fumed while she begged and denied his charges and pleaded for her life. She could not understand Desdemona. Although she had played the part several times before, she suddenly felt locked outside the person who was Desdemona. She could not feel with Desdemona's heart or think with her mind or breathe the air she breathed. She wanted to become angry. She wanted to fight back as she had fought back nine years ago. She wanted to hurt him as he was hurting her. She had done it once, and she thought she had succeeded well enough. She had started to tell him this morning that she sometimes regretted it. No, she could not be Desdemona.

And then his hands were about her throat, and she fought a losing battle for her life. Isabella would have fought a dirtier fight. At the very least she would have used her knee on him to sap his strength and distract his mind. But she was Desdemona, and a few minutes later, when Emilia had burst into the room and all was noise and confusion, she managed to speak again before she died.

"'Nobody,'" she said in response to Emilia's question as to who had done this to her. "'I myself. Farewell. Commend me to my kind lord. O, farewell!'"

There had been no farewell nine years ago and no kind words. He had come to use her services late in the evening, when she should have been home from the theater, and she had not been there. He had stayed until she came, at three o'clock in the morning. She had been to supper and cards with Lord and Lady Stapleton and a group of their friends. Lord Stapleton had wanted her to spend a week of the summer at their country estate, participating in an outdoor performance of some suitable play, yet to be decided upon. She had been obliged to refuse—regretfully enough.

And then she had gone home to find Jack, white with

fury, up and waiting for her and quite unwilling to listen to her story. She had been with a man. How stupid did she think he was? Did she think he did not know very well that she was as much a whore as she had ever been? He wanted her to admit it. For once in her life, he wanted her to tell the truth and admit that she had been with a man.

They had yelled and fought for a long time before she gave him the answer he wanted, spitting it in his face for the satisfaction of watching his expression. Yes, tonight, she had told him, and countless other nights before it. Did he think he was man enough to satisfy her alone?

The look on his face had been very satisfying. And the way he had stalked from the house without another word.

No, there had been no farewell between her and Jack. She had left London the next day. She had left England within the week.

" 'She's like a liar gone to burning hell,' " she heard Jack say now. " ' 'Twas I that kill'd her.' "

"Oh, Isabella," Anne said with a sigh, "I wish I could act even half as well as you."

Isabella, opening her eyes and sitting up, felt very much a fraud.

"It is not too bad," Claude said dubiously. "You, of course, are wonderful, Isabella. Jack, you must learn your lines. You have always been the last to learn your part, and I daresay I cannot expect you to break with tradition. But you could have some consideration for the state of my digestion, you know. Anne, well-done, but remember that Emilia is not a gentle soul."

"I will try, Claude," Anne promised. "I remember how I did it last time. I pretended I was Kate Hardcastle. Is that what you do, Isabella?"

"Precisely that," Isabella said. Though there was really no pretense in it. She sometimes thought she actually did become the characters she played.

"But it was easier last time," Anne said, "because Kate was someone I admired and wished to be like."

"I have to leave," Jack said. "I promised to take Juliana

outside for a walk or a wade in the snow as soon as I finished here. I have scarcely seen her all day."

"You sat by her at breakfast and luncheon," Claude said with a grin, "and according to Stanley's boasting about that snowman, you were building it together this morning. But you have scarce seen her. Is true love not amazing, Isabella?"

"I think, Claude," Anne said gently but firmly, "that we should not tease poor Jack. It is not kind. Go to Juliana, Jack. I am sure she is eagerly awaiting your return."

He went, saving Isabella from having to contribute to that particular line of conversation. He would take Juliana outside, she thought, and perhaps have to keep her warm with an arm about her. He would surely find the opportunity to steal a kiss, as he had the day before beneath the sprig of mistletoe and later beneath the kissing bough.

Jack and Juliana. Married. Living together. Sleeping together. Having children together. Growing familiar with each other and comfortable together. Growing old together.

"Come, Isabella," Claude said, offering his arm, "you have worked hard enough for one day. You have earned some tea and the creamiest cake on the tray."

"Oh." Isabella laughed. "Lead me to it, sir, and I promise to do it full justice."

Anne walked on her other side. "I remember in the last play," she said, "that I had to allow Alex to kiss me. I thought I would surely die, and yet he was my husband. It must be one of the most difficult parts of your job to have to allow actors who are strangers to kiss you. Like Jack. Not that he is exactly a stranger to you, is he? Grandmama says that you had met before."

"Yes." Isabella smiled. "We had a passing acquaintance many years ago, before I went to France.

Ah, Jack. A passing acquaintance!

Anne laughed. "I can well imagine that you would not forget Jack," she said. "He is too handsome for his own good, I sometimes think."

No, Isabella thought. No, she had not forgotten Jack. She

would never have forgotten him even if she had not set
eyes on him for the rest of her life after that bitter quarrel.

Jack did not find Juliana after the rehearsal and did not
see her again until dinnertime. Bertrand and Rose Fitzgerald came calling again during the afternoon, presumably to
see Ruby and Freddie and their nephew, Robert. Certainly
they spent a dutiful twenty minutes in the nursery.

"Come along, Julie," Howard said to his sister when he
had found her reading a book in the library. "Fitz and Rose
are in the nursery. I suggested to Freddie that he send over
to the rectory to invite them. Life must be very dull there
all day long." He grinned. "Let us visit the children ourselves."

Juliana frowned. "Since when have you grown fond of
children?" she asked.

"Don't be dense," he said, taking her book from her and
closing it without thinking of first marking the page. "I am
going to take Rose for a walk again, but I will need you and
Fitz to act as chaperons."

"But I cannot come," she said. "Jack is going to take me
walking as soon as he has finished rehearsal."

"Julie," he said, grasping her by the wrist and hauling her
to her feet, "that rehearsal will go on for hours as this
morning's did. We will be back long before the time comes
for you to do your billing and cooing with Frazer. Is he
Jack now, by the way? I see that progress is being made.
Come on. Do this for me. Just for half an hour."

Juliana wanted both to go and to stay. She had been
pleased with herself for the last day. Her courtship was progressing well, and she was becoming easier around Jack.
By Christmas Day, she was sure, she would be in love with
him. And yet the lure of spending half an hour with her
brother and Rose and Fitz was very strong. She had so enjoyed their walk yesterday morning and the little while they
had spent together at the lake. She had been able to relax
and forget herself. She had been happy.

"Howard," she said, "I do not want Rose hurt. Are you

not being rather too particular in your attentions? Perhaps she will not realize that this is but a Christmas flirtation."

He drew her in the direction of the door. "Julie," he said, "I am going to walk with her for half an hour, in company with her brother and my sister. Perhaps I will roll her in the snow. Perhaps if I am very clever I will be able to steal a kiss without arousing Fitz's wrath. I hardly think she is likely to expect a declaration tomorrow."

Well, for half an hour, Juliana thought. That was all. She wanted to be ready when Jack came from his rehearsal. And she wanted to be looking pretty for him. She did not want to have to greet him with bright red cheeks and nose.

But Fitz wanted to walk down to the marsh to see if any of the smaller lakes were frozen over well enough to allow for skating within the next day or two. There were, apparently, several boxes full of skates in the stables. And then the two men had to test the ice at the edge and coaxed the two young ladies to come slip and slide with them. Howard succeeded in taking a tumble with Rose so that she landed full on top of him. But Fitz did not notice the quick kiss they exchanged, Juliana saw, because he was busy trying to slide backward and was trying to persuade her to take his hands and slide toward him.

And then Howard decided that they should walk the distance to the triple-arched bridge so that they could stand over the center arch and see the famous view of the house.

By that time Juliana had almost forgotten the necessity of returning to the house within half an hour or an hour at the longest. She was talking and listening and laughing and clinging to Fitz's arm because her boots did not have good enough grip to allow her to walk comfortably on snow. She was enjoying herself so much that she kept convincing herself that not too much time had passed after all. Besides, as Howard had said, the rehearsal would probably go on far longer than Jack had expected.

There were two ways back to the house, both obscured by snow. But Fitz and Rose were both familiar with them. They would take separate routes back, then, Howard suggested. He and Rose would go one way and Fitz and Julie could go the other way. They would see which was the shortest route.

Juliana wondered for a moment if she should make some objection. But Fitz did not, and he must surely know that Howard was looking for a few minutes alone with Rose. She was being silly, she thought. Doubtless Rose was old enough to guard against being hurt by a little harmless flirtation.

And so they went their separate ways. And Juliana found herself talking and laughing with Fitz just as merrily as before and holding his hand instead of his arm, their fingers laced tightly together.

They soon lost sight of the other two among the trees and had to slow their pace as they waded through snow almost knee deep. But it seemed exhilarating and funny rather than uncomfortable to feel snow slipping inside their boots.

And then his hand tightened on hers, and he drew her to a halt. Juliana looked at him in surprise as he swung her around and against him. He kissed her swiftly and open-mouthed. Her own mouth opened involuntarily, and he thrust his tongue inside.

And then he was looking into her shocked face and laughing again. "That was for yesterday," he said. "I did not have the courage to draw you beneath the kissing bough."

She stared into his eyes.

He looked rueful suddenly and set his forehead against hers. "I ought not to have done it, ought I?" he said.

"No," she whispered.

He released her immediately, and they trudged onward. They did not talk or laugh anymore. But they still walked with hands joined and fingers laced.

Chapter 13

It was the day before Christmas Eve. There had been a little more snow, enough to keep what was already on the ground looking fresh. And it had remained cold, invigoratingly so, most of the guests at Portland House agreed, especially as it had ensured that the ice on the smallest of the marshy lakes was safe for skating. A few learned scouts—Fitz, Perry, and Stanley—had pronounced it so, though the last two had declared that perhaps the center of the lake should be avoided just in case.

Skating had always been a rare but wonderful treat at Portland House. And there had always been enough skates for everyone and a whole army besides, Jack explained to Juliana. No faint-hearted member of the family or guest could ever plead the excuse that there just were not enough skates to go around. And they came in all possible sizes, too.

"Then I will thank my good fortune that I have a different and quite unassailable excuse," Lisa said, tapping her swollen abdomen significantly. "On the only occasion I attempted to skate, I spent more time on my back than on my feet."

"And Zeb says I may not skate this year by any persuasion," Hortense said with a sigh. "I have assured him that I have never in my life taken a spill on the ice, but he has to play the autocrat. I do wish someone would change the wording of the marriage service so that it was the husband who promised obedience to the wife. It would make a great deal more sense."

"But it would be less fair, dear," her great-aunt Emily

said. "Women have wiles by which to get their way. Men have no such assets. And so we give them the illusion of dominance by promising them obedience."

"Then why am I not skating?" Hortense asked.

"You can help strap on all the children's skates, my love," her husband said. "And you can help breathe life into the fire and keep warm by it while the rest of us freeze our fingers and toes and noses."

"I can scarce wait for the delight such an afternoon promises," Hortense said, tossing a look at the ceiling.

They were to wait until the afternoon. Although the duchess loved to see her family and guests enjoying themselves, she also insisted on organizing that enjoyment for herself. And, of course, they were to enjoy themselves with a musical concert on Christmas Eve and with theatricals on Christmas Day. Practices and rehearsals were essential. Each scene had its rehearsal in the morning. And the music room was fully occupied all morning, too—Her Grace had noticed that it had stood empty for much of the day before. She organized definite time allotments for her musicians today and left nothing to personal inclination.

But the afternoon was to be free for skating. All the children and a large crowd of adults were to go. Rose and Bertrand Fitzgerald had walked over from the rectory. The bonfire and the jugs of chocolate had been such a success during the afternoon when they had all gathered the greenery that both were to be repeated this afternoon.

And so they set out, a large and cheerful crowd, as usual, Freddie and Bertrand carrying the big box of skates between them. Zeb stopped a snowball fight by barking at a group of children, including his own twins, and warning them that if they were covered with snow by the time they reached the lake, they would have to dry off at the fire and merely watch the skating.

The procession proceeded almost sedately.

Jack walked to the small lake with Juliana on his arm. He set about amusing her with stories of London that were fit for a young lady's ears. She did not appear to have a great deal of conversation herself this afternoon, but he did not particularly mind having to do the bulk of the talking himself. It kept his mind occupied.

And he needed to spend time with her, he decided. Although he was often in her company, he always had the strange feeling that he was neglecting her. Perhaps it was because his mind was so preoccupied with Belle and what had happened between them nine years ago.

He had even dreamed about her again last night. She had been asking him, hands on hips, eyes flashing, voice filled with contempt, if he thought himself man enough to satisfy her. And he had felt those humiliating tears on his cheeks again as he had stretched out his hands to her and pleaded with her. He had had no experience, he had told her, except what he had gained with her. What was he doing wrong? How could he better please her? What did she want that he did not know to give her?

Thank heaven the dream had been inaccurate, he thought now, his mind working quite independently of his voice, which was chatting to Juliana. In reality, he had merely stalked out without a word. And had not seen her again or exchanged another word with her for nine years.

"You were with Fitz and your brother and Rose when they inspected the ice and pronounced it safe for skating?" he asked now.

"Yes," Juliana said. "We did not have skates, of course, but it seemed solid enough underfoot. There was a great deal of snow on the ice, of course."

"It has been swept clear for this afternoon," he said. He looked ahead to where Juliana's brother was walking, Rose's arm drawn through his. "I believe there is a romance brewing or a flirtation in progress," he said, grinning. "Were you playing chaperon, Juliana? His sister and your brother? It must have proved quite daunting—for them."

"It was all perfectly innocent," she said quickly. "They were not alone for a single moment. But Howard is a gentleman, anyway. He would not—compromise her."

Her cheeks were rosy from the cold. Jack could not tell if

they were also flushed with embarrassment. He covered her hand with his own. "I am sure he would not," he said. "I was merely teasing, Juliana. If he had meant disrespect, I am sure he would not have asked you and Fitz to accompany them. He did ask, I assume?"

"Yes," she said. "And I am sorry we were so late back. Fitz—M-Mr. Fitzgerald wanted to come to this lake, and then Howard wanted to go to the bridge, and the snow was deep and slowed us down. I was dismayed to find that so much time had passed."

She had apologized profusely the day before, too. He had not minded her absence. It had given him a chance to recover after that first rehearsal with Belle.

They were almost the last to arrive at the lake. Already the box of skates had been attacked and a few children in a frenzy were trying to find a pair that fit. Ruby, with a forcefulness that would have done justice to the duchess, was creating order out of chaos and forcing everyone to line up so that she could match skates to feet.

Some children, already matched, were whining for mothers to help them lace the blades over their boots. Mothers obliged. Davy, the first to step on the newly swept ice with his skates, promptly climbed an invisible ladder to heaven and landed heavily on his bottom. Younger cousins, never having heard about compassion, screeched with mirth. And then the same younger cousins came to grief in much the same way.

"There are going to be some stiff and sore limbs tomorrow," Jack said as he took a pair of blades from Ruby's hands and measured them against Juliana's feet. "Perfect. What a dainty foot you have. Let me help you lace them."

Doing so, of course, gave him the opportunity to view and even to touch her very pretty and trim ankles—something he did appreciatively and in as leisurely a manner as he dared. It was something one might expect of a rakish gentleman, something he expected of himself. And yet it was something he did quite dispassionately on this occasion. He derived a certain aesthetic pleasure from what he did but not even the slightest sexual stimulation.

She was, of course, like a tiny and exquisite child. No, hardly that. Like a doll. Like someone he still could not quite imagine being carnal with.

"Have you skated before?" he asked her, taking her hand after he had strapped blades to his own boots. "I do hope not." He grinned at her. "Then I will have to hold you tightly while I teach you."

She looked into his eyes and smiled brightly at him. It was an unexpected expression after her quietness during the walk. It was almost as if she was deliberately changing her mood, Jack thought. He was reminded of her behavior in the ballroom when he had been hanging decorations on the chandeliers—and in the drawing room after the kissing bough had been hung.

"Then perhaps," she said, "I could pretend that I cannot, Jack."

Yes, definitely like that afternoon with the unexpected, almost defiant flirtatiousness. He suspected that it was normally quite out of character. He wondered if she did it because she was attracted to him and wanted to mask her shyness or whether she did it because she knew she had to marry him and was trying to prepare herself for what she suspected was to come after the marriage.

He must ask her before the day was out, he decided. Tomorrow was the day on which he had told her he would make his formal offer to her father—unless she had found by that time that she could not like him. It seemed to have come so fast. Tomorrow! After tomorrow there would be no going back. There was no going back now.

"But you do skate in reality?" he said, leading her to the edge of the bank and stepping down carefully onto the ice before turning to hand her down beside him. "All the better. You can hum a tune, and we will dance—a waltz. Have you ever waltzed?"

"Only with my dancing master," she said.

"It is a little more tricky on ice," he said. "You have to dance a little closer to your partner so that you can feel the rhythm of his movements."

Her eyes responded to the flirtatiousness of his remark

but not to the more risqué suggestiveness of his words, he noticed. He was touched by her innocence. He really had grown fond of her during the week. And he must grow fonder. She would be quite chilled by the time they left the ice. He would have all the excuse in the world to set an arm about her shoulders at the bonfire and hold her close. And it would be almost expected of him to take her among the trees after they had warmed themselves with the chocolate in order to steal kisses.

He must take her a little beyond the chaste kisses they had shared thus far. By tomorrow he wanted to feel some physical desire for her as well as the fondness he already felt. If only he could feel desire for her, he thought, if only he could become aroused by her this afternoon, he would feel safe. Or at least hopeful for the future. If he was fond of her and if he wanted her, he could make a marriage of it.

He must make a marriage of it regardless.

They skated slowly for a while, hand in hand, "getting their skating legs under them," as Alex put it. Most of the children could not skate, but all were gamely trying and were slithering and wobbling about the ice, clutching an adult's hand or coat. Davy had got over his early humiliation and was now showing off by skating fast and even executing a few inelegant pirouettes. Meggie and Kitty, Jacqueline and Marcel were quite steady, though cautious on their skates. Kenneth was wobbling along between Meggie and Kitty, holding to a hand of each.

The adults could all skate. Connie and Sam, unencumbered yet by children, skated together, Jack saw, as did Howard and Rose. There was another couple, he thought, who were going to be slinking off among the trees before returning to the house. He just hoped that Juliana's brother was intent on flirtation and not seduction with Rose. Jack was rather fond of her. But of course seduction in the outdoors with several inches of snow on the ground was not a strong possibility.

Isabella skated, first with Stanley and Celia, and then with Perry and Fitz. Jack kept his eyes away from her and tried to do likewise with his mind, as he had done since

leaving the house. It was understandable that seeing her unexpectedly again had upset him considerably for a few
days. It was understandable, too, he supposed, that he
wanted her again. She was an unusually lovely woman, and
it was not his habit to ignore the appetite he felt for a beautiful woman. It was something he was going to have to
learn to do very soon. It would be unpardonable to be lust-
ing after other women once he was married to Juliana.

It was something he was trying to learn immediately. He
was trying to ignore his very powerful awareness of Belle's
proximity.

It all happened very quickly, as such things usually do.

The children had all been given strict instructions, repeated more than once, to stay close to the edge of the lake
and not to venture near the center. It was really quite safe
right across, the adults had agreed among themselves, but it
was best to be overcautious when one was dealing with so
many exuberant children.

Anyway, each child was well chaperoned. The rule
would not be at all difficult to enforce.

But as sometimes happens, one of the children, one too
small to have understood the warning, also escaped attention for a short while. Kenneth had relinquished the hands
of Meggie and Kitty in order to pursue Robert and Freddie,
but he could not catch up with them since he moved along
with a strange combination of slides and crawls. And then
he spotted a snake of snow that the breeze was blowing
across the lake and made off in its direction. By some
strange chance no one was observing him. Alex and Anne
were busy helping Catherine to skate gracefully on one leg.

But no child in that gathering could go unobserved for
very long. Marcel spotted him and shouted out to him in his
piping, penetrating voice.

"Come back here, Kenneth," he called. "We are not to go
out that far."

Even as the attention of several adults turned his way,
Marcel decided that the best thing to do when dealing with

such a very small infant was to go after Kenneth himself. He zoomed across the ice toward him.

"I shall take you back to your papa," he said. "Take my hand. You are quite safe."

Isabella called out. Anne clapped both hands over her mouth and froze to the spot. Alex yelled and skated off toward the two children.

But all seemed well. Kenneth, who had come to adore Marcel during the previous few days, laughed at him and obediently took his hand. Marcel turned and smiled at his audience.

"He is quite all right," he called. "It is quite safe out here."

But there was a loud crack, very like the report of a gun, even as he spoke. Alex yelled once more. There were several screams. Marcel pushed Kenneth to the ice and shoved him in the direction of Alex, who caught him up just as there was another crack and Marcel disappeared half through the ice. He clung to the ice with his gloved hands, his eyes grown as big as saucers.

"Don't move!" Jack roared. "Get Kenneth back to the bank, Alex. Don't move, Marcel."

Without conscious thought, he was tearing at the straps of his blades and dragging them off his boots and then at his greatcoat to remove it and thrust it behind him. All the while he was moving closer to the boy. He had not removed his eyes from him, and Marcel's eyes had focused on him.

"Don't move." Jack lay down on the ice, spread-eagled, distributing his weight as widely and evenly as possible, and inched toward the dangerous crack in the ice and the hole into which Marcel had fallen from the waist down. "Just stay calm. I am coming for you." He was talking quietly, conversationally.

And then he had his hands firmly clasped about the boy's wrists.

"Just relax," he said. "Don't try to help." And he drew the boy toward him, having to exert rather more pressure than he would have liked in order to pull the lower part of his body over the lip of the ice. "Good boy. That's the way. We will have you safe in no time."

He knew that the ice was going to go. He could sense it. He had to use a great deal of self-discipline to move slowly so that at least the child would be safe. And then Marcel was out of the water and lying flat along the ice— at the same moment as Jack saw with his peripheral vision the crazy zigzag of cracks that shot out at all angles from the center that was his weight.

He jerked the boy around by his wrists and sent him skimming and twirling across the ice toward what seemed to be dozens of waiting arms. Jack had forgotten about all the other people on the ice, and he had become totally deaf to all the sounds they must have been making—if they had been making any. Perhaps they had all been silent, holding their breaths.

But the thought hardly had time to form in his mind before he was plunged into an icy bath that closed over his head. He came up gasping and convinced, in some panic, that he would never again draw air into his lungs. The shock of the cold would surely stop his heart.

But the other adults had been busy. Alex had come as close as he dared with Freddie behind him, and they were hurling him a line made of numerous scarves tied together.

"Catch it, Jack," Alex called. "We will haul you out. Don't panic, for God's sake."

It was not as easy as it might have sounded to grab hold of a length of scarf with fingers that had turned instantly numb in the water. But then it would be too stupidly pathetic to drown in the smallest of the marsh lakes, Jack thought. As boys, they had scorned to swim in it after the age of ten because even in the middle the water barely covered their heads when they stood upright. It would be almost as shameful to die here as to do it in his bathwater.

His mind forced his fingers to close about the scarf. After that he followed the advice he had given to Marcel and relaxed and allowed his cousins to pull him out. Not that he felt a great deal better when he stood finally on firm ice at the perimeter of the lake. He felt it altogether possible that he would die of cold even if the danger of drowning was past.

"To the fire, man," Alex was saying to him, "and get rid of as many clothes as possible."

"Thank goodness for the fire," Anne was saying, Kenneth clasped in her arms. "Oh, Jack. Dear Jack."

She was crying, Jack realized. Not that he could hear her. His teeth were clacking too loudly. Not only had he never been so cold in his life, but he had never suspected that it was possible to be so cold and still be alive.

"M-m-marcel?" he asked.

"At the fire already," Alex said, hurrying him in its direction. Freddie was propelling him by the other arm, Jack realized suddenly. "Isabella took him and ran."

Jack's hands were too numb to be of any use to him. While his face registered the blessed hope of warmth from the fire, it was Alex and Freddie and Ruby who stripped him of his coat and waistcoat and shirt, and it was Hortense—sobbing as if she would never stop—who took off her cloak and rubbed it vigorously over him to dry him from the waist up.

"What would I have told Mama?" she managed to jerk out between sobs. "And Zeb keeps telling me that I must avoid excitement. What would I have told Mama?"

"Y-you would have t-told her that I d-drowned in a t-teacup of water, I suppose, H-hortie," he said.

"It would be best not to talk, Jack," Ruby said, her voice as firm as ever, quite in command of the situation. "Here. Drink this chocolate. No, you cannot hold the cup. I will hold it for you."

And so he suffered the indignity of being fed his chocolate, his teeth clacking against the cup, some of the liquid trickling down his chin. The warmth of it felt very welcome as did the heat of the bulk of it that found its way down to his stomach. Someone wrapped his blessedly dry greatcoat about his shoulders. The heat from the fire was beginning to make his flesh feel like living flesh again, though he felt lamentably cold and soggy from the waist down.

Rationality began to return. Juliana was hovering in the

background, looking frightened. Fitz had an arm about her waist. A few of the children were crying. Ruby was pouring him another cup of chocolate, and from the martial look on her face, he guessed that he was going to have no choice about drinking it. Belle was on her knees beside the fire, her cloak wrapped tightly about Marcel, from his head to his feet—Jack guessed that the child's clothes had been all stripped off—and was holding a cup to his lips. Her head was bent over him. It was very obvious that there was no one else in the world for her at this moment except her son. Jacqueline was standing quietly beside them, her eyes reddened. If he had been in control of his body and his voice, Jack thought, he would have called her to his side and set his arms about her. She was looking utterly forlorn.

And then Freddie—dear, gallant Fred—not even looking back to observe Ruby's approving nod, was removing his own greatcoat and stooping over Belle to wrap it about her and drawing them both to their feet. He held his arm about her and turned her to hurry her in the direction of the house.

Jacqueline stood and watched them go.

"Can you walk, do you think, Jack?" Alex sounded rather anxious.

"If I cannot," Jack said, "are you planning to toss me over your shoulder, old chap? I think I will manage."

And manage he did, standing on legs that were painful with the cold, allowing Alex and Ruby to help him on with his greatcoat and to do up the buttons, and then setting off in the direction of the house, a silent Juliana trotting along at his side, and a subdued family trailing along behind just as if they were members of a particularly somber funeral procession, Jack thought.

"You were wonderfully brave," Juliana said. "I have never been more frightened in my life. You saved Marcel's life."

"He saved Kenneth's," Jack said. "We are going to have to make a hero of that little boy once he has been thawed out at the house."

"We sent the servant running back to the house with instructions to have hot baths waiting for the two of you," Perry said.

"That will feel like heaven," Jack said.

And then he felt a little body nudge against his side and looked down to see Jacqueline walking beside him, head down.

"Jacqueline." He touched the top of her head. "He is quite safe, dear. Just a little cold. He will soon warm up."

He was jolted by the misery in her eyes when she looked up at him. "I thought he would die," she said. "Mama calls him our ray of sunshine, and he is. I thought he would die. And then I thought you would die. I did not want you to die." She sobbed painfully.

"Come, Jacqueline." Anne had moved up on her other side and spoke with warm sympathy. "Take my hand, sweetheart. We will go and see Mama and Marcel as soon as we reach the house. He is a wonderfully brave boy, your ray of sunshine."

But Jack had stopped walking. He stooped down and lifted Jacqueline into his arms. She wrapped her own about his neck and clung to him as he walked on, her face hidden against the capes of his greatcoat.

"I would not have let him die," he murmured against her ear. "And I was in no danger, just very cold."

He felt warmer despite the uncomfortable wetness of pantaloons and stockings and boots. He felt warmer, just holding her.

Chapter 14

Marcel protested when he was first brought back to the house that he did not want to lie down and have a sleep. He wanted to put on dry clothes and play. But his body had been chilled, and Isabella watched him grow visibly sleepier as he sat in his hot bath while she swished water over him.

"I could not ask for a braver head of my family," she said, smiling at him and beginning to feel the aftereffects of shock and terror on her own system.

"It was nothing, Maman," he said, pausing to yawn hugely. "He is just a little baby and did not know he was being bad. They will not spank him, will they?"

"No," she said. "They are too happy to have him safe and sound." He was little more than a baby himself, her five-year-old Marcel. Maurice would have been proud of him today.

Marcel protested feebly after he had been dried and dressed, but he sat on the edge of his bed, yawning, and declared that to please his maman he would lie down and perhaps have a little sleep. He drank down the hot milk the duchess had had sent up, made a face because it tasted funny—there was a draft of something in it, Isabella guessed—and lay down immediately.

But Anne came hurrying into his room before he had gone quite to sleep. Alex was a few steps behind her.

"You are still awake, Marcel?" she said, bending over him and then slipping her arms beneath him to hug him tightly when she saw that he was. "You are a brave, brave

boy. You saved my son's life today, and I will love you forever for it."

"It was nothing, Aunt Anne," Marcel said, but he was
beaming with sleepy pleasure, Isabella could see.

"It was everything," Anne said firmly. "Now you must
have a good sleep and then submit yourself to being hugged
by every adult in the house, you wonderful boy."

"Now that is something to look forward to." Alex smiled
down at Marcel and extended his right hand. "I will leave
the hugging to the ladies. Let me shake your hand, Marcel,
and commend you on an act of extraordinary courage."

Marcel lifted his hand and looked as if he might well
burst with pride.

"And thank you for my son's life," Alex said. "That will
be the best Christmas gift I will receive this year, lad, and
one I will always remember."

They did not stay. Anne, teary-eyed, hugged Isabella and
they left.

Marcel was sleeping within minutes, Isabella's hand
smoothing back his hair. She sat gazing at him for a while
longer, shaking at the memory of the sound of cracking ice
and the sight of Marcel plunging half beneath the ice. And
the agonizing and seemingly endless minutes while Jack
edged toward him and pulled him free just in time.

Jack! She had seen the ice give way. She had seen him
disappear under ice and water. And part of her had heard
the commotion of his rescue and his arrival at the fire. But
she had been totally engrossed by her maternal instincts.
She had had no attention to spare for anyone but her son.

Not even for Jacqueline. She was ashamed now to realize
that she had been unaware of her daughter from the moment of the accident on. And, of course, Jacqueline was not
the sort of child to push herself forward for attention.

Marcel would doubtless sleep for a few hours. Isabella
leaned forward to kiss his forehead and then got to her feet.

She found Jacqueline in the bedchamber she shared with
three of the other little girls, sitting cross-legged on her bed,
hugging a pillow against her. Isabella sat down and set an
arm about her thin shoulders.

"He is warm and sleeping," she said. "Were you as frightened as I was, *cherie*?"

"Yes, Mama," the child said.

"And I could not comfort you because I was too concerned about getting him warm and bringing him back here," Isabella said. "I am sorry, Jacqueline."

"It is all right, Mama," her daughter said. "I know that if it had been me, I would have had all your attention. Marcel was very brave. Everyone is saying so."

"Yes, he was," Isabella said. "We are fortunate that he belongs to us, are we not?"

"Yes," Jacqueline said. "He is our sunshine."

Isabella smiled and hugged her. It was something she often called him, just as she often called Jacqueline the soul of her family. "You came home with the other children?" she asked.

"I came with Mr. Frazer," Jacqueline said. "He carried me and I put my arms around his neck and he held me tight because I was sad."

Isabella felt a great lurching in her stomach. Jack! He had saved her son's life and then comforted her daughter.

"Will you have a sleep, too?" she suggested. "It would probably make you feel better."

"I am going to read to Catherine," Jacqueline said. "I like doing that, Mama, and she likes to listen."

"Well, then." Isabella hugged her again and kissed her. "I shall see you later. You know that I love you every bit as much as I love Marcel?"

"Yes, Mama," her daughter said gravely. "I know that."

And so, Isabella thought, closing the door of the nursery behind her a few moments later, there was one thing left to do. He had saved Marcel's life at great danger to his own. She drew a deep breath. Good heavens, he might have died. She had turned away from him with Marcel as if his own life meant nothing at all to her. She had paid no attention to him at all.

He might have died for Marcel. For her son. She shivered and forced herself to descend the stairs.

* * *

Jack lay on his back with his hands clasped behind his head. He dug his heels into the mattress and pointed his toes straight up and watched the small tent he had made of the bedclothes. He swiveled his ankles and pointed his toes outward in order to widen the tent. And then he yawned with what he hoped might be tiredness but which was undoubtedly merely boredom.

A half-empty glass of once-warm milk—*milk*, for God's sake!—lay on the table beside the bed. It was true that it was laced with brandy and therefore more interesting than it would otherwise be, but he strongly suspected that it was laced with something else, too. He could taste the bitterness of the something else, and he did not doubt that his suspicions were well-founded since his grandmother had confessed to him that she had prepared it with her own hands.

He positively refused to be drugged merely because he was a great hero—Wellington could not have had a more enthusiastic welcome home when he returned from Waterloo than he, Jack, had had earlier on his return to the house. The memory of it made him grimace. His mother had actually had a full-blown fit of the vapors and had had to be revived. What would she have done without her sole prop and support? she had asked of the gilded ceiling when she had begun to recover consciousness. His mother enjoyed the myth that she would be destitute and forced to live in the gutter of the nearest street if he should be inconsiderate enough to die before her. In reality she had an independent fortune and an impressive house of her own in London. And she had Hortie and Zeb if all else failed.

Jack yawned again until his jaws cracked. And so he was enjoying the rewards of heroism. He had been banished to bed and dared to set one foot to the floor until dinnertime at the very earliest. His grandfather had blustered, his grandmother had organized, and his mother had wept. And he had crept meekly along to his bed.

For a fleeting moment he regretted that invitation to spend Christmas with Reggie and his bevy of beauties. He would quite probably be in bed at this moment if he had gone, just as he was now, but he would definitely not be bored.

He was starting to feel warm again at last. His bath had felt like a little piece of heaven—no one had ever suspected that heaven might be a bathtub full of hot water instead of flowery fields full of cavorting angels playing harps. And he had to admit that the blankets weighing him down—his grandmother had had an indeterminate number of extras piled on him—were completing the process. And perhaps, after all, he was feeling just a little drowsy. It would certainly pass the time if he could nod off for an hour or so.

He awoke with a start when someone tapped on his door and did not open it to bring in fresh coals for the fire or to lay a hand on his fevered brow. Whoever it was tapped again.

"Come in," he called, and turned his head to see who it was.

She opened the door quietly, stepped inside, closed it with her hands behind her back, and stood against it.

"They said you would be sleeping," she said. "And so I said I would speak with you later. But I was passing on the way to my room, and I thought . . ."

"Belle," he said, "you look as if you are ready to collapse."

She came hurrying across to the side of the bed and stood looking down at him. "I had to thank you," she said. "He might have died. He might have been dead now and cold." She drew a steadying breath through her mouth. "I will always be in your debt."

"That suggests all sorts of interesting possibilities." He grinned at her.

But her face was pale and her eyes were troubled, and she did not even scold him for the levity of his words.

"Belle." He reached out a hand to her, and she took it and raised it to set the back of it against her cheek.

"Jack." She closed her eyes. "Thank you seems absurdly inadequate. You might have died. You very nearly did."

"Nonsense," he said. "The water is rather shallow in that particular bit of marsh, Belle. I would have had to make an

effort to drown there. It was just a rather cold dunking.
Nothing worse than that."

"Jack," she said, her eyes still closed, "don't belittle what
you did. You might have died for my son." She turned her
face to set her lips against his hand.

"Belle," he heard himself say, "go and lock the doors."

She would, of course, refuse and take her leave. And this
moment would be at an end. Mercifully so. He did not need
this. Neither did she.

She released his hand and crossed the room quietly to
lock both doors—the one into the corridor and the one into
his dressing room. And then she came back to the bed and
looked down at him with calm, accepting eyes.

Good God! He realized suddenly that she was prepared
to pay the debt she had just spoken of if he chose to exact
payment in the expected manner.

"That is not what I meant," he said to her, and reached
up with both arms to grasp her waist and bring her tum-
bling across his body to lie at his far side on the bed. He
leaned across her and folded the top covers over her so that
she would not be cold. He kept one arm beneath her neck
and about her shoulders and turned her against him. All
the formidable pile of blankets was between them.

He kissed her gently on the lips and cheeks and eyes. "It
was not what I meant, Belle," he whispered to her. "I would
never force you against your inclination. I never did that. It
was never against your will. Was it? You never did it just
because you needed the money?"

He wished he had not asked the question. The answer
could well kill him.

"It was never against my will." She was looking into his
eyes in that very direct way of hers. She wrapped an arm
about his waist on top of the covers. "You know it was not,
Jack. Oh, you know it was never for the money."

Why, then? But he would not ask the question aloud. Either way, he did not want to know.

They lay gazing at each other, warm, comfortable. He
could easily fall asleep again, Jack thought in some surprise. He did not find her presence in his bed sexually

arousing. Only something far more seductive and far more dangerous than that. But he would not think of the danger. Not now. He would take this strange gift of a time out of time and not analyze it until it lost all its wonder.

"Belle." He was stroking his hand over her head, over the silky smoothness of her golden hair. He did not want to ask it. But he needed to put the past to bed. He needed to understand it so that he could move on into the future and finally put behind him the pain he had carried about for nine years.

"What?" she asked softly.

"Why did you do it?" he asked. "You must have realized that I would be remorseful, that I would need to beg your pardon for some of the things I had said to you. You must have realized how devastating it would be to find you gone without trace when there was so much that needed to be said. Why did you leave me?"

He thought for a while that she would not answer him. But she spoke eventually. "It was time, Jack," she said. "The good times were gone. You were destroying me. The only way I could restore my self-esteem and my self-confidence was to leave. I could not just break with you. I would not have had the strength. I had to go where you would not find me and tempt me to come back."

"*I* was destroying *you*." His hand stilled on her head. "Do you not know what it did to me, Belle, to know that you could not keep from the beds of other men? To know that I was not man enough to satisfy you?"

She closed her eyes at last. "We say terrible things to hurt those we care for," she said. "Jack, you satisfied me utterly. Always."

"Then why?" He still spoke quietly. He could hear the pain in his voice. Pride seemed to have deserted him. "Why the other men?"

"It was what you wanted to hear," she said, opening her eyes again. "You would never believe me when I denied it. And in that last bitter quarrel, I wanted to hurt you. I wanted to hurt you as deeply as you had been hurting me

for weeks, maybe months. I believe I must have succeeded."

"What are you saying?" He was whispering again.

"Jack," she said, "I have lain with two men in my life.
One of them was my husband."

It was his turn to close his eyes. He should have been
feeling relief, pleasure, triumph, happiness. But there was
only deep pain, pain that touched dangerously close to despair. A simple lie had destroyed everything, had blighted
nine years of his life. And now? There was no now except
for perhaps this particular moment of time. There was nothing beyond this room and this hour. No future.

"But before me?" he asked.

"Before you?" Her voice was puzzled, though he did not
open his eyes to look at her. "You know there was no one
before you, Jack. You know that I was a virgin that first
time."

His eyes snapped open.

"You did not know?" Her eyes widened. "But there was
my gaucheness, my pain. There was the blood on the
sheet."

"How could I know?" he said. "It was my first time, too.
Was there blood? I did not see it. You made up the bed
very tidily."

They stared at each other, and then both laughed rather
shakily.

"Why?" he asked when they had sobered again. "Were
you in such desperate straits, Belle? Was it a dreadful decision—to sell yourself to me?"

"I was surviving," she said. "And I was finally doing
what I had always wanted to do and what I had known for a
long time I must do. I went with you because I wanted to.
Because I lo—Oh, why not say it? I gave myself to you because I loved you and was a foolish, hopeless romantic. I
loved you more than I have loved any other man, Jack,
even—Well, I was fond of Maurice and he was good to
me."

He tightened his one arm about her shoulders, and with

the other hand brought her face against the blankets over his chest.

"I never knew it, Belle," he said. "God help me, I never knew it. And perhaps you never knew that you were my love and my life."

"No." The word was a whisper of sound against his chest.

"Is such a thing possible?" he said. "We were together for a year. We talked in that time. It was not all just bed with us, Belle. We talked and we laughed together. Did we never talk of anything important? How could we not know the most important thing of all about each other?"

"We were young," she said.

"Is that it, then?" He buried his face in her hair and kissed the top of her head. "Are older people wiser?"

"I do not know," she said.

They lapsed into silence for a while. Jack found himself wondering idly if anyone knew they were here together in his room. There would be hell to pay if anyone did. Alex would blacken both his eyes and break his nose and relieve him of all his teeth just as an appetizer. But Jack did not care what anyone thought. He did not have her here to take his pleasure of her. There was no pleasure in this. None.

"It was all my fault, then," he said. "I was insufferably possessive. I was jealous of anything and anyone that took you from me. I was jealous of your career and growing success. I was jealous of all the men who so justly admired you. It was all my fault."

"No, Jack." She shook her head against his chest. "I was often selfish. I was ambitious and often stayed away when I knew you would be wanting me. I thought I should be able to have both my career and you. I had not yet learned that the people in our lives are always more important than the things. I had to make room for my acting—I always will—but it should not have predominated. And I did lie to you. And then left you without leaving even a letter behind to explain that I had lied. I wanted you to continue hurting as I continued to hurt."

"Ah, Belle," he said.

"The fault was not all yours," she said, "or all mine. I believe we were equally contemptible and equally vulnerable."

They held each other rather tightly as if they thought to eradicate all the bitterness they had both endured.

"It was an impossibility anyway," she said. "It had to end sooner or later. I was your mistress, and the fact that I had chosen to be an actress destroyed my small claim to gentility. You were the grandson of a duke. Let us not make a grand tragedy of it, Jack. I just wish I had been honest with you. I wish we could have parted on amiable terms."

"We could never have parted amiably," he said.

"No." She sighed. "I suppose not." She drew back her head and looked into his eyes and smiled. "It was all a long, long time ago. We have gone our separate ways since then. We each have our very different lives now. Happy lives."

"Yes," he said.

"And now," she said, "perhaps we can have gentle memories of that year. We have gained something."

"Yes," he said.

"I am glad it was you who saved Marcel this afternoon," she said. "I will remember that with deep pleasure. And that it was you who brought Jacqueline home. You carried her. You held her tight, she told me. You have been good to her this week."

"I love her," he said, surprised by the truth of his words. "Because she is yours, I suppose. And because in her own right she is very special."

"Yes." Tears sprang to her eyes, and she bit her upper lip for a few moments. "She is very special and very precious to me. Oh, Jack." The tears spilled over, and she hid her face against the blankets and his chest again. "Oh, Jack."

"The events of the afternoon are catching up with you, I believe," he said. "It is all over, Belle, and really no great harm has been done. Just relax for a while. Close your eyes and relax."

He should suggest that she go to her own room and have a rest, he knew. But he could not let go of the moment himself, even though it was bringing him little pleasure. He was holding her, and they were alone and quiet together. It was all they would ever have. He would not feel guilty for clinging to the moment with both arms and with all his will and all his heart.

He was amazed less than five minutes later to realize that she had taken him at his word. More than that. She was sleeping, warm and relaxed in his arms. He closed his eyes and willed memory of this moment to be burned indelibly on his mind.

She knew as soon as she awoke that she had not slept for long. But she had slept deeply so that for a moment she did not know where she was. But she did know that there was a deep happiness and an equally deep misery awaiting her when full consciousness returned. A strange mixture of opposites.

And then she was fully awake, and she knew that instinct had not failed her. She was on Jack's bed, in Jack's arms, thick blankets between them. He had loved her all those years ago. He had been possessive and jealous, not because he had feared he was not getting worth for his money, but because he had loved her. And today he had saved Marcel's life and had carried Jacqueline home in his arms and comforted her. And then when she, Isabella, had come to thank him he had drawn her down onto his bed and held her and talked with her instead of making love to her. He must have known that she had offered herself in gratitude to him. And it would have been making love. She would have given herself with love.

She was glad, though, that he had not accepted her unspoken offer. She would have cherished memories of this day.

But there was the deep misery, too. This was all they would ever have, this moment. And she had already stayed far longer than was wise. What if Marcel was awake and they were looking for her? What if they were looking for her for another reason? What if someone came knocking at his door?

And there was misery, too, in knowing that she had still

not told him the whole truth. And never would. And so she would carry the guilt away with her from Portland House to sadden her future as the last nine years had been saddened.

But at least the bitterness was gone.

She opened her eyes. He was looking at her. She smiled.

"I slept," she said unnecessarily.

"I had forgotten," he said, "how quickly and easily you can do it. It used to annoy me considerably as I lay wakeful.

"I know." She continued to smile. "You used to wake me up—to punish me, as you used to say. It never was punishment."

"Wasn't it, Belle?" He touched the backs of his fingers to her cheek.

She disentangled herself from the bedclothes he had wrapped about her, sat up, and got out of the bed on her side.

"I hope I can leave without being seen," she said. "This is very shocking."

He had got out of bed, too. He was wearing only his pantaloons. She could see more fully how he had lost his boyish slightness of form and had acquired muscles in all the right places.

"I shall poke my head out and make sure that my whole family is not queued up out there waiting to visit," he said.

She laughed.

"Belle." He was holding out a hand to her. "This is goodbye, dear. It is the last time we can be together like this, chaste as this has been. Let me kiss you once more. Please?"

She went to him without hesitation and spread her hands on his chest and leaned against him. She raised her mouth to his as one of his arms came about her waist and the other about her shoulders.

She opened her mouth to him and gave from the depths of her heart and of her love for him. For the last time, he had said. *This is good-bye.* And so she said good-bye wordlessly and lingeringly.

She was shaken by the time he lifted his head. She had

always known that she still loved him and always would, but she had not known that she loved him with a love as raw and as new as it had been on the day she had allowed him to take her to that cheap and shabby inn.

"Belle," he said to her, "I loved you, my dear. No woman was ever loved as deeply and as passionately as I loved you."

Past tense.

She smiled at him and moved away from him.

"Poke your head out of the door, please, Jack," she said.

"At your service, ma'am." He made her an elegant bow and turned toward the door.

Chapter 15

Christmas Eve. It should have been a day of relaxed preparation for an even more relaxed Christmas Day. But at Portland House, of course, it became probably the most frenzied day of the year.

There were rehearsals for each of the Shakespeare scenes that would be acted next day. There were practices for the evening concert—the duchess spent all of an hour in her private sitting room with her daughters and her sister, drawing up a program. There were children to amuse—one could not expect three nurses to contain their exuberance all day long without a break. There were gifts to wrap and food baskets to be taken to several villagers and poorer cottagers. And, of course, there would be church to attend at night, after the concert.

And for Jack there was a young lady to speak with and her father to consult—depending upon what she had to say to him first. For Jack it was to be one of the most important, most fateful days of his life.

He procrastinated. Or perhaps procrastination was forced upon him. Juliana and Howard were scheduled to practice in the music room directly after breakfast—she was to play a pianoforte solo, and the two of them were to sing a duet. Almost as soon as Prue was listed to take their place, Jack was due to attend rehearsal in the ballroom. And then a mere half hour after that it was his own turn for the music room—he was to play Bach on the pianoforte. Half an hour after that, he was to be joined by his five old partners in song—Grandmama had insisted that Grandpapa's Christmas would be incomplete if there was no madrigal on the concert program. They had searched diligently for a song with a minimum of fa-la-las and hey-nonnys and had succeeded. Instead they broke after every verse into a glorious burst of echoing cuckoos.

The rehearsal was something of an ordeal. Jack knew his part, or would know it by tomorrow, anyway. Why learn a part too early, he had always said, only to forget it and have to relearn it? He was even acting it well enough, according to Claude. But he would have preferred not to have to do it at all. He had said good-bye to Belle yesterday afternoon in his bedchamber, and he had meant it. No more reliving the past, trying to make sense of it. Sense had been made of it. His own stupidity and jealousy and her lie had ruined everything. But at least now he could let go of the bitterness. She had not merely used him. She had loved him. But it was all in the past. It was over. It was gone. Today he was to offer marriage to a lady of whom he had grown fond in the past week.

He did not enjoy the closeness to Belle forced upon him by the rehearsal. He did not enjoy kissing her and knowing that it was not Othello kissing Desdemona, but Jack kissing Belle.

He could have sought out Juliana in the half hour between the rehearsal and his music practice. Thirty minutes was a long enough time for what needed to be said. But his mind was still too agitated after the rehearsal. He found his steps taking him toward the nursery instead.

Two infants—Rachel and Rupert—hurtled toward him as soon as he opened the door and threatened to bowl him over. But they were needed for a game of "Ring Around the Rosy" with some of the other little ones and soon made off again.

Marcel was smiling sunnily at him. Jack strolled toward him and ruffled his hair.

"How are you this morning, lad?" he asked.

"Well," Marcel said. "I am going outside soon with my friend Davy and my friends Meggie and Kitty and their papa. We are going to make snow angels."

"Be sure to guard against those trickles of snow down

the neck," Jack said with a chuckle. "They can be a mite uncomfortable."

Belle's son had been brought down to the drawing room early last evening by the duchess herself, and all of them assembled there had applauded him then hugged and kissed him if they happened to be female or shook his hand and slapped his back if they were male. Anne had cried all over him again, and Belle had made discreet dabs at her eyes with a handkerchief. The duke had wheezed and growled and taken the boy's small hand into his great paw and left a shiny golden guinea on the little palm when he released it.

The child had been wide-eyed and rosy-cheeked. He had behaved well. There had been not a single hint of a swagger or a boast. And then the duchess had taken him back to the nursery.

Jacqueline was painting. She was quietly absorbed in her task, but she looked up when Jack rested a hand on her shoulder, and her eyes brightened.

"You have talent for this, too," he said, looking at four figures skating on ice, arms outstretched, scarves flying. "You are a clever girl, Jacqueline." He went down on his haunches and watched her finish the fourth figure by adding a bonnet with a fur brim.

She washed out her brush with deliberate thoroughness and set it down on the table with the paints. Then she turned and wrapped her arms about his neck and set her cheek against his.

"Please?" she said. "Please take me to the music room. Mama will not mind. She did not scold last time. Please may I go?"

He chuckled. "The music room is so busy all day today that it may never recover," he said. "But it happens to be my turn next. And I do not need all of half an hour to practice one Bach fugue. Come along with me, then."

But she did not immediately release him. She squeezed his neck a little tighter and kissed his cheek.

"Thank you," she said.

And so he played his own piece for no longer than five minutes—his grandmother would have a heart seizure, or more likely would threaten him with his grandfather's heart seizure if she knew. Jacqueline played for twenty-five minutes while he listened, still almost awed, though he knew by now what to expect.

He had not even realized how much time had passed until a tap on the door heralded the arrival of Alex, Perry, Prue, Connie, and Hortense for the madrigal practice. Jacqueline, who was between pieces at the time, hastily returned the violin to its case.

"One escapee from the nursery?" Alex asked with a smile for her. "Have you been watching Jack and correcting his fingering, Jacqueline? You have pianoforte lessons?"

"Yes, sir," she said.

"Come," Jack said, holding out a hand to her, "I'll take you upstairs and then come right back to sing."

But a thought struck him as they reached the landing outside the nursery. Doubtless a rash thought. Certainly one he should have checked out first with both his grandmother and Belle. But he spoke it right out.

"Would you like to play at the concert this evening?" he asked. "I am sure you would be the star turn even though everyone else is adult. You could take my place on the program. Would you like to?"

Her eyes were wide and shining when she looked up at him, and he realized suddenly how he had allowed his tongue to run away with him. Belle would have his head. And it was very obvious to him that all her fears were very well-founded. Here was a child who wanted and needed to share her talents with other people.

"Yes," she whispered. "Oh, yes, please."

Dash it all, he was not at all sure it was going to be possible. His grandmother might object. Belle might well plant him a facer.

"I shall see what I can arrange," he said, squeezing her hand and standing to watch as she whisked herself into the nursery.

He raked the fingers of one hand through his hair and blew out his breath from puffed cheeks. Time to go practice cuckooing. And then time to seek out his grandmother and

Belle. And then time to have a word with Juliana and more than a word with Holyoke.

What a glorious Christmas Eve, he thought. He wondered what Reggie and his beauties and his guests were up to at this precise moment. Sleeping in all probability since they would have been carousing for half the night and otherwise busy for the rest of it.

Juliana and Howard had dutifully practiced through most of their half hour in the music room. Juliana did toy with the idea of talking heart-to-heart with her brother, but it seemed that he was preoccupied with his own concerns. As soon as their practice was over, he was going to take himself over to the rectory.

"No, I cannot come with you," she said when he asked. "I—Jack—I have to stay here."

Howard frowned. "Do you think they will let me take her walking alone for a short while?" he asked. "They are an amiable couple, are they not, the Fitzgeralds?"

"Howard," Juliana said, "you will not compromise Rose, will you? Please? I like her."

He stared at her. "A few more days and I will never see her again," he said. "I don't know if I'll be able to stand it, Julie."

"She is a governess, Howard," Juliana said. "Papa—"

"Damn Papa!" he said irreverently. "Her sister is married to Lynwood. Her father is a gentleman."

"Oh, Howard," she said, her eyes widening, "are you seriously considering—"

"I do not know what I am considering," he said, still frowning. "My thoughts are in a whirl, Julie."

It was definitely not the time to try to talk to him about herself. Besides, there was nothing really to talk about. She liked Jack and found him attractive and was falling in love with him. Everything was progressing smoothly and satisfactorily. Except that Fitz had kissed her that once and turned her world upside down. And she had turned to him instinctively at the lake yesterday in the midst of all the upset, and he had set his arm comfortingly about her waist.

And had said never a word to her. The normally cheerful and talkative Fitz had been silent.

All morning she had known that this was the day. And she knew what she was going to say. She was happy with what she was going to say. And so when Jack asked her after luncheon if she cared for a stroll in the gallery, she smiled warmly at him and told him she would fetch her shawl.

They did stroll for a while, the whole length of the gallery, her arm through his, his hand covering her own.

"Well," he said, drawing her to a halt and smiling down at her. "The moment of decision has come, Juliana. I told you I would not press the point if you could not like me by today. Today has come."

"Yes," she said. "I do not dislike you, Jack."

His eyes were different, she thought. Today they did not look old or cynical any longer. Today they looked merely kind. A lover's eyes? Or a fond uncle's eyes? It was a strange thought to leap to mind at such a moment.

"That is a start at least," he said. "Can you bear the thought of marrying me, Juliana?"

"Yes," she said.

"Is it a thought only to be borne?" he asked.

She was not quite sure what he meant.

"Do you wish to marry me?" he asked. "If you were perfectly free at this moment to make a perfectly free choice, would you choose to marry me?"

"Yes," she said.

"Why?" he asked her, his eyes very intent on hers. The soft kindness had gone, but the hard cynicism had not come back, either.

She had not expected the question. Surely it was not necessary. "Because you are Papa's choice," she said, "and because you have been kind to me, and I have come to like you. I have seen how good you are with children, and that is important. And because—well, because it is time to marry, and I believe you will be a good husband and I want to try to be a good wife." It sounded all very lame.

"Do you have a fondness for me?" he asked.

"Yes." She did. It was no lie.

"And for no other man?" he asked.

"No." Her heart beat uncomfortably fast. She was unaccustomed to lying. She wanted to ask him all the same questions, but she dared not. She was a woman. It was not her place to question a man. But what if he was marrying her only because he felt it his duty to do so? What if he had not come to like her during the week? What if he did not have a fondness for her? What if he had a fondness for another woman?

He bent his head and kissed her. A warm, gentle kiss with slightly parted lips. A more skilled kiss, she guessed, than Fitz's almost fierce assault had been.

"You are willing for me to arrange a settlement with your father, then?" he asked after he had finished the kiss. "And to allow the announcement to be made tomorrow— probably during the evening? You are quite sure, Juliana?"

"Yes," she said. "Yes, I am quite sure, Jack."

The kindness was back in his eyes. "Then you have made me the happiest of men," he said.

She found the conventional words strangely disappointing. They were more like a shield between them than a window into the state of his own feelings and inclinations. Had she really made him happy? She wished she knew. Oh, she wished she knew.

"I am happy, too." She smiled. "I am very happy."

"I believe," he said, "I had better go in search of your father."

"Yes," she said.

But she could not go to join her mother and grandmother in the salon when he escorted her back downstairs. They knew very well what was going on and were tense with well-bred excitement. So was the duchess and Jack's mama. She could not go and sit with them and converse on mundane matters and pretend that nothing out of the ordinary was happening.

She went scurrying off toward the ballroom, expecting it to be empty since all the rehearsals had been scheduled for the morning. But Isabella was in there alone, doing voice exercises that sounded strange to Juliana's ears.

"Oh, I am so sorry," she said, and would have fled out again if Isabella had not stopped and smiled at her.

"Oh, do come in," she said. "It is time I stopped for today."

Juliana was the last person she wished to speak with. She had had a wretchedly restless night, tossing and turning for hours wondering uselessly what might have happened if she had not fled nine years ago but had faced him with the truth. And when she had fallen asleep, she had dreamed of Marcel clawing at the edge of the ice and slipping beneath it with agonizing slowness. She had woken up several times, gasping for air just as if she were the one drowning.

And now today she was having to face the fact that it was all finally, finally over. It had been over for nine years. She had forgotten about him and got on with her life. She had done wonderful things with her life in nine years. But only now today did she realize that until yesterday it had not been over at all.

Yesterday they had admitted to having loved each other all those years ago. And yesterday they had said good-bye.

The last person she wanted to talk with now was the girl he was going to marry. And yet she was an innocent girl and a sweet one. And doubtless she was deeply in love with Jack. What woman would not be if he set his mind to courting her?

"I did not mean to disturb you," Juliana said, but she advanced farther into the room. "I was looking for a quiet place."

"Well." Isabella still smiled. "You may have this room to yourself if you wish."

She watched the girl draw a deep breath and release it slowly. "Do you ever feel so close to panic that you want to scream and run?" she asked.

"Yes," Isabella said. "Yesterday at the lake. Has something happened?"

"Only what has been expected all week," Juliana said.

"He is speaking with Papa right at this very minute. They are talking about a marriage settlement. Tomorrow our betrothal will be announced—at the ball, I believe." She smiled brightly.

Isabella felt rather as if a knife had been plunged into her stomach and was being turned. "And you feel panic?" she said. "Is it just the natural panic that anyone feels on such an occasion? You do not have real doubts?"

"How could I?" Juliana said. "He is everything any woman could dream of, is he not? He is handsome and wealthy and charming and kind. He is quite different from what I expected when I first saw him. I thought then his eyes were hard and he was cold. But it is not so. I like him exceedingly. And I loved what he did yesterday, though I am sure any of the men would have done the like had they been closer. I believe I could not be more fortunate than I am. And he says I have made him the happiest man in the world."

Ah, Jack. The knife twisted again. Why had she decided to come back to the ballroom after luncheon? Why had she not gone to spend the whole of the afternoon with her children? She knew why, of course. She had been upset over the duchess's begging her to allow Jacqueline to play at this evening's concert. It was all Jack's doing, she suspected. And she could see it all beginning for her daughter—the lure of pursuing excellence, the compulsion to demonstrate that excellence before an audience.

"Are *you* happy?" she asked quietly. She did not want to know the answer. Either way, she did not want to know.

"Howard admires Rose Fitzgerald," Juliana said quickly. "I have walked out with Fitz—with Mr. Bertrand Fitzgerald a few times so that Howard could spend some time with Rose. I like Fitz. He is very easy to be with. I laugh with him and do not have to think about what I should talk about next. He is—unthreatening. But he kissed me down by the bridge two days ago because he had not kissed me beneath the kissing bough the day before that. It was nothing. It was nothing at all. And he works for a living even though he is a gentleman. He is a steward. Papa would never . . . It is nothing, is it, Isabella? I am just being silly. I wish I had some of your experience and some of your poise."

Oh, dear. Oh, dear heaven, she did not need this.

"No amount of experience enables a person to answer all questions, Juliana," she said, "especially for someone else. I am sorry."

And yet she felt desperate to give advice. *Don't marry him*, she wanted to say. *Not unless you love him with all your heart. And even then. Don't marry Jack. Not Jack. Please don't.* Just as if he would marry her if he did not marry Juliana. The woman he had once loved—past tense. The woman who had been his mistress.

What a terrible irony it was that Juliana had chosen her as a confidante.

"You must do what is right for you after everything has been taken into consideration," she said. "That sounds like very dull advice, and it is not an answer at all. But I cannot give you an answer, Juliana."

The girl smiled rather wanly. "I do not need an answer," she said. "The matter is already decided. I said yes, and he went to talk to Papa. It is as you said. It is the natural panic anyone must feel to know that the whole of the rest of her life has been decided for her. Did you feel such panic?"

"Yes," Isabella said.

"But you had a happy marriage?"

"Yes." It had been happy. She had liked and respected Maurice, and he had adored her. She had decided when he did her the almost incredible kindness of marrying her that she would make him happy. And she had. Although she had pursued her career during her marriage, at Maurice's urging, she had learned also during those years that the people in her life were more important than the things. Maurice, Jacqueline, Marcel—they had been very dear to her. And the memory of Jack. "Yes, it was a very happy marriage. Because I wanted it to be. Because I set myself to making it happy. Some things happen to you in life, Juliana, like falling in love. But far more things you can make happen. You can control your life to a large degree if you wish instead of being at the mercy of whatever happens. And there, I did not mean to preach."

But Juliana was smiling. "Oh, you really are wise," she said. "I knew you were. I like that. You had a happy marriage because you wanted it to be happy and because you set yourself to make it so. You have made me feel so very much better. I am going to be happy, too. And I am going to make Jack happy."

The knife turned one more time.

"It is so very hard to know if he is happy now," Juliana said. "Do you think he is? As an impartial observer, do you think so?"

"He is a gentleman," Isabella said. "He will be good to you, Juliana."

"Yes." Juliana smiled. "Yes, I know he will. Thank you for listening and advising. I wish I could return the compliment as real friends should do. But you are so—complete and self-possessed. You do not have problems, I am sure."

"You think not?" Isabella said.

"I am sorry," Juliana said. "You lost your husband. It must be hard to be without him. But you have your children and your beauty and your acting and your fame. I can scarcely wait to see you act tomorrow evening."

"The other characters are good, too," Isabella said, on familiar ground again and moving them in the direction of the door. "Perry makes a marvelously evil Shylock, and Alex is an infuriatingly domineering Petruchio. And Jack is a very tortured, sad Othello. And Freddie"—she laughed—"is a deliciously excitable Gratiano, though he has a tendency to come out with his lines at the oddest moments. Anne is doing wonderfully well at thinking her way into Emilia's mind. Tomorrow evening is going to be fun." *Part* of tomorrow evening.

She laughed determinedly as they left the ballroom, and Juliana joined her.

Chapter 16

The music room had been set up formally with the pianoforte and other instruments arranged in the middle of the room and empty chairs set in a circle about them.

"Just as if we were attending a concert in Mayfair at the height of the Season," Charles Lynwood muttered to his wife. Martin was to be master of ceremonies, a position he had thought quite superfluous. But he could see now that this was one of the duchess's grand occasions. He wished fervently that he had prepared introductions. He coughed nervously and looked down at the program in his hand.

The duke looked his usual gruff self. The duchess looked regal. Almost everyone else looked sheepish, since almost everyone else was to perform.

"It never seemed fair to me," Prudence whispered to her husband, "that Grandmama and Grandpapa never took part in any of our concerts or theatrical performances and yet the rest of us were given no choice. We should have rebelled, should we not?"

"I thought so when I first married you, Prue," he said. "And yet tonight I find myself preparing to sing a baritone solo. My brothers would not stop laughing for a month if they knew. If you ever tell them, I will throttle you. There is definitely something about your grandmother. I have not yet fathomed out quite what it is."

The three children who were to perform were apprehensive and wide-eyed and sat very upright on the edges of their chairs. Davy and Meggie had been granted the privilege of participating in the family concert by virtue of the fact that they were past the age of ten—they were to play a duet on the pianoforte. Jacqueline was only seven but had had a personal invitation from Her Grace to play the violin.

All the other children were present, too, with the exception of Kenneth, who was asleep in the nursery. They would enjoy the music and the singing, the duchess had said, and besides it was Christmas and Christmas was a family affair.

Jack sat beside Juliana, her arm resting on his. They were to be married in the spring at St. George's, Hanover Square, in London. Viscount Holyoke, it seemed, felt it necessary that his daughter make her appearance in society and her curtsy to the queen before her marriage. They would marry in May. In five months' time. There would be plenty of time to adjust his mind fully to the new reality in his life.

The very beautiful new reality in his life. She was dressed this evening in delicate pink, and her cheeks were flushed to match. Her hand was small and dainty on his arm. He had been amazed to learn from her father that she was nineteen years old. He had had to adjust his whole thinking about her. She was not an infant barely out of the schoolroom. She was a woman.

Everyone knew, of course, that his offer had been made today and accepted, that a marriage settlement and preliminary wedding arrangements had been made. Everyone knew that the announcement would be made tomorrow—at the ball, it had been decided. Everyone had known a week ago that it was inevitable, but now it was general knowledge that it was all official. No one had said anything, of course. It was understood that the announcement was to come as a surprise tomorrow.

"You are nervous?" Jack covered the little hand on his arm with his own.

"If my heart beats any faster," she said, "it may well burst right through my chest."

"I know the feeling." He chuckled.

And he glanced at Jacqueline, sitting very still and pale on her chair beside Belle. She was obviously nervous, though she appeared to be more in a trance than in the jitters. Was she regretting her decision? Had he done her harm in suggesting she perform publicly when she was so young? She was looking almost pretty in a blue party dress with a matching large bow in her dark hair. She was going to be a beauty when she grew up, he realized in some surprise.

He kept his eyes off Belle—lovely Belle in her simply styled white silk gown. She had one arm about the shoulders of Marcel, who was swinging his legs and looking about him with bright interest.

And then his grandmother gave her regal nod, and Martin got to his feet, looking as if his neck cloth might be tied too tightly. Prue started flexing her fingers. Her harp solo was to open the concert.

Everything proceeded smoothly. Prudence had not lost her touch, Jack's fingers did not tie themselves in knots on the keyboard, Juliana's voice did not shake during her duet with Howard, the six madrigal singers succeeded in keeping to their separate parts and cuckooing merrily and by some miracle finishing together.

And then it was Jacqueline's turn.

There was some amused, indulgent titters when she lifted one one of the violins to her chin and took up the bow. They seemed to dwarf her. And there was a polite hush as she stood for a few moments staring at the floor in front of her feet.

Jack found himself sitting forward in his chair, letting Juliana's arm drop away from his. His heart was thundering in his ear. *Come on,* he was telling the child silently, *forget we are here. Show us what music is all about.*

She lifted the bow to the violin and closed her eyes.

She played Beethoven as she had that first evening he had heard her. She played with passion and abandonment, her whole body moving with the beauty she created with the violin. Jack knew that she had forgotten her audience. And then he forgot it, too. There was nothing but the music and Jacqueline. There was a soreness in his throat and at the back of his nose that he did not recognize for what it was even when he blinked back tears.

There was silence for a moment when she finished playing—and then applause that was far more than just polite, and exclamations of surprise and appreciation.

Jack did not clap. He sat forward in his chair, smiling at Jacqueline while she looked startled and then blushed scarlet and then set down the violin and bow carefully. When she looked up again, her gaze was directed at him, and she gave him one of her rare smiles. He held out his arms to her and she came to him and he hugged her tightly.

"You were magnificent, Jacqueline," he said.

"Thank you." There was an unusual excitement in her voice. "Thank you for letting me."

"You have an amazing talent for a seven-year-old," he said. The room was falling quiet again.

"I am *eight* years old," she said. And then her eyes widened, and she slapped a hand over her mouth. "Oh, I forgot. I was not supposed to say."

And she turned to hurry back to her chair beside her mother.

Martin got to his feet, consulting his program as he did so. But before he could start to introduce the next performer, Isabella jerked to her feet and hurried from the room. Martin waited politely until the door had closed behind her.

Jack would not afterward have been able to say who performed next or what the item was.

I am eight years old. I was not supposed to say. He stared sightlessly at his mother and his aunt as they sang their duet, the soprano part rather too high-pitched for his aunt. *I am eight years old. I was not supposed to say*.

"Excuse me," he said quietly to Juliana beneath the sound of the applause that followed the duet. "I will be back."

There were two footmen in the hall.

"Which direction did the Comtesse de Vacheron take?" he asked one of them.

"The ballroom, sir," one of them said, pointing. "She did not take a candle, sir, though I called after her."

Jack did not take one, either. He did not even hear the footman's words.

I am eight years old. I was not supposed to say.

Alex shifted uneasily in his chair.

"I have a feeling that all hell could be about to burst its bounds," he muttered close to his wife's ear.

She looked at him with eyebrows raised in inquiry.

"It was Perry, was it not," he said, "who commented on the fact that Jacqueline Gellée looks more like a member of our family than some of our own children?"

"Why would she be told to say she is seven when she is eight?" Anne whispered, looking puzzled.

"Because eight years and nine months ago Isabella was not married to de Vacheron," he said.

"Oh, Alex." She looked distressed. "It is none of our concern."

"But she and Jack were lovers," he said, as if she had not spoken.

She stared mutely at him.

The room was growing quiet again. Martin was on his feet.

She had gone to the ballroom by sheer instinct. After she got there, she thought it would have been better to have gone to her room. She could have locked the door and been safe there. But perhaps she did not want to be safe. Perhaps she knew that there could no longer be safety.

The ballroom was in darkness. But there was the light of moon and stars and the peculiar light of snow beaming through the French windows. The curtains were not drawn across them.

She hurried across the ballroom to one of them, as far from the doors as she could go. She braced one hand against the window frame and the other on one of the handles and rested her forehead against the cold glass. She closed her eyes.

Somehow she could neither think nor feel. It was as if a

deadweight had filled her from her toes to the crown of her head. She waited.

She heard the door open and then close again—quietly. She had braced herself to hear it slam. And then she heard his footsteps echo hollowly on the bare floor as he came toward her. She knew it was he. It could be no one else. Her shoulders hunched involuntarily in anticipation of his touch.

She turned before he reached her and set her back and her head against the wall. She set her palms against it, too. And she looked at him.

He came to stand in front of her. He did not touch her. He set one hand on the wall beside her head and stood the length of his arm away from her. She thought for a while that he would not speak, but she could not break the silence herself.

"How long after you left me was she born, Belle?" he asked at last. His voice was quiet.

She could not answer. She could not force her lips apart or sound to come out. But he waited.

"Six months," she whispered.

He was still and silent for so long that she grew frightened. But she could not move or speak again.

"Jacqueline," he said softly. "Not a French name for a French husband, but *Jack*eline."

"Yes." Her lips formed the word, though she heard no sound.

He closed his eyes. "Belle," he said. And then he bowed his head forward until his forehead was resting on her shoulder. "Ah, Belle."

Her stomach lurched when she heard his first sob. She stood very still, biting hard on her upper lip while he cried until tears she had not known she was shedding trickled from her chin down her neck. She tipped her head sideways and rubbed her cheek against his hair. She took her arms away from the wall and set them about him. She held him thus for a long time.

"Why?" He had lifted his head and was looking into her face in the near-darkness again. "Why, Belle?"

"I had to go away," she said. "Don't you see that, Jack? I could not have lived through the degradation of staying. I would always have been your whore, and she would have been your bastard. Your first question would have been to ask me whose she was. For my own sake, I had to leave. And especially for hers."

"I *loved* you," he said. "You were my life."

"I believe you," she said, "though I never knew it at the time. But it was not a good love, Jack. It was a jealous and possessive love. It was a love without trust or respect."

"And your love," he said, "was without compassion. You took my child from me, Belle. You did not even tell me. You let another man give her his name."

"It was not a good love," she said sadly. "It had to end."

She had never seen his eyes look so unhappy. "Love does not end, Belle," he said. "Love deepens and grows and matures. Or it sours and grows bitter and cynical and parodies itself in lust and promiscuity. If you had told me you were with child, perhaps we both could have taken a step forward in our love."

"And perhaps not," she said. "Love does die, Jack. We do not love each other any longer."

His face moved closer so that she had to press her head back against the wall again. "Ask me in an eternity or two how I feel about you," he said. "The answer will be the same then as it is now and as it has been since I first got to know you in Hyde Park. I love you. You are the only woman I have ever loved and the only woman I ever will love."

"Oh," she said. It was an agony of sound.

"I have had a daughter for longer than eight years," he said, "and have not known it because you kept the knowledge from me."

She could only stare mutely at him.

"You are right," he said. "I loved poorly. I loved as a young man loves, surprised by love and scared by it. I had not learned to enjoy it. I had not learned to loosen my clutch on my love. I was still afraid that if I did so, it would

fly away. But it flew away anyway. I have been amply punished, Belle. I lost you. And I lost my daughter."

"Don't make me believe now," she said, "that I did the
wrong thing, Jack." But she did believe it. She had made
the wrong decision. "I would not be able to live with that
knowledge. You will never know how hard it was to leave
you and go to a strange country when I loved you and when
I was with child by you. The loneliness and the aching
heart, Jack. When I grew larger with her . . . When she was
born . . . It was only the knowledge that there had been no
real alternative for me that kept me going. Don't tell me
now that I was wrong."

He searched her eyes for a while longer and then
straightened up and half turned away from her. He ran the
fingers of one hand through his hair.

"I wonder," he said, "if any other two people who pro-
fess to have loved each other have ever made such a
damned mess of their lives. Do you think it is possible?"

She did not answer him. She doubted it. She very much
doubted it.

"Jacqueline is my daughter," he said. "I have a daughter.
I still feel as if a strong fist has slammed against my stomach and robbed me of breath. I am a father."

She could remember with a dreadful ache the day
Jacqueline was born, with masses of dark hair to proclaim
her paternity. She could remember the almost overpower-
ing temptation to send for Jack even though she was in
France and he was in England.

What would have happened if she had given in to temptation?

"Belle," he said, "I am going to acknowledge her. I am
going to provide for her. I am not going to have my daughter . . ."

"No," she said.

He turned his head to look at her.

"You are betrothed to Juliana," she said. "She is a very
sweet and very innocent and very vulnerable young lady."
And she did not love Jack.

He had no answer to give her.

"We are going to have to return to the music room," she said. "Separately. We are going to have to hope that no one will make anything particular out of the fact that we have been absent together. There is church to attend afterward. There is Christmas Day to live through tomorrow. You must do nothing to upset anyone else, Jack."

"She is my daughter," he said.

"Yes."

He continued to stare at her for a while. Then he nodded briskly and straightened his shoulders. "I will return first," he said. "I will say nothing. Don't worry."

She watched him stride purposefully across the room away from her. And she knew again, as she had known several times over the past ten years, what despair felt like.

Juliana sat beside Jack in the pew at church. Their arms were touching. They were packed in rather tightly since there were so many of them from Portland House to take up the pews. Mama sat on her other side and then Papa and then Grandmama. Not Howard. Howard was sitting in the front pew at the other side of the church with Rose—and with Mrs. Fitzgerald and Fitz.

Juliana looked at them rather wistfully. There had been a terrible row between Papa and Howard just before dinner— an entirely private row—because Howard had offered for Rose at the rectory and had been accepted before coming home to consult Papa. But Papa had given in, of course— he had had no choice really. And it was not such a dreadful match. Rose was a gentlewoman and unknown to either Papa or Howard until this afternoon, her father was heir to a modest estate and fortune and had been able to offer a small dowry with Rose.

So Rose was to be her sister-in-law. And that meant she would meet Fitz in the future, not only when she came to Portland House with Jack, but sometimes when she visited Howard and Rose. She let her eyes rest on Fitz for a moment—so much less handsome than Jack, yet good-looking and good-humored. And so easy to talk with and laugh with.

But it was Christmas. She concentrated her mind on the sound of the church bells pealing and on the sight of the church full of worshipers waiting for the rector to come in and begin the service. Christmas was a wonderful time. And she was with her newly betrothed. Next year she would be married to him. Perhaps by next year she would be . . . But even the thought made her flush.

She turned her head to smile at Jack. But his head was turned slightly to the other side, and she could see that he was watching little Jacqueline, Isabella's daughter. She was sitting one pew ahead of them with her mother.

He was fond of the child. Juliana had noticed that before. And now she understood why. It was Jack who had discovered how splendidly she played on the violin and had persuaded the duchess to allow her to play at the concert.

He felt her eyes on him and turned his head to look down at her.

"She is very talented," Juliana whispered.

"Jacqueline?" he said. "Yes."

"I think," she said, "she must resemble her father. She looks nothing like Isabella, does she?"

His eyes were still on hers for a moment. "No," he said. "I believe you must be right."

And then the congregation was rising for the entrance of the rector.

Christmas. A child being born. None of it had ever meant a great deal to him. There had been the games and the presents when he was a boy, the carousing when he became a man. He had always avoided the church service whenever he could. It was invariably tedious. Always the same story, always the same carols. Always the same child being born.

But tonight a child had been born to him. His feelings were still raw with the wonder of new fatherhood. His eyes kept straying to her. His heart kept yearning toward her.

Christmas had come to Mary and Joseph, not with unalloyed pleasure as it came to most people these days. There had been pain and discomfort and anxiety. But at the end of it all, joy. Joy more intense because it had come out of those other things and despite them.

Joy was different from pleasure, he was discovering. There had been nothing pleasurable about this evening's discovery. It had been an excruciating agony, in fact. But it was an evening of joy nevertheless. He had become a father tonight. A child had been born to him. A thin, quiet, solemn, immensely talented little eight-year-old. She was his daughter.

And so he celebrated the coming of Christmas at church with his family and Juliana's in pain and joy.

And finally in pleasure, too.

The service had begun late, far too late for the younger children, but they had all come, except for Kenneth. Most of them were asleep before the Reverend Fitzgerald had got even half launched into his sermon. Isabella bent over Marcel and lifted him onto her lap and rocked him, though he was clearly asleep even before she started. Jacqueline sat upright for a while longer and then let her head fall sideways against her mother's shoulder. Twice it slid forward, and she jerked awake.

The second time she looked over her shoulder and caught Jack's eyes. He smiled at her and crooked one beckoning finger from his lap. Then he got half to his feet, bent over the pew in front, and lifted her over the back of it and onto his lap. Isabella turned her head, startled.

And so his daughter snuggled against him and despite a tendency to insomnia—*which she must inherit from him,* he thought suddenly—she was soon fast asleep and warm and relaxed and trusting in his arms.

It was pure pleasure, pure joy.

It was Christmas.

Chapter 17

Gift giving on Christmas morning was a rather private affair, each smaller family being left to organize its own gathering place and its own little celebration. They would all gather together in the drawing room later, of course, to give the servants their gifts, to share a drink and a mince pie with them, and to sing a few Christmas carols.

Jacqueline and Marcel came to Isabella's room and climbed onto the bed with her and shook her while she pretended to sleep and then explained to her what day it was when she pretended to have forgotten and then demanded their presents—or Marcel did anyway, bouncing on his knees on the bed.

"Presents?" Isabella frowned. "Hm, presents. Now, did I remember to bring them from London? Or were they in the bag I left in my dressing room at home and forgot to have carried down to the carriage?"

"Mama." Jacqueline smiled and slid under the bedclothes to lie beside her mother.

"Maman!" Marcel bounced, in an agony.

"Ah, yes, I remember now." Isabella smiled. "I did bring that bag. But where on earth did I put it? I do not remember to have seen it since we arrived."

"Mama." Jacqueline was giggling.

"Maman!" Marcel was too unsure that he was being teased to dare laugh.

"I suppose," Isabella said, sitting up and swinging her legs over the side of the bed, "I had better go into the dressing room here and look." She picked up a pillow and swatted Marcel with it as he resumed his bouncing.

She loved Christmas morning, though last year there had been a sadness because it was their first without Maurice. There could be no warmer feeling than watching one's own children caught up in the magic of opening parcels and exclaiming in wonder over new toys and books and clothes. She always made them take turns opening, one parcel at a time, so that it would last longer.

"Well." She laughed and looked about rather ruefully at the mess of wrapping paper and bows on the bed and the floor surrounding it when they were finally finished. "Do you suppose we should tidy up?"

Jacqueline knelt up on the bed and wrapped her arms about Isabella's neck. "Thank you, Mama," she said, "for the doll and the dress and the muff and books and hair ribbon. They are lovely."

Marcel was down on his elbows on the bed, bottom elevated, cheek almost against the covers, seating a toy soldier on a toy horse while numerous others were scattered about among the debris.

Isabella laughed again. "I shall go and get dressed quickly," she said, "and then we will clear away and move to the nursery. Agreed?"

"Yes, Mama," Jacqueline said. She was putting her doll neatly to bed.

"Charge!" Marcel said, and the horse took a dive while the soldier went soaring through the air.

The nursery was deserted, all the other children being off with their parents somewhere else in the house and the nurses having been given the day off. Marcel was all impatience to be dressed so that he could get back to playing war. Isabella lingered over Jacqueline, clothing her in her new yellow frilled dress, brushing her hair until it was smooth and shining and tying it with the new yellow ribbon, fussing over it until the bow was just so.

Jack's child, she thought, looking at her daughter's image in the looking glass. The cherished memento of her year of love. Not that she always, or even often, thought of Jacqueline that way. Jacqueline was a person in her own right. As was Marcel. She had been afraid throughout her pregnancy with Marcel that she would be unable to love Maurice's child as she loved Jack's, but of course her fears had been unfounded. They were both her children and both precious persons.

"May I go and play with my doll, Mama?" her daughter asked now.

"Of course." She smiled and followed Jacqueline out into the empty nursery. Perhaps she should take them downstairs to the drawing room. That was probably where everyone was gathering by now, and they would enjoy the company of the other children and the excitement of Christmas morning with the whole household. Selfishly, she wished she could spend the rest of the morning alone with them. With her children. Her world.

Ask me in an eternity or two how I feel about you . . . I love you. You are the only woman I have ever loved and the only woman I ever will love.

No. It was over. He was not part of her world now, though once he had been almost the whole of it. It was her children who gave her her reason for living now. Perhaps when she went back to London, she would pursue more aggressively her acquaintance with the Earl of Helwick. But she would think of that tomorrow. Not today.

The door opened suddenly, and she lifted her head to see who was coming. But her children were before her.

Marcel whooped and darted across the room. "Come and see," he said, his voice high with excitement. "Come and see what I got. You may play with my soldiers if you wish."

Even Jacqueline went tripping across the room with an uncharacteristically childish exuberance. "This is a new dress," she said, "and a new bow. In my favorite color. I have a new doll."

And then they both stopped and stared with heightened interest as he brought his arms from behind his back.

"Presents!" Marcel shrieked. "For us?"

Jack grinned. "Why would I be bringing presents for you?" he asked.

"Because it is Christmas," Jacqueline said, and his grin softened to a smile as he turned his attention to her.

Isabella's heart turned over painfully. He should not be here. He should be with Juliana. Or with his grandparents and his mother. Or with his sister and his nephew and niece. He should not be here. But Jacqueline was his daughter and had been kept from him for eight years.

He looked across the room, still smiling. "Happy Christmas," he said.

"Happy Christmas." She could not quite smile back.

"Which is mine?" Marcel was bouncing again, but on his feet this time. "Let me have it."

"Marcel," she said, embarrassed.

But Jack was laughing. "The big one is yours," he said, "and the little one is Jacqueline's. Let us go over to your mother, and you may open them."

He looked like a boy himself, Isabella thought with a pang, his eyes dancing with merriment.

Marcel's cricket bat and ball were unseasonal, he explained as the boy opened his parcel and exclaimed with delight. They were also not new.

"They were mine long ago when I was a lad," he said. "They were up in the attic. I went up there last night and found them and worked on them to make them look a little newer." He ruffled Marcel's hair. "In the spring, someone must teach you England's game."

"You?" Marcel said.

Jack smiled. "Perhaps," he said.

He must have worked a long time, Isabella thought. Both ball and bat looked clean and new. Marcel had pestered her during the summer for a cricket bat. She had said perhaps next year—the perennial parental answer.

It was Jacqueline's turn. She had held the small parcel patiently in her hands, savoring the mystery before opening it. She unwrapped it slowly and then stared at it with big eyes.

"Let me pin it on your new dress," Jack said, such tenderness in his eyes that Isabella felt the rush of tears to her own. He pinned the brooch carefully to Jacqueline's dress.

Where on earth, Isabella wondered, had he found on such short notice a diamond-studded brooch in the shape of a violin, a silver bow across its silver strings?

"Thank you," Jacqueline said. "I will always wear it." And she lifted her arms to hug him about the neck.

He was in no hurry to leave. Marcel wanted to play war and before many minutes had passed the two of them were down on the floor, Jack lying full length on his side, his head propped on one hand. He was organizing infantry to withstand the charge of Marcel's cavalry.

"I think they should be set in square like this," he said. "That is how foot soldiers withstand attacks from men on horseback. And they almost always succeed. Did you know that?"

"I shall blow them apart," Marcel declared excitedly.

Jack chuckled.

And then Jacqueline was on the floor, too, sitting against Jack while he set his arm about her shoulders, his square being ready to do battle. She was showing him her books, and he was doing an admirable job of dividing his attention between the two children so that neither would feel neglected.

Like any good father with his children.

Isabella sat and watched, her throat aching with unshed tears. When she had first seen him with the parcels in his hands, she had feared that he had brought gifts for Jacqueline only and that Marcel would be severely disappointed. And she would have expected that all his attention would be given to his daughter.

But he was chuckling as he looked down at his demolished square of soldiers and explained to Marcel that in reality the cavalry would not have found it nearly so easy because horses will not charge a square of fixed bayonets.

"Horses are a great deal wiser than men," he said. "Shall I revive this army? It is cloudy outside today," he said as he rearranged his soldiers, in line this time. "I thought we would not see the sun at all. But I can see it here in Jacqueline's dress and bow. Is she the prettiest girl I have ever seen or is she the prettiest girl I have ever seen?"

"You said the same thing twice," Marcel said, laughing gleefully.

"That must mean she is the prettiest girl I have ever seen," Jack said while Jacqueline looked at him with bright eyes.

It was such a cozy, domestic scene, Isabella thought, trying to impose reality on her mind. Tonight his betrothal to Juliana was to be announced. Tomorrow she and the children must go back to London. But she knew it would not be the end. Everything in his eyes and his voice and his manner this morning told her that he was going to pursue his acquaintance with their daughter. And that he would be equally kind to her son.

And his manner last night . . . She would never forget how he had lifted Jacqueline over the back of the pew in church and held her on his lap so that she could sleep. And how he had closed his greatcoat about her and carried her for the long walk home and kissed her when he set her down on her bed in the nursery before leaving her to Isabella's and a nurse's care.

She had never suspected that Jack could love a child, even his own.

"We should go downstairs," she said. "Everyone else will be in the drawing room, and we will be expected."

"Yes." Jack sounded reluctant. "Yes, so we should. Shall we put the army safely back in its box, lad?"

"I am going to tell my friends about my presents," Marcel said, jumping to his feet.

"But first the army gets put to bed," Jack said firmly.

It was a Christmas morning she would treasure in memory for the rest of her life, Isabella knew.

It was a chaotic day. There were children all over the house all day and children outside the house. There were brief rehearsals in the ballroom during the afternoon and then the setting up of chairs and arranging of the stage by the men of the family, the duties of the servants being kept to the minimum for the day. The orchestra for the ball arrived from London and had to tune up their instruments and practice briefly while chairs were being scraped across the floor and children were darting among legs—legs of people and legs of chairs. And late in the afternoon guests began to arrive from London and had to be greeted on the terrace by the duchess, despite the cold weather, and then shown to their rooms by family members and—as like as not—a darting child or two. Howard walked to the rectory with his parents and Juliana, and they brought all the Fitzgeralds back with them.

There was a great deal of kissing going on beneath the kissing bough.

"Quite shameful," the duchess's sister declared, smiling benignly when she caught Connie and Sam at it.

"That is what kissing boughs are for," the duchess added briskly as Howard and Rose took Connie and Sam's place.

Freddie was worried about his costume for the play. Actually it had been decided to act without costume, with the exception of Isabella, who had brought with her what she would need. But Freddie could not decide whether to wear a plain white waistcoat, as he had been forced to do for their last play since he was merely a servant in that, or to wear something a little more elegant—his word.

"Fred," Alex said, patting him reassuringly on the shoulder. "what is the most splendid waistcoat you possess? The very most splendid?"

Freddie frowned. "That would be the red one," he said. "Ruby says it is orange but it is really red, Alex. Damme but it is a fine waistcoat. Everyone turns a head to look at it."

"I'll wager they do," Alex said. "Wear the red, then, Freddie, my lad. The audience will love it."

Freddie looked pleased until he had a thought. "I will not take attention from Isabella?" he asked. "I would not wish to do that, Alex. Isabella has brains. She is a fine actress. I ain't got brains."

"Trust me." Alex squeezed his shoulder. "And wear the red."

"It will certainly look elegant, Freddie," Anne added kindly, almost causing Alex to break out in a quite inappropriate grin.

Claude was suffering from his usual wild despair preceding a family theatrical performance. The only thought that was keeping him sane this time, he told anyone who cared to listen—mainly his wife—was that no one would notice anyone else on stage except Isabella, and she was superb.

"That oaf, Freddie," he complained. "He remembered one of his lines this afternoon and then insisted on calling Portia 'O learned judge' at least fifty times. *At least* fifty!" He took out a handkerchief to mop his brow.

Christmas at Portland House moved to its climax.

For the last couple of days, Jack had watched the rehearsals of all the scenes that were to be performed. And he had been forced to the conclusion—no longer reluctant— that Isabella was indeed a great actress. And yet on the night, after dinner and after the arrival of all the more local guests and after everyone had been seated in the ballroom and the performances began, he soon realized that until tonight she had not been acting.

Tonight, although his own scene came last and he was feeling the usual sick flutters of nervousness lest he make an utter ass of himself when he finally appeared onstage, he watched and he listened. And was so enthralled by the confident, intelligent Portia that he fell in love with her on the spot. And then he was so intrigued by the shrewish, sharp-tongued Katherina that he wanted to jump up onto the stage to tame her himself. He wanted to kiss her silly. And when she appeared in the later scene from the play, tamed by her Petruchio, he was only momentarily saddened by her loss of spirit. Then he saw her eyes and knew that she had learned a most valuable lesson. The eyes were intelligent, keen, and amused. And he knew that the audience saw it, too. Katherina had not been tamed at all. What she had done was learn wisdom. Poor Petruchio did not know what was in store for him.

Devil take it but she was good, Jack thought, shaken suddenly when the sound of loud applause brought him back to reality and he realized that he was on next.

He might have had a hand in the making of her, he

thought. He might have encouraged her in her career—
though she had not needed encouragement, as matters had
turned out—and at the same time have given her the stability of his love. But he had been young. He had had no wisdom at all.

And so he had lost his chance to be a permanent part of
her life.

And now he was about to act out a scene with her in
which he must play the part of another idiot. Othello had
killed in a jealous rage. He, Jack, had not exactly killed
Belle, but he had killed everything that was beautiful in his
own life and had almost destroyed her in the process.

He grew cold at the realization that during that final
quarrel and when she had fled from him, she had been with
child by him. With Jacqueline.

That brooch! He had given it to Hortense as a gift years
ago and had gone begging for it last night, promising to replace it with something bigger and better when he got back
to London. By some miracle she had had it with her. But
then Hortie always carried around all her jewels with her,
much to Zeb's discomfort and their mother's hysteria. Hortie had thought the brooch was for Juliana and had looked
puzzled when it had turned up pinned to Jacqueline's dress
this morning.

Alex knew. Jack had met his eyes this morning when
Jacqueline was showing the brooch to their grandmother.
Not a word had passed, but Alex knew all right. And Anne,
too, judging by the look of wide-eyed sympathy she had
given him a moment later. Dear Anne!

"Jack!" Claude hissed. "This is not the time to go wool-
gathering, man."

Jack jumped up on the stage. He could not recall one single line of his part. He hauled a deep breath of perfumed air
into his lungs.

Isabella was wonderful. Juliana had had no idea that
watching someone act could so transport one beyond oneself that one could actually shed tears. She had admired Isabella as Portia and had been amused by her as Katherina.

She wept for her as Desdemona, waiting for her husband to come home, having premonitions of death, knowing that he was angry with her but not knowing the cause. And she watched, aghast and upset, as Othello wept over her sleeping form and kissed her and convinced himself that he must kill her, though he loved her.

Jack was good as Othello. One would almost swear that he really loved her, and one's heart felt torn in two with watching the two of them, so much in love, so unable to communicate meaningfully with each other. And so the scene moved to its tragic outcome, and Juliana wept. Wept for the innocent and sweet Desdemona and for the guilty and misguided Othello. And wept for the world beyond innocence, where love did not always bring happiness, where there could be so many misunderstandings and tragedies because people would not talk openly with each other—even with those they loved.

"Magnificent," she heard her father saying as applause broke out all around her. "Not quite what one might expect of Christmas, perhaps, but great acting is always relevant."

Juliana felt bereft. For a few moments she could not even applaud. Fingers touched the back of one of her hands, and she looked up at Fitz, seated beside her. Howard and Rose's betrothal had been announced by the rector at dinner, and their two families were seated together for the plays.

Juliana remembered that she had been feeling depressed even before the scene from *Othello* began. Though depression was not quite the word for the way the play had made her feel. It was a feeling a little more exalted than depression.

"Is she not wonderful?" she said.

"The best our world has to offer, I believe," he said. "Shall we stroll somewhere else while the ballroom is being readied for the ball?"

The ball! There was a sinking feeling in Juliana's stomach. Would the announcement be made at the beginning, at the end, or in the middle?

She ought not to stroll anywhere with Fitz, and from the look in his eyes, she knew that he knew it, too.

"Thank you," she said. "That would be pleasant."

"Where?" he asked when they were outside the ballroom, and she knew that neither of them would be content to follow the crowds to the drawing room or the hall or one of the salons.

She led him upstairs to the gallery. It was in darkness apart from the light that was coming through the window.

"The announcement is to be made tonight, is it not?" he asked, linking his fingers with hers and crossing to one of the windows with her.

"Yes," she said.

"You must be very happy."

"Yes."

"Are you?"

She drew breath to answer again, but said nothing.

"Are you?" he asked again, his fingers tightening about hers.

"No." Her voice was a whisper.

"Why?" he asked. "You do not like him?"

"I like him," she said.

"Why then?" he asked.

But she had no answer to give.

"Julie," he said, "I love you. I am far less eligible than Jack, and your father would not give you to me in a thousand years. But my grandfather has asked me to go there to live and to manage his estate now that his longtime steward is about to retire, and the property will be mine one day. It is hopeless, is it not?"

"Yes," she said.

"If I were as wealthy as Jack," he said, "and if I were the grandson of a duke, would you marry me, Julie?"

"Oh, Fitz," she said, "those things do not matter to me at all. But I did not mean to love you. I did not expect to. I just liked you tremendously and enjoyed talking and laughing with you. And then—and then I loved you."

She was in his arms then, and he was holding her very tightly and rocking her and finally seeking for her mouth with his own. She sighed and surrendered to the temptation of the embrace.

"What are we going to do?" he asked at last, his cheek against the top of her head. "Do you want me to have a word with Jack before it is too late? Or with your father?"

"No," she said.

"What then?" he asked. "It is too late, Julie? You have to go ahead with it?"

She was terrified then by the weight of the decision on her shoulders. It was something no one could do for her, and there was no comfortable choice. There was no one to hide behind—not her father or her grandmother or Jack or Fitz. It was something she had to decide for herself.

Though that was not really true. She did not have to make any decision at all. It had been made already. Her father and her grandmother had chosen for her, and she had accepted their choice. Jack had been very fair to her. He had given her a week in which to make a free choice, and she had done so. She had said yes.

She could not hurt Jack, though she did not believe he loved her exactly.

Fitz did. And she returned his love. Oh, yes, she did. She loved him with all her heart. He was her friend. And far more than that.

Yes, there was a decision to make.

"Fitz," she said, "take me back downstairs. We will be missed."

"Yes," he said, offering her his arm. "I am sorry, Julie. I have upset you. I really just want you to be happy, you know. And Jack is the devil of a fine fellow."

"Yes," she said, taking his arm and laying her head very briefly against his shoulder.

Chapter 18

There was a curious feeling of calm resignation. The announcement of his betrothal was to be made during the ball. He had known that almost from the moment of his arrival at Portland House a week ago, but there had been a large number of activities between then and now. There had always been something else on which to focus his mind. The ball—the culmination of the Christmas week of activities— had always been in the future.

It was in the future no longer. It was beginning. Family and guests were starting to gather in the ballroom again. The members of the orchestra were tuning their instruments. Soon the dancing would begin.

Within the next two hours he would be an officially betrothed man. His grandfather and Juliana's father were to make the announcement just before the supper dance began. Not that there was any secret involved, of course.

He had changed into his blue and silver evening clothes, and was using his charm without conscious effort on a number of ladies who appeared dazzled by the fact that he had acted with the great de Vacheron. He was waiting for Juliana to arrive. He was to dance the opening set with her.

He hoped that Belle would choose not to come to the ball, though there would be many disappointed guests if she did not. He rather thought she might stay away. He did not believe she was quite indifferent to him. Being present at the ball at which his engagement was announced might be painful to her, or embarrassing at the very least.

This was the end, he thought. Or a little past the end. From this evening on all his devotion was going to be directed to Juliana. He turned and smiled as she appeared in the doorway, looking flushed and bright-eyed and dainty and not a day older than sixteen. He reached out a hand to her and bowed as she took it.

"I have had no opportunity to tell you how lovely you look this evening, my dear," he said. "I will be the envy of every other man present."

She looked at him with those bright eyes, and he could see her swallowing awkwardly. His smile softened.

"You are nervous," he said. "And so am I. But all will be well. You look exquisite."

"M-may I speak with you?" she asked.

There was something wrong. He realized it immediately. Something more than mere nervousness.

"Yes, of course, my dear," he said, leading her toward the door and to one of the anterooms outside the ballroom. He ushered her inside and closed the door firmly behind them.

"What is it?" he asked.

"Do you love me?" She had turned to face him and looked at him now with wide and fearful eyes and flushed cheeks.

Deuce take it, she had got wind of the fact that he had been spending time with Belle. He would not hurt her for the world.

"I have a fondness for you, Juliana," he said. "Yes, I love you." He did not altogether lie. There were many kinds of love.

"Oh," she said.

"Did you fear that I did not?" He possessed himself of her hand and held it between both his.

"I hoped you did not," she said. And then she looked stricken and tried to remove her hand from between his. "Oh, I am sorry. Do forgive me. You were right. I am very nervous. I—Forgive me."

"Why did you hope I did not?" he asked.

"I—I did not know what I was saying," she said, her eyes on his hands. But she looked up at him again, and he saw the transformation he had seen in her on a couple of occasions before. The docile, obedient young girl gave place to a determined woman. She had used the determination in order to flirt with him on those other occasions. This evening she used it differently.

"I like you," she said. "Even though at first I thought you cold and—and something of a rake, I have come to see that you are kind and honorable. I think I even love you in a way. I know you would make a good husband. I know I could not do better. But I do not want to marry you."

Jack felt the stirrings of painful hope.

"Can you tell me why?" he asked gently.

"Yes," she said. "I want to marry s-someone else."

"Who?" He raised his eyebrows. "Am I permitted to know?"

"Fitz," she said defiantly.

"Fitz?" He could not have been more surprised. Fitz did not seem the romantic sort of figure someone of Juliana's exquisite beauty would be attracted to. And yet he knew she had spent a fair amount of time in Fitz's company during the past week. It had just never occurred to him . . .

"I love him," she said, making a valiant but very obvious effort to control panic. "I—I love him."

He was still holding her hand. "And you wish me to release you from your promise?" he asked. "You need not look so fearful, Juliana. It is done. I would not want an unwilling bride."

"I do not want to hurt you." The little girl was back. Her eyes filled with tears.

He brought her hand to his lips. "Juliana," he said, "I am not hurt. Believe me, I am not. I would have been honored to have you as my wife, but you must not fear that my feelings are deeply engaged. I have a fondness for you. My heart will not be broken at the loss of you."

He was not accustomed to delivering diplomatic speeches. He hoped he had said nothing to offend or hurt her.

"There is no great harm done," he said. "No official announcement has been made even though everyone expects one. I shall find your father and have a word with him."

"No," she said, and he could see that she had put the young girl behind her again. "I will speak with Papa. I will not have you take any of the blame. None of it has been yours. You have been—very good to me. If I had not met Fitz, perhaps . . ."

He chuckled. "Somehow," he said, "I do not find it particularly flattering to be considered second best to Fitz. Not that I have anything at all against him. Is it a match your father will permit?"

"Not willingly," she said, her chin coming a little higher. "Perhaps not at all. But I am nineteen. In two years' time I will be able to choose my own husband. I do not mind waiting if Fitz does not."

Jack smiled and raised her hand to his lips again. He liked this girl-turned-woman. She reminded him in some strange way of his grandmother, and not only in stature. He rather thought she was going to mature very well, indeed.

"Fitz is a fortunate man," he said. "I wish you well, Juliana. From my heart I do. I shall speak with my mother and my grandparents. There will be no hostility from them and no embarrassment for you, I promise. The announcement will simply not be made. No one can complain, since the whole thing has been a closely guarded secret. Or so our grandmothers firmly believe." He grinned at her.

She bit her lower lip and then smiled back. "Thank you for being so kind," she said. "It is more than I deserve."

And that was that, Jack thought, leading her from the anteroom, staring down the knowing smirks of a few impertinent cousins, and taking her into the ballroom to her parents' side. Her arm was trembling on his, he could feel, but when he glanced into her face, he could see that she was not about to crumble.

He bowed and took his leave of them. His mother was talking with a group of guests. Jack detached her from them and led her to the doorway, where his grandparents had just arrived and had just given the signal for the first sets to form.

Two minutes later the four of them were in the library, and Jack was lifting his grandfather's foot to a cushioned stool.

"There is to be no announcement tonight," he told them without preamble—his grandmother was already grumbling about a hostess being absent from her own ball. "There is to be no betrothal and no marriage between Juliana and me."

For once the duchess was speechless. The duke growled deep in his throat—it might have been a cough. Jack's mother sat down abruptly on the nearest chair and opened her fan.

"Jack," she said. "How could you? How could you do this to your mama and to your grandmama and grandpapa?"

"It was a mutual agreement between the two of us to end our betrothal before it became official, Mama," he said firmly. "I hope you do not believe that I would do anything as dishonorable as break off a betrothal myself."

"It is Bertrand Fitzgerald, I suppose," the duchess said with surprising calm. "I thought they were enjoying each other's company altogether too much, those two. I feared that love might gallop up on them unawares. Holyoke will never agree to the match. She is a foolish girl."

"I think not, Grandmama," Jack said. "I see her more as a determined young lady who is beginning to realize that she has a life to live and that she should have some hand in ordering it."

"Ah," his grandmother said with unexpected docility.

His mother had found a handkerchief somewhere about her person and was dabbing at her eyes with it. "Poor Jack," she said. "Jilted and heartbroken."

Jack clucked his tongue. "Neither, Mama," he said. "I told you it was mutually agreed upon. I believe that I have said all that needs to be said. Let me escort you back to the ballroom."

But he said something else to them when they were all on their feet. Something that was going to have to be said sometime. It might as well be now.

"There is a child upstairs," he said, "who is a member of this family. Your granddaughter, Mama. Jacqueline Gellée is my daughter. Mine and Belle's. I want you all to know because I intend to acknowledge her."

Surprisingly it was the duke who broke the stunned silence that followed his words. Not just with the usual wheezings and rumblings, but with words.

"And high time, too, my boy," he said sternly. "She is

eight years old. You deserve to be horsewhipped for leaving it so long."

"Yes, Grandpapa," Jack said.

"And it would seem to me that there is probably someone else to be acknowledged, too," His Grace added.

"Yes, Grandpapa," Jack said.

Marcel had fallen asleep almost as soon as his head touched the pillow. It was his second late night in a row, and the excitement of the day had exhausted him.

Jacqueline was still awake, though she was not complaining. Isabella might have gone away and left her. But she sat on the edge of her bed, smoothing a hand over her head, glad of the excuse to stay in the nursery rooms after all the other mothers had hurried away to prepare for the ball.

She was not going to go down to the ball. She had told the duchess so, and Her Grace had not pressed the point. Her guests would be disappointed, she had said, but the dear comtesse had worked extremely hard to put on a magnificent performance and must be weary. If she should change her mind, she would be very welcome to come down to the ballroom. Very welcome, indeed.

She had squeezed Isabella's hand and kissed her cheek. His Grace had wheezed and declared that he was honored to have entertained her in his own home.

They were Jacqueline's great-grandparents, she thought, humming quietly and unconsciously one of the lullabies she had sung to her children when they were babies.

Tomorrow they were going to return to London, though they had been invited to stay longer. Marcel would be disappointed to leave so soon. He had played for hours today with the other children and their various Christmas presents.

There was a tap on the half-closed door of Jacqueline's room, and both of them turned their heads to look.

"Not sleeping yet?" he asked, coming inside.

It was not fair, Isabella thought. Did he not understand that she would not want to see him again this evening? It was enough that she had had to act out that very intimate scene with him. She had found it very difficult to convince herself that she was Desdemona and he was Othello. Reality had kept intruding.

"No," Jacqueline said. "I just came to bed."

"Well." He clasped his hands behind him. "I see your doll is still awake, too. Perhaps you should try putting her to sleep."

He looked quite undeniably gorgeous, Isabella thought, stealing a glance at his pale blue satin coat with the silver embroidered waistcoat and silver pantaloons and very white linen and lace. He had used to come to her sometimes after a formal social event, dressed as splendidly as this, and she had used to feel the great social gap between them.

"I will sing her a lullaby," Jacqueline said. "I saw you acting with Mama."

"Did you?" He smiled. "Did you know that your mama is the greatest actress in all England? And in all France, too? I was honored to act with her."

He had never ever praised her acting before. And though he did so now only for the benefit of their daughter, there was a curious warmth in Isabella's heart.

"If I take your mama away," he asked, "will you be able to sleep?"

Jacqueline nodded. "Where are you taking her?"

"Not far. She will be here when you wake up in the morning," he said.

"All right." She closed her eyes.

But she opened them again and raised her arms to Isabella and puckered her lips. Isabella bent over her and kissed her. And then Jacqueline lifted her arms to Jack and invited his kiss, too, just as if it was the most natural thing in the world to do.

Isabella looked at his eyes as he bent over their daughter and kissed her—warm and tender eyes. She wished he had not come. She did not want to feel this pain now. There had been too much pain in the past week—all self-induced. She had been the one who had decided to come here.

"Good night, Jacqueline," he said softly.

Chapter 19

"I am not going to the ball," she said when they were outside the nursery. "I am tired. I am going to my room. Good night."

But he held out his arm for hers and after looking at it for a few moments, she took it. Let him escort her as far as her room, then. All this was her fault. She had no one but herself to blame for the unexpected suffering this week was bringing her.

"Where are we going?" she asked when he did not pause outside her door but walked on past it.

"To my room," he said.

"No."

"Yes," he said, and she did not argue further.

His room looked very familiar, as if she had shared it with him on numerous occasions. She had lain with him on his bed for an hour or so one afternoon and had slept there for a few minutes, his arms about her.

"I have to go," she said. "You have to go downstairs. They will be waiting for you."

But he had turned just inside the door and set his hands against it now, one on each side of her head.

"There is no betrothal, Belle," he said. "There is to be no marriage. Juliana asked to be excused from it so that she can be free to marry Fitz—Bertrand Fitzgerald."

She pressed her head back against the door. His words numbed her. She could not immediately react.

His mouth came against hers, open, and her own opened involuntarily and her arms came around him as his came around her and drew her away from the door.

"Jack." She drew her head back from his, fighting for sanity. "They will be expecting you downstairs. The ball is beginning."

"I have more important things to do," he said, his mouth against hers again. His hands were at her back.

"What are you doing?" She pulled her head back.

"Undoing your buttons," he said. "Don't ask why, Belle. I am undressing you. I am going to make love to you. On that bed. As I have been wanting to do for days. No, for years. Don't fight me. Don't say no. Kiss me so that you do not have the chance to say no."

"Oh, Jack." It was half a sob.

He kissed her.

There was an achingly erotic mixture of familiarity and unfamiliarity. He was Jack, wonderfully and unmistakably Jack with his ability to touch her with hands and mouth and tongue and body and ignite her to sizzling desire at the same time. And yet he had learned more and different touches, and he had learned to build and control and prolong her desire so that it did not shatter too early or too often and thus weaken the ultimate yearning. It was Jack's body that both she and he stripped of the splendid evening clothes, but it was the muscular body of a man now rather than the slender form of a boy.

"Belle." He was lying on top of her on the bed, propped on his elbows, gazing down at her, his dark eyes heavy with passion—ah, so familiar even after all the years. "My love."

He was pushing her legs wide with his own. She lifted hers to twine about them. She knew this part with him—the long foreplay until they both pulsed with desire and then the pause, the taut moment in which they both savored in anticipation the wonder and the pain and the frenzy and the release that were to come.

"Jack." She whispered his name. "I have always loved you. I always have."

He smiled at her as his hands slid under her and lifted her to him. He smiled at her as he came inside her, long and hard and deep. She smiled back.

And then he lowered his head to the pillow beside her and began to move in her. In the old remembered way. Slowly at first, withdrawing almost completely, pushing back inward his full length. Slowly so that they could both feel the sheer enjoyment of what they did together.

And then finally the urgency. The sudden return of desire, almost unbearable in its intensity. The urgent shared rhythm, the reckless approach to insanity, and the sudden crashing through to nothingness, to emptiness, to beauty, to peace. To heaven. To that momentary glimpse of what heaven must surely be like.

And the full weight of his body pressing her into the mattress. So familiar it might have last happened yesterday. She lifted a hand to play with his hair and rested her cheek against the side of his head.

He sighed and moved off her, keeping his arms about her as he did so. "You know that puts me to sleep," he said. "Did you want to be squashed for the next hour or so?"

"Yes," she said.

He smiled at her. "The old answer," he said.

She smiled back at him and closed her eyes. She felt so deliciously sleepy. She wanted to go to sleep. She did not want to have to face reality yet and the knowledge of what she had just done.

She wanted only to fall asleep, feeling loved—the old seductive feeling.

"Belle." He kissed her nose. "You are not going to fall asleep. It is very flattering, of course, but we have to talk."

"I do not want to talk," she said. "I want to sleep."

"I want to talk." He kissed her mouth. He was still marveling at the sameness and the difference in her. The girl he had fallen in love with was gone, together with her girl's body. A woman had taken her place with a woman's shapely form. but she was unmistakably Belle as she had always been.

"I will not be your mistress again," she said. "I have grown past that, Jack, and I never intended it in the first place. I was very naive and very romantic. I thought we

were becoming lovers because marriage was impossible between us. I did not realize I was making myself into a
whore. But never again."

"Good," he said. "Let us discuss making an honest
woman of you, then. When shall we do it? Next week? I do
not believe I can wait longer."

She opened her eyes at last. The dreamy sleepiness of a
woman who has just been well loved had gone from her
eyes to be replaced by unhappiness.

"It is impossible for us, Jack," she said. "I am respectable now, and I am genuinely welcomed by kind people like your grandparents and your whole family. But there
are invisible boundaries past which I cannot go. I know. I
live with those boundaries every day of my life. I would not
be allowed to marry a member of this family. You would
not be allowed to marry me."

"I believe," he said, "my grandfather is going to use a
horsewhip on me if I don't marry you, Belle. If it is half as
heavy as his hand used to feel when we were boys, I am
squirming already."

She was looking at him with wide, dismayed eyes.
"Jack," she hissed. "they do not *know*?"

"I told them a short while ago," he said, "my grandparents and my mother, that Jacqueline is ours."

She closed her eyes and grimaced.

"That was when Grandpapa made his ominous remark
about horsewhips," he said.

"Jack," she said, "how will I ever face them?"

"With me at your side," he said, lifting a hand to run his
fingers through her golden hair. It had lost none of its shining silkiness in nine years. "I think we had better marry
here, Belle. You and the children can stay here while I ride
neck or nothing back to London for a license. My family
would never forgive us if we slunk off somewhere else to
marry secretly."

"Jack." Her eyes were agonized. "We cannot. Oh, you
know it would never work. We are quite incompatible."

He kissed her and lingered longer than he had intended.
He wanted to find the right words.

"I meant what I said to Jacqueline," he said. "You are the greatest actress I have ever seen, Belle. I suppose I knew it ten years ago, and I was terrified of losing you, terrified that you would grow beyond me and not need me any longer."

"Jack—" she said, but he laid a finger over her lips.

"I did not know how to fight something inanimate," he said, "so I made it animate. I convinced myself that it was the praise and the admiration you craved and the attention of men. Belle, I was very young and very much in love and very insecure. I know now that you need your career. I would never ask you to give it up."

"You would never be able—" But his finger stopped her words again.

"Yes," he said, "I would. I have seen how much you love your children, Belle. There is not the smallest sign of neglect in your treatment of them or any sign that they suffer from the fact that your time is divided between them and the theater. I have acquired a little wisdom over the years, I believe. I know now that it is impossible and undesirable to possess another person every moment of every day. I know that one has to give freedom to the person one loves and trust that she will give love freely in return. Give me a chance."

"Oh, Jack." There were tears in her eyes. "I was just as foolish. I loved you and I wanted you, but when I realized the true nature of our relationship—long before you ever put it into crude words—I tried to wean myself away from you. I told myself that things were more desirable than people, more predictable, more reliable. I was terrified of losing you, and so I would not let myself trust you. I used to stay out after my performances to convince myself that I did not have to go running back to you. I used to have supper with other gentlemen to convince myself that there were other charming, attractive men in this world. And then when you used to get angry and started to get suspicious and started to call me names, I told myself that I had been right about you all the time."

"We were a couple of prize idiots," he said.

"And then I suspected and then knew that I was with child," she said, closing her eyes again and setting her forehead against his chest. "And I could not trust you with the knowledge. And so I ran. And deprived you of the chance to decide for yourself if you wanted Jacqueline or not."

He raised her chin and gazed into her eyes. "I think we need to forgive ourselves, Belle," he said, "and then forgive each other. Shall we?"

She nodded, tears in her eyes.

"And then I think we need to get on with our lives," he said. "Together. Married. We have two children to raise. I want to be a father to both of them, Belle."

"Marcel—" she said.

"To *both* of them," he said firmly. "And I hope to one or two more in time."

"Jack," she said, her eyes luminous, her voice wistful. "Is it possible, then?"

"It is Christmas," he said, smiling. "All things are possible at Christmas."

"But Christmas will be over soon," she said. "It does not last all year."

"But it comes again next year and the year after and the year after that," he said. "Besides, why should I not be able to keep my Christmas Belle with me all year?"

"Your Christmas *what*?" She laughed. "What a dreadful pun, Jack. A shudderingly bad one."

He chuckled with her. "I thought it rather clever," he said.

"Next you will be talking about ringing it," she said.

"Belle." He rubbed his nose against hers. "Will you marry me? On the understanding that I will not let you out of this bed until you say yes?"

She drew a deep breath and let it out slowly. "I'll marry you, Jack," she said. "I have loved you for ten years and have fallen in love with you all over again this week. How could I possibly say no?"

He tightened his arm about her so that she was against him from shoulders to toes. "I forgot to mention," he said, "that I was not going to let you out of this bed even if you said yes."

They laughed together again. But he released her suddenly and unexpectedly and rolled away from her to sit on the edge of the bed.

"On second thoughts," he said. "There is something even more important than that, Belle. And don't argue with me. I am adamant. I am practicing to be a tyrant like my grandfather. I will give you half an hour."

"Half an hour?" She sounded mystified.

"To get ready for the ball," he said.

"Oh no," she said, dismayed. "No, Jack, I—"

"Twenty-nine and a half minutes," he said. "You can do it, Belle, and you will. Your very best performance ever, love."

She was sitting beside him, naked and beautiful and very tempting. She opened her mouth and then closed it again. "It will have to be, won't it?" she said.

The ball had been in progress for longer than an hour. There had been no apparent unpleasantness, though somehow word had got around to all the family members that there was to be no announcement that night.

Juliana and her family were still present. And Juliana had even danced with Fitz. If anyone had known the real reason for the break with Jack, he or she might have noticed the intensity with which they spoke at first and the dawning hope with which they gazed at each other for the rest of the set. But almost no one knew—though rumor had it that Jack had not been the one to prevent the announcement's being made.

It was just a pity, some of them said, that Jack was too upset or too embarrassed to put in an appearance.

And it was a pity also that the comtesse was too tired to come down and dance. The Christmas ball would have been complete if all their number had been gathered in the ballroom.

"Perhaps—" Anne said, looking up at Alex.

He drew her closer to his side and smiled fondly at her. "I fear you are too much the romantic, love," he said.

But at that very moment a stirring of interest drew their attention to the doorway. Jack stood there, handsome and immaculate as ever in blue and silver and white, with Isabella on his arm, glorious in shimmering blue satin.

Jack looked about him until he spied his mother. By some happy chance she was with his grandparents.

"Chin up, my love," he said. "Five pounds on it that their first reaction will be to tell me what a lucky fellow I am."

"Stepping out on a stage was never as difficult as this," she murmured as he led her across the room, smiling the dazzling smile that had used to make him murderously jealous of its recipients.

"Mama, Grandmama, Grandpapa." He made them an elegant bow and was aware of Belle dropping into a deep curtsy. Fortunately the music and dancing made it almost a private moment. Clearly it would be in bad taste to make a public announcement tonight. "May I present to you the mother of my daughter. The love of my heart. My future wife."

"Oh, Jack." His mother was fumbling for her handkerchief. "Dear boy. My dear comtesse."

"Not too far in the future, I hope," his grandmother said sharply. "It is already a shameful nine years late."

The duke wheezed and frowned ferociously. "Good evening to you, Comtesse," he said. "All I can say to you, Jack, my boy, is that you are a lucky fellow."

Jack looked at Isabella, and she looked at him. And they smiled at each other with amusement and affection. And with such open love that the other members of the family, shamelessly curious and shamelessly spying, knew very well what top secret announcement they were to be surprised with within the next day or two.